MUSKOKA PROMISE

CAROLYN MILLER

CHAPTER 1

The music spilling from her car stereo blared its special blend of pain and angst. Anna Morely twisted the dial to pump up more volume. Once upon a time she might've laughed at those tragics who loved this kind of song. Now she understood their heartache. Once upon a time she had lived in a bubble of perky happiness. Now she knew that happily-ever-afters were never guaranteed.

As her car passed the Muskoka Shores community church, she averted her face. She hadn't stepped inside since Toni's wedding six months ago. Even then it had only been a slip in, slip out, hope-nobody-noticed-her kind of deal. Not that she'd gone to support Toni. Nope. It'd been for a far more shallow reason: to satisfy her curiosity, and confirm the fact that she no longer had anything in common with those people who'd once called her their friend.

The car crept past the rest of downtown. She rolled her eyes as she passed Brandi's Bookstore and Gifts—apparently Brandi had found love at Christmas—then past The Coffee Blend, where Suzy's son Dylan had struck up a romance with young

Rochelle. Ugh. What was wrong with this place that everyone seemed to be finding romance except for Anna?

Was there something wrong with small town Muskoka Shores? Or was there simply something wrong with Anna? Why couldn't she be the one to find love? She still couldn't believe that Serena had bounced straight from Anna's two-timer of a loser cousin and now kicked-from-the-family Dwight, to Joel, aka Mr. Perfect, and married him less than a year later. Then Toni had done the same with Matt, and Staci had married James after a year, too. It seemed all her former friends only had to snap their fingers and hello, Mr. Right suddenly appeared, as if God had zapped the perfect man for them straight down from heaven.

But as for Anna? Not so much. Not at all, actually. Every guy she'd ever liked had instantly fallen for someone else. Which left her wondering why they didn't like her. Wondering if it would always be this way. Wondering if something really was wrong with her whether people would even have the guts enough to tell her. Maybe God just didn't love her, or thought she couldn't be trusted with another person's heart. But then, these days it was getting harder to believe God was real, too.

A car passed, and she glimpsed a laughing face that reminded her a little of Jackie O'Halloran's. Anna's stomach clenched, her fingers gripping the steering wheel more tightly. Don't even get her started on Jackie and Lincoln Cash, the Hollywood megastar, who apparently had bought a house here in Muskoka Shores just so he could be closer to his girlfriend. His girlfriend, who used to be Anna's friend, who had *known* how much Anna wanted to meet him, but had basically lied about him and kept her relationship a secret. On Anna's worst days she hoped they'd break up and she'd be proved right, that the Hollywood hunk had zero in common with Miss Holier-than-thou Jackie. How could she have ever thought Jackie was her friend? She would never forgive—

BEEP!

A honking from behind snapped her attention to the here and now, and she slammed on the brakes, barely missing an elderly woman using a Zimmer-frame as she crossed the street to the Nuthouse, away from the pedestrian crossing. Protest snarled within, but she clenched her teeth. She might not be the nice person she used to be, but she'd recently been made aware that venting every stray thought only led to a cloud hanging around her, which apparently others did not want to see. Or so her mom had said, bless her. But come on. Why didn't the old lady use the pedestrian crossing like a normal person? What gave the elderly the right to do what they wanted, like normal rules didn't apply to them, simply because they'd lived on planet Earth longer than most? Talk about a sense of entitlement.

She rolled her eyes at herself, and forced herself to pay attention. The streets were a lot busier these days thanks to the recent profusion of tourists here to see the spring flowers which had brought Muskoka to life again. She might've grown up here, and was used to the seasons of change, but she'd always appreciated spring. Given the heaviness of Muskoka's long winters the town council had done what it could to entice visitors with its range of festivals, celebrating everything from cranberries to pumpkins to Christmas. Even so, it was still a long winter season. The spring freshet—the spring thaw—was always a time to celebrate, even if it meant the winter melt led to occasional flooding in lower lying areas of Muskoka. Spring was a time of renewal, of flowers, of joy, new life, as the days grew longer with the promise of summer.

Not that she'd be celebrating. Not that there was much to look forward to this summer at all really, especially as she'd spent much of the past year eating her feelings, so her swimsuit didn't fit, and she had zero desire to look like a whale in those too-tiny clothing store changerooms in an effort to buy a new one.

She sighed, her soul's heaviness weighing her down into apathy again. She hated being this person, the one who complained and felt sorry for herself, the person always spoiling for a fight, her soul a tangle of barely-contained snarl and bite. But it now seemed entrenched as part of her personality, and a habit that was now far too hard to break. She probably would turn out to be as grim-faced as her mom's sister, Aunty Adelaide, whose pulled-down mouth reflected the sourness and low "that'd be just my luck" expectations with which she faced the world…

"Ugh!" And that was enough introspection for the day. She turned the volume up even higher.

"Why….?" She sang along to the words on her playlist. Sing the words, sing her emotions, sing her questions, the plaintive question of the 80s song like the soundtrack to her life. Sometimes it was better when she could get those things out of her head, so they didn't live within her anymore, and the dark thoughts didn't keep circling, circling, circling—

BUMP!

She slammed on the brakes, and the car skidded to a stop, her body humming with fear. What had she just hit? Her fingers shook as she steered to the side and put the car into park. *Dear God, help!* She hoped it wasn't a person. *Please, Lord, no!*

A car pulled up behind her, the door opened, and someone got out. She drew in a shaky breath, bracing herself as she glanced up through the window.

A man who looked to be of a similar age to her gestured for her to lower the window.

No, sir. She locked the doors. She'd seen how these kind of things rolled. Lower the window and it was an invitation to get car-jacked. Or worse.

He put his hands on his hips, like he was getting impatient. Well, too bad.

Except... *Had* she seen him before? His face drew the slightest tug of familiarity.

As the music kept thumping, she lowered the window the tiniest crack, hoping he wasn't about to squirt her with tear gas or pepper spray. Which was unlikely, probably, considering it was mid-morning in Muskoka Shores, and there were lots of people around, but you never knew. People couldn't be trusted these days. There were plenty of shady people disguised as nice folk wandering around. But considering the sheer volume of people around, maybe she was safe. "I hit something," she yelled over the music, and pointed to the front.

He nodded, then moved to the front of her car, bending to peer at her front bumper before gesturing for her lower the window more.

She shook her head. Who knew who he might be? Women could get kidnapped in broad daylight. It'd happened before. Hello? She'd spent much of the past six months binge-watching true crime shows and knew a thing or two.

Then he drew out a badge and held it close to the window. She peered at it, then exhaled, as she recognized the insignia of the Ontario Provincial Police. Fine, then. She powered down the window, and the officer frowned, his dark eyes holding a fierce intensity as he pointed to her dash and said something.

"What?" she yelled over the music.

"Turn off the music," he yelled back.

Oh. She punched it off, and the sudden silence made her blink. "Um, sorry."

"You should be. Nobody should be listening to that." He shook his head.

"Excuse me?" Was he questioning her taste in music? Didn't he know Annie Lennox was a queen?

"You heard me. Now show me your license and registration, please."

Huh. She didn't think plains-clothed police asked things like that. "Are you a detective?"

"Yes."

"What did I hit?"

"License and registration, please," he repeated, his tone holding the faintest sigh.

She wasn't about to argue anymore. For all her crimes, she'd never actually been arrested for anything. Not that she had ever committed any crimes, apart from not going to church any more. Oh, and not talking to her friends.

He cleared his throat, and she startled back into action. "Um, sure."

She grabbed her handbag from where it had fallen into the passenger footwell and searched its contents for her wallet. "I know it's in here somewhere."

He drummed his fingers on top of the doorframe of her car, the sound like heavy raindrops, persistent and annoying. But asking a police officer to stop doing that would be like asking to get arrested, right? So she kept her lips zipped, as her cheeks heated, her pulse spiking as she kept hunting for her wallet. Where *was* it?

"Miss? You do have your license, don't you?"

"Of course I do," she said, more snappishly than she wanted —or that he wanted, judging from the sudden narrow-eyed glare. "Sorry. I know I have it, because I never leave home—and obviously would never dream of driving—without it. I just don't understand where it is." Had she left it at the grocery store? Fear clenched her chest. Maybe someone right now was using her credit card to fill up their car, or buying a one-way ticket to Hawaii! And she really didn't need to be working as hard as she did just to pay for someone else's vacation. She drew in a shaky breath.

"Miss?"

She ignored him, dumping her bag's contents on the

passenger seat, wincing as she tucked the pack of tampons below a fold out vinyl shopping bag printed with dogs. "It's definitely in here somewhere!"

"Miss!"

"What?" Her gaze swerved to him.

He'd raised his eyebrows—probably because of the waspish note in her voice again—and was pointing to the passenger footwell. Where her dark purple wallet was hiding, out of plain sight from her position in the driver's seat, until she leaned forward like she was doing now. She snatched it up and passed it to him, but whether she had done so with too much force or not, the momentum sent the wallet flying straight out the window to thud into his chest.

He coughed, and now she *really* hoped he wasn't in a bad mood because Clumsy Woman actions were likely to have put him there now.

"I'm so sorry!"

He handed the wallet to her, and she took it, gingerly. "I'm sorry," she whispered again.

"Your license?"

Ugh. Tears sparked to the back of her eyes, and she slowly slid out her license and showed it to him. He tugged it from her fingers and walked back to his vehicle, and she slumped over the steering wheel, her head on her arms. At least whatever she had hit couldn't have been too important if he was not making a fuss about that or radioing for an ambulance. Still. Could this day get any worse?

New heaviness pressed on her shoulders, and she sagged, then the horn blared its loud *beep*, jerking her upright, her cheeks firing with fresh flames. A glance in the revision mirror showed him glaring back at her, and she shook her head, hoping he understood her shrug and upraised hands as the apology that it was.

She slumped against the back of the seat, the spilled contents of her bag silently mocking her: pathetic, scatter-brained, loser. So she sighed and did what any self-respecting woman would, and started sorting through it, peering at the expiry dates on old coupons, wincing at the large number of candy bar wrappers, which she quickly stashed in the car's plastic trash bag. Random coins and notes she placed in the appropriate spots of her wallet, the pens she stashed in the zipped side pocket where they were supposed to be next to the notepad she kept there for goodness-knew-whatever reason. Maybe for the day she'd write the great Canadian novel. Another eye-roll.

Ugh. Her mom had never understood how Anna could fail to live up to the family's high standards of organization and elegance. But the older Anna got the more she realized that there were many inexplicable things in this world.

Anna closed her eyes and listened as the sounds of other vehicles went past. How many of them knew the loser in the car was her? Who would be gossiping about her now? How she hoped none of her former friends were driving past right now. Or worse, any of her mother's friends, who would then think it their duty to inform her mom about the latest misdemeanor of her only child.

A yawn escaped. Last night's late bedtime, after watching a documentary about the true kidnapping attempt of Princess Anne, had been a bad idea. She'd known that at the time, but had justified the late hour because as an adult she didn't need to bend to anyone else's bedtime rules and could live her life her own way, thank you very much. But maybe there was something in going to bed earlier, especially when what she watched had a troubling tendency to pursue her through her dreams, so she never slept well these days. She hadn't slept well for months, really. So maybe if this took any longer, she could snatch a few moments and gain a micro-sleep...

"Miss?"

Her eyes flew open as she jerked upright again, her hand

hitting the steering wheel so the horn blared again. "Oh my gosh! I'm sorry. I really didn't mean to do that. Or do it the other time." Could any person be more idiotic than her? She pressed against her eyes where stupid tears begged to fall. "I'm really sorry."

When he didn't say anything for the longest time, she peeked through her splayed fingers, and glanced up at him. He was biting his bottom lip, his mouth twitching like he was trying to hold in a smile. He was laughing at her? The one handsome man she'd had any interaction with in the past however-long was laughing at her?

She swallowed, put on dignity like she was her mother, and lifted her chin. "I don't think an apology is worth laughing about."

He made a sound like a smothered chuckle, and handed her license back to her. "You need to pay more attention to the road, Miss Morely."

"You know my name?" How—? Oh. She mentally slapped herself. He'd just looked at her license. "Forget I said that."

This time, he didn't try to hide the smile. "The paint cans of this world will thank you."

"I beg your pardon?"

He pointed to the front of her car. That's right, the whole reason she was in this mess was because she'd hit something. She hurriedly opened the door, not realizing the car door had hit him until he drew back, wincing, as he shook out his hand.

"Oh my gosh! I'm so sorry. Please don't arrest me. I just wanted to see what damage was done." She covered her mouth with her hands. "But now I've damaged you, and I'm so—"

"Sorry, I know." He sighed, and moved, and she exited the car, taking care to give him a wide berth as she moved to the front.

Her nose wrinkled. The front grille of her red Mazda was now decorated with a black spray of paint. "I hit a paint can?"

"It got you good." He pointed to the paint. "You'll need to get that cleaned as soon as possible."

"You mean like with a hose?"

"I mean like at a car detailers." He shook his head. "Water won't fix that."

Her shoulders slumped. More money she didn't have.

He coughed, his feet shifting. "I, uh, probably shouldn't mention this, but my brother owns a car repair business in town, and could probably deal with this for you."

Oh. That was… unexpectedly kind. "Thanks, but unless he does it for free, I can't afford it."

Mom had never understood why Anna didn't save more. Anna didn't understand where her wages went, either, apart from on her mortgage. All she knew was that there was never as much in her bank account as she'd like to keep her in the manner to which she'd grown up and would now prefer to be accustomed. But then, maybe if she'd chosen a more challenging career than receptionist at the local medical center, she would have more income to match her degree. But Mom's unsubtle hints at marrying for money like she had, marrying someone like Kyle Crayling, the son of her best friend, was a degree too far, even for Anna.

The police officer shrugged, like he really didn't care, which forced herself to paste on a wobbly smile and pretend to feel more nonchalant than she was. "At least it was only a paint can. Although why one was in the middle of the road, I don't know."

"People can be careless sometimes."

"So true."

But judging from the way he was looking at her, maybe the careless person he was referring to was the one standing not three feet from him. She winced, wrinkling her nose, and dropped her gaze. "Again, I'm really sorry. I hope your arm is okay."

"Me too."

She met his brown gaze then, the intensity there causing a whole-body shiver, and she backed away. "So, um, is that it? Can I go now? I'm sure you have more important things to do than think about random paint cans and clumsy women."

His gaze lasered onto hers, and his chin dipped. "Drive carefully now, Miss Morely."

She nodded, murmured a, "Thank you. You too," then winced again at the utter stupidity of that last comment. *You too?*

The corner of his mouth ticked up for a beat then flatlined again as he crossed his arms.

Okay, when a girl noticed a police officer's muscly arms it was probably way past time to go. She hopped back into her car and sank into her seat, as the awkwardness of that encounter sent shivers through her again. Ugh. How embarrassing could one woman be? She started the engine, and it jerked forward, causing him to leap out of its way. *Dear heavens.* She mouthed another "sorry" and waited for him to move—no way was she going to hurt that man again—then checked over her shoulder, and carefully, and very *very* slowly, rejoined the traffic heading from Muskoka Shores.

Tom Woodmore shook his head as his gaze followed the red Mazda. Well, that was unexpected. His mouth begged to smile, but he'd been so out of practice it was like he didn't know how to do it anymore. But Miss Anna Morely was certainly... interesting. What his mom would call colorful. Unusual. And a local. He'd had to check her address when he'd looked her up in the system. And if he hadn't been the law and she wasn't so obviously troubled, and if he'd come across her in a different life, then he may have done something about it. But he was, and so was she, and he'd come across her in this context, so anything more was not to be. Even if her antics had been the first to make his heart fizz a little since Meghan's death. And he couldn't shake the feeling that they'd met somewhere before. But asking a woman that kind of question while he was on duty was a recipe for a harassment case, so he'd let it slide. But still, it'd be interesting to know…

"Hey God?" he prayed aloud as he closed the door to his vehicle. "I guess You knew that would happen. But anyway, thanks for the reminder that I'm not completely dead."

Like he'd felt for the past three years since the accident that had stolen Meghan's life. Since then, he'd existed in a strange half-world where work consumed his life with the occasional break for family. It had helped moving back two years ago and having his folks close by, his brothers as mainstays of the community, one owning the local mechanics, the other working in the fire brigade. They'd drawn him from sinking into the abyss known as grief, their faith and his extended family demanding he not live shackled in the past. Still, it was nice to know that his mom's claims of Tom working too hard weren't so true that he hadn't noticed a pretty girl. Not that he was supposed to notice them. Not when he was paid to notice other things.

He rejoined the traffic, and moved through the tourist traffic to the main road as he resumed his rounds. A cherry tree filled with pink blossoms flashed past, the brief moment of beauty releasing the band around his chest. Spring in Muskoka was his favorite time of year, and considering he'd had over thirty of them now, apart from a few when he'd been in the city, he considered himself something of an expert in the matter. It was like as soon as winter ended everyone relaxed, their shoulders dropping an inch or more, like they were as happy as the wildlife about the thaw. Of course, he didn't love it when the winter thaw resulted in major flooding like what had happened a few years ago. But that was just part and parcel of what could happen when one lived in God's own country.

His radio squawked, alerting him to an accident on the 169, so he swung the car around, lights flashing, as he navigated through back streets to join the highway. Normally this would be the highway patrol's role, but the Muskoka station's proximity meant they were sometimes called in to support. Policing here saw the usual challenges, his work as a detective leading him into all kinds of things he hadn't encountered in the city.

Cottage country held a few unique challenges, such as those trying to take advantage of the many wealthy people's cottages that lay vacant through much of the year. Then there was dealing with those living strange existences in the backwoods, living off the grid for various reasons, some for drugs, some for fraud, some mere recluses. Learning to discern the difference could mean the literal difference between life and death. Working here in Muskoka also meant stepping in occasionally to help with certain encounters with wildlife, which had seen him work closely with his firefighter brother, Marc, after a few vehicles came off second best with the occasional bear, deer, or moose.

And, as he neared the accident and pulled off the road, judging from the looks of this one, it was another deer or moose strike. Tire tracks showed the vehicle's slide into a tree where the Toyota's bonnet lay crumpled against the trunk. It reminded him of a similar incident on New Year's Eve, where he'd assisted local paramedic Michael in helping a woman who was supposed to attend a wedding but instead had been stuck in the car for who-knew-how-long. The magazine writer from Toronto had since visited Muskoka Shores—and Michael—more than a few times. Yeah, the police station was as bad as a barber's for spilling the tea and small-town gossip.

The rescue engine was nearby, and just as he'd suspected, Marc was there, using the jaws of life to help extract the white-haired occupants. One of the highway patrolmen was there too, thus negating Tom's need to be. He nodded to him then waited for Marc to finish being a hero, joining the others waiting as the newbie cop, Cole Jones, directed traffic.

"All good?" Tom asked, as the redheaded cop pointed to the diversions in place.

"Some people have no clue." Jones shook his head as another driver vented their feelings at the delay.

Yep, welcome to the world of policing, where they were often considered the bad guys and an inconvenience to many—until their help was needed. His colleague's exasperation drew an almost-smile as his mind flicked back to his own encounter with a hapless motorist not thirty minutes earlier.

"Whoa." Marc dusted off his gloves, eyeing Tom with a furrowed brow. "Is that what I think it is?"

"Depends what you think it is," Tom countered, hands on hips.

"Did I just see a smile on your dial, bro?" Marc whistled. "I haven't seen one of those for years."

His brother's tease drew an instant frown.

"No, no, don't do that. You look almost human when you don't frown."

Tom ignored him, nodding to the Toyota. "They gonna be okay?"

"Cuts and bruises more than anything. A few hours at the hospital and they'll be right as rain."

He nodded, offering a silent prayer of thanks it wasn't more serious, then lifted a hand to Michael, the paramedic, who offered his own nod in return.

A quick check revealed it was a moose that had spooked the city driver. Which was fair enough. Encountering a moose would spook most people.

His lips twitched as his fickle mind flicked back to the earlier incident, and he wondered what effect a moose might have on Miss Morely. She might be a local, but if she was that jumpy with him over a paint can, he could imagine she might have a full-blown panic attack at an unexpected moose meeting. Not that it was a smiling matter, but still, his job meant he had to find amusement where he could. And Marc was right. It had been a long time since anything—anyone—had drawn his smile.

He wasn't needed here, so he drove back to the station, and was soon immersed in his routine. But not back with the same heavy state of heart. Because for the first time in a long time, he felt a sense of anticipation.

For just like when he went fishing with his dad on Lake Muskoka and a fish might appear on his dad's fish radar so he paid attention and looked for it, so Tom had a feeling, a sixth sense, that this morning's incident was just the same. Now he'd noticed her, he had the weirdest sense he could soon expect to bump into her again.

Miss Anna Morely was a local after all.

CHAPTER 2

"Ah, Anna. It is good to see you again my dear, even if I'd prefer to see you at the house than in this place."

Anna smiled at Mrs. Heather Crayling, her mother's best friend for a million years, as she peered cautiously around the medical clinic. The Craylings lived in a huge lakeshore estate just outside the next town, in a mansion that gave grand English manor vibes of the Jane Austen kind. They did so much for the surrounding community, helping the poor, helping the homeless with low-cost housing, and Heather was involved in many charities both here and in the city.

"You have an appointment with Dr. Lewisham, yes?" Anna asked, checking her computer.

"I do. Is he running very late?"

"No. I think he must've heard you were coming, so he's running pretty close to time."

"Oh, that makes a nice change. I do understand that sometimes doctors have emergencies, but sometimes I wish unexpected things did not crop up."

Anna nodded, inwardly smiling at the complete lack of awareness Heather Crayling displayed in that statement.

"I do hope we'll see you out at the house again soon, dear."

Anna nodded, and murmured something non-committal. Maybe if it was only their house, and not their Lodge. She might like the Craylings, and what they did for those poor souls they cared for by providing low cost housing on the acres they owned nearby, but there was something unsettling there too. In her line of work Anna came across all kinds of people and knew not to judge too quickly, but some of the people she'd met when she'd last visited a fundraising event at the Lodge seemed a little… strange.

"Oh, and I'm sure your mother has mentioned something about the upcoming fundraising Summer Ball, but just in case she hasn't, I do hope we can count on seeing you there. I know Kyle is always very happy to see you."

Ah. Mom might've mentioned something, but Anna couldn't admit to a lack of awareness about Heather's pet fundraising project for the year. Mom's too. And Kyle was nice, but she had no desire to promote any thoughts of a closer connection with him. "It'll be a great night," she said, as diplomatically as she could.

"It always is," Heather said complacently. "You know we love our soirees." Heather gave a tinkly laugh, as Anna's smile dropped at that last word.

Once upon a time, she had loved to attend evening get togethers at Serena's with their friends for what Serena had termed her soirees. But that had all changed with the arrival of Joel in Serena's life, and the way the other girls had soon found boyfriends, and their conversation had changed, from innocent talk about movies and men, to marriage, and babies and other things Anna could never relate with. Then, when she'd finally objected, Jackie had self-righteously told Anna to stop complaining. Yeah. Easy for someone in a relationship to say. Especially for someone in a relationship with the man that

Anna had been dying to meet, who then kept it a secret from her…

Mrs. Crayling took her seat in the waiting area while Anna's internal turmoil raged on. How could Jackie have ever pretended to be her friend when she kept such a big secret? That, as much as anything else, made her question the genuineness of her friends, and even their Christian beliefs. How could someone call themselves a Christian when they didn't act in the way they said they would? It didn't seem fair then, and it still didn't seem fair now. And Anna had close to zero desire to attend soirees of any sort, anywhere. She didn't trust the people who did that kind of thing anymore. So, protest as her mom likely would, Anna would simply have to find an excuse to avoid being involved in the Craylings' latest event.

The clinic was its usual busy place, and she continued with taking payments, answering the phone, making appointments, calling to remind people of appointments, and rescheduling when necessary. Her mother had been a little ashamed she had chosen this career, insisting that Anna had the smarts to "be a nurse, at least." But the sight of blood made Anna squeamish and always had, so nursing wasn't for her. Here at least she got to low-key help people, even if the pay wasn't great. At least she was being useful.

The door opened and a familiar face walked in. Rachel Taylor. Anna ducked her head, wishing she could hide, but Gabby, the other receptionist was on her break, leaving Anna to deal with all and sundry. Including former friends. Wonderful.

"Hi Anna."

Anna forced herself to look up. Mature she wasn't, but there was an awkwardness with her former friends that she still didn't know how to deal with. And Rachel had always had a propensity for truth bombs that made her a little unlikeable sometimes.

"I have an appointment with Dr. Morgan."

Anna nodded, her gaze sliding away, her mouth unsmiling. "She's running ten minutes late. Take a seat."

Rachel hesitated, but Anna couldn't afford to care to see what she wanted, and instead focused on the next phone call on her list, quickly dialing the numbers. "Hello, Mrs. Thomas. I'm calling about those results. Dr. Strauss would like you to schedule a non-urgent visit as soon as possible." Emphasis on the non-urgent. So many people freaked out otherwise.

When she glanced up again, Rachel was sitting in a plastic chair opposite, her gaze on Anna, and when Anna met her eyes Rachel's smile was gentle. Hmm. Weird. Maybe something was going down with Rachel. She seemed a lot less nervy than Anna remembered.

She continued with phone calls and payments, then Dr. Morgan came in, and called for Rachel to go in.

Rachel drew close to Anna's workstation, offering her another calm smile and a murmured, "It's good to see you, Anna. I've missed you," as she passed by.

Heat drew to the backs of her eyes, forcing Anna to blink back tears. It wasn't fair for her former friends to sabotage her working day like this with unexpected kindness. Maybe Rachel really did feel unwell because she was acting in a manner most unlike the hectic outspoken woman that Anna had always known.

A savage pang for her old friends drew tightness across her chest. But no. They'd made their feelings clear, and so had she. It was called boundaries, and knowing who was toxic and had to be kept from poisoning one's life. She had no time for those who clearly didn't like her, or want her in their life.

Except right now, Rachel didn't feel like a toxic member of that former crowd at all.

. . .

THE NEXT FEW hours passed as they usually did, with the hustle and bustle of patients, crying babies, anxious elderly, and all those in between. One of the good things about her job here was that there was a clear distinction between work and home. When she finished for the day, she was done, unlike some of the doctors, like Dr. James Wells, who often took their patients' files home or would follow up from home. She guessed his wife, the *New York Times* bestselling novelist Staci Everton, wasn't too concerned, as she'd said in the past, she worked from home herself. Whatever. Anna was thankful she didn't have to worry about that herself.

She said goodbye—Gabby was locking up tonight—and drove to the Nuthouse. The store selling all things nuts and candy was open again for the tourist season, and she had just enough time to grab a bag of her favorite post-work snack— milk chocolate-covered dried orange slices—that was the perfect accompaniment to Netflix true crime shows and ice-cream. She'd caught up on all her shows after binging most seasons of everything she'd wanted to watch, along with a few things she hadn't. Funny how pulling away from those who thought they knew better than Anna about how Anna should live her life had allowed so much more time to do fun stuff like watching TV. Even if sometimes she might wonder what they were up to, and whether they'd found someone else to fill the Anna void. Despite what Rachel had said, they probably hadn't even noticed she was gone, too busy living their best lives while she stumbled on in hers.

She collected the jumbo pack of chocolate orange slices then stood upright, and almost toppled into someone standing behind her. "Oh my goodness, I'm…"

For the love of snickerdoodles. Not again.

"Let me guess. You're sorry?" The police officer from yesterday offered a rueful twist of lips. "And here I could've sworn your license said Anna Morely."

"You remember?"

Ugh. How could he have forgotten uber-klutz her? It had taken hours to get over the waves of embarrassment from yesterday's encounter with the poor man, another reason why she'd stayed up so late. Watching dumb shows on TV had proved a very necessary distraction from the images that had kept slide-showing through her mind. It wasn't any wonder he was backing away. No, wait. That was her.

"Forget it," she muttered, then pivoted on her heel and hurried down the aisle. Heat swarmed her body, embarrassment shimmering in radiant waves as regrets renewed. Once upon a time she'd known how to talk to a man without acting like a thirteen-year-old. Now, her confidence and trust in people was gutter-low, which was why isolating herself made so much more sense. When it was just her and the TV, she didn't have to worry about saying the wrong thing. It just was, so she could be too. Just Anna.

She reached the end of the aisle, relieved to see he wasn't following—like, come on, as if he wouldn't be trying to get as far away as possible from her—then hurried down the next aisle to the checkout. Only to see him there ahead of her.

He glanced over his shoulder, nodded, and she turned abruptly away. Looked like there was plenty of thirte-year-old Anna left inside, after all! She snatched up a bag of trail mix, like she'd suddenly morphed into a hiking junkie, which she obviously wasn't.

She waited until he paid, then finally shuffled across to pay. "Just the oranges," she mumbled, putting the trail mix aside.

The cashier smirked, but said nothing. It wasn't like he didn't know what she always bought here, anyway.

After paying with her phone, she moved outside, the early evening light holding a pinkish tinge. The lake would look beautiful at this time of day. Maybe instead of hiding inside she could afford to live a little and have a picnic. Well, maybe not literally afford, and maybe not a picnic, but she was pretty sure she'd seen a pizza voucher among the handbag detritus yesterday.

She paused, hunting through her bag, and sure enough, a "buy one get one fifty percent off the next" voucher for her favorite pizza store lay there, tempting her. Her hips said she sure didn't need two pizzas, but seeing it was only three quarters of the usual price, it made sense as she was technically *saving* money, especially as she'd put the second in the freezer.

Seriously. Why was she always second-guessing things? She was an adult, and didn't have to explain her actions to anyone. Except maybe the doctor at her next checkup, but she'd be sure to schedule that far enough away so that she'd have a chance to work off the extra weight. Which meant maybe she should schedule it for next year.

Whatever. Now she'd thought about it, she *really* wanted pizza. Now. So she ordered online, then returned to her car, and waited for fifteen minutes so their "freshly made" promise could be kept, then crossed the road, and went inside.

Mmm. Baking bread, garlic, oregano. Some of her favorite scents filled her senses as she moved to the pick-up area.

"Name?"

"Anna."

The server checked his docket. "Are you sure?"

She stared at him. "About whether my name is Anna?"

"Yeah."

She squinted at his nametag. "Well, Jerry, is that your real name?"

"Uh, yeah."

"Are you sure?"

"Yes." He bit off the word.

"Well, I'm sure my name is Anna. And I'm sure I ordered my pizzas and I sure want them. Now."

"Yeah, but…" He frowned at the docket.

"Yeah, but what? Haven't you started cooking them yet?"

"No, we cooked them. It's just someone else came and picked them up already."

"What?"

He showed her the docket. "They ordered the same as you."

"Are you kidding me? Don't tell me their name was Anna as well." Look at her, sarcasm queen.

"I, uh, I don't know."

Her fingers clenched. Normally she'd just turn around and leave, but because she'd paid online, someone had just waltzed off with her dinner that she'd already paid for. "I hope you're going to refund me."

"Um, yeah. I suppose."

"You suppose?" She nearly snarled the word.

"Is there a problem here?" a new voice said.

"Would you mind your own—?" She whirled around. Her eyes widened, then she spun back and closed them, her body stiff. Was this a nightmare? She cracked open her eyelids, peeked sideways. Nope. If only she could disappear.

"I, uh—"

"Forget about it," she shot at the clerk. Arguing over eighteen dollars wasn't worth the agony of having to explain things and embarrass herself yet again.

She opened the door and strode away, ignoring the calls of "Anna!" and "Miss!" from behind her, as her cheeks flamed. Yes, she knew that was a stupid overreaction, but how many people acted with poise and dignity all the time? Well, apart from Heather Crayling and Anna's mother?

She reached her car and climbed in, tossing up the choices of what to do. The whole point of going to the lake seemed spoiled now, the idea of a solo picnic no longer appealed. Especially now she wore another layer of fresh embarrassment. Who knew who else she might see and expose her pettiness to? She couldn't trust herself, the tension inside like a living, breathing thing. She should probably go home and protect the world from her meanness, but she'd wanted to make the most of the sunset, and her home was not exactly positioned to best capture lake views. Still, that was probably the safest option, the best one to avoid snarling at any others and then feeling guilty about it. She'd go home and binge on true crime and her chocolate orange slices and ice-cream instead, and hope that the combined sweetness somehow found a way inside her heart.

TOM KNOCKED on the door and waited. Everything screamed this was a dumb idea, except for a tiny, quiet part that had propelled him on. He hadn't been one hundred percent sure if it was even the right address, but then he'd seen the car out the front, and felt an inkling to try. She obviously didn't like him, or want to see him, so he hoped this might prove a peace offering.

It was crazy how after living in the same place for a few years he hadn't come across her until now, then seen her three times in two days. Except something persistent insisted he *had* seen her before. But when? He couldn't remember, not for the life of him.

He knocked again, listening harder. Then, just as he raised his hand a third time, the door suddenly swung open, the swiftness of the movement almost causing him to lose his balance on the pizza boxes. He gripped them more firmly. "Hey."

"What are you doing here?" Anna's eyes widened. "Have they made a complaint?"

"A complaint?"

"About me. Look, I know I wasn't very gracious, but how would you feel if someone just walked off with your food that you'd already paid for?"

A little ticked, but nothing warranting the steam he'd seen pouring from her ears.

"But if they have complained, well, I hope they know I'm sorry, and don't plan to ever lose my cool again, and—"

His lips twitched.

"—and why are you smirking? Did I say something funny?"

"Are you always this fired up about stuff?"

"Excuse me?"

He willed his lips to bend down. "Look, Anna—"

She arched a brow.

"—I mean Miss Morely—"

The eyebrow lowered.

"—I have your food here, and it's getting cold."

"What? Why do you have it? Do you do pizza deliveries now?"

"Only on certain occasions."

"Oh."

She straightened, and he noticed the lines of weariness that had smudged her makeup. Even still, she looked better than his day had felt.

"How did you end up with it?"

He shrugged. "I'm a detective. Solving problems is what I do."

Some of the tension in her face dissipated as she tilted her head, studying him. "Is that so?"

He dipped his chin. "I talked to the guy, he explained what had happened, and just as we were speaking, lo and behold, in walks this older woman complaining she had the wrong order. She'd picked it up by mistake."

Her nose wrinkled. "So it's cold now?"

"Actually, I got them to make new ones." He leaned in slightly. "I figured you probably didn't want to eat pizza that had been half-eaten already."

"Hmm. No wonder you're a detective, figuring out stuff like that."

A chuckle pushed out despite his best intentions. "Are you always this snarky?"

Her lips pressed together, and she ducked her head. "I don't mean to be. I'm just so tired and frustrated about lots of things."

He knew the feeling. Clocking off today had been a joy, his new case teasing at his thoughts meant he'd been glad to put off thinking about it for a few hours longer. "Anyway," he shoved the pizza boxes at her, "here's your meatlovers and supreme. A nice choice, can I say."

She accepted the boxes, her face still tentative. "Um, thank you?"

He stifled a laugh. This chick certainly didn't make things easy. "You're welcome." He stepped back, back to his vehicle where his own pizza waited. "Have a good night."

"Uh, you too," she murmured, clutching the box in front of her.

"I hope your friends enjoy."

"My friends?"

He gestured to the pizza.

Her nose winkled. "Actually, it's just dinner for me. But not all at once," she rushed to add. "It's for a few nights. And maybe for some lunches too."

He bit back a smile at her explanation. "I'd eat a whole pizza if I could," he admitted. "They might mess up the occasional order, but it's the best I've eaten in years."

She nodded. "It's why I like to freeze one, then have it later."

Huh, good idea. "Which one were you going to freeze?"

"I don't know. I like them both, so maybe I'll half and half them, then freeze the other halves."

Forget good, that was a great idea. "I might just do the same."

"What have you got?"

"Chicken supreme and vegorama."

"They're my next two favorites."

He shrugged, the action seeming to propel words from his mouth. "You could always join me. I was going to the park to watch the sunset—"

Her mouth fell open.

"—but then I got waylaid."

"Delivering pizza?" she asked, her lips curled on one side.

"Look who could be a detective," he teased.

She ducked her head, her cheeks pink. "I, uh, I probably shouldn't."

A thin spear of regret shafted through his chest. "Because you do drugs and don't want to ruin your reputation?" he teased some more.

Her gaze shot up to meet his. "No. Why did you say that?"

Yeah, why had he? Honestly, it was like he didn't talk to people all the time. He usually could read people like a book. Even a blind person could see the woman was still nervy and tense. "I, um, I was joking."

"Just so you know, I've never done drugs. Not even weed. So I really don't appreciate the insinuation—"

"Whoa." He held up his hands. "It was a joke, a bad joke, but definitely not an insinuation. I'm sorry."

Judging from her stony expression, he guessed that would be a solid no to his invitation. "I guess I'll see you around then."

She licked her bottom lip.

He took a step back. "Unless you happen to feel like watching the sunset from near the bandstand in the park." His lips flicked up in something that would likely cause his brother to have a heart attack if he were to see.

"Um, thanks."

He didn't need to be a detective to recognize the "no" in that tone. He jerked his chin, swiveled, and moved away. Back to where his pizza lay waiting, slightly cooled and less appetizing now.

But because he believed in making good on his word, he drove to the lakeside park. He parked, picked up his pizza and a can of cola, and moved to a concrete table and bench near the rotunda, and watched the sky meld into Lake Muskoka. And as he ate his pizza, he swallowed the tiniest amount of disappointment.

CHAPTER 3

Why was she doing this? No clue. Blame the measure of inexplicable in her DNA. Anna parked, the pizza she'd just microwaved back to maximum heat in the box on the passenger seat, the aroma tantalizing her tastebuds. Call her crazy, but saying yes to meeting the detective felt fraught with danger. Not because she didn't trust him—police weren't perfect, but they probably had to try harder than most to be seen to be above the law. But because she didn't trust herself. Her heart was a fragile thing, inclined to leap ahead of reality and make assumptions not based on truth. And it had been a long time since her reality had witnessed a handsome man inviting her to have dinner. Even if it had sounded more like a pity invitation than anything real. While once upon a time she'd probably been desperate enough to accept a pity invitation, these days she was trying to have enough self-respect to not feel such a need.

From here she could see his broad back, the way his shirt hugged his shoulders, the way he really did seem to be checking out the sky. Just like she had wanted to.

How bizarre that she would encounter someone who seemed to enjoy the same things she did. She wondered what he would do if she plonked herself and her pizza next to him.

She swallowed. Here went nothing, then. A twig cracked as she moved to him, and he turned as she slid onto the bench seat, near but not too close, and placed the pizza boxes on the table.

"You came." Surprise lit his face, his voice textured in something that sounded like pleasure. "I wasn't sure you would."

"I'm not sure I should be either, seeing I don't even know your name."

He blinked. "Oh, man. I thought I'd said something."

"You flashed a badge, but I didn't get your name."

He held out his hand. "Tom Woodmore."

She eyed it, then gently touched it with her own before dropping it instantly. Too much heat lay there. "Anna Morely."

His eyes crinkled. "I know."

Of course he did. She sighed. "Anyway, it's a pretty night, and believe it or not, and at the risk of you thinking that I'm a stalker, I actually was going to do this myself."

His lips twisted. "Great minds, huh?"

She nodded. Already she could feel some of the tension leave, the angst and pressure of the past hour dissipating in the beauty of the sky. Although she was conscious of a new tension thrumming below the surface as her heart begged to run ahead with what eating with this man might mean. So it was probably best she start eating now. She opened the box, nearly salivating at the smell.

He groaned as she picked up a slice of meatlovers. "That smells so good."

Mmm. Her taste-buds exploded with happiness, as she kept her eye on the lake and swallowed her mouthful. "It *is* so good."

For a moment, they both concentrated on eating, on watching the lake, and in the serene beauty of the scene she felt some of the tension leave. She usually felt so edgy, but this was nice. Better than nice. And the fact she was eating here, with a man, even though he'd seen the raw side of her several times now, felt a little wondrous.

But no, she told her hormones firmly. *We're not getting carried away. This was a pity invitation, remember?* Maybe if she didn't look at him, and just concentrated on the pretty sky, then she might survive the meal with her heart intact.

She finished her first slice, started on the second. Supreme this time. Too bad if he thought women were supposed to eat daintily. That so wasn't her. *Not that we're trying to impress him, remember?*

A flock of birds arrowed across the sky, merging with the thin ribbons of cloud that the sun's lowering rays had painted gold. She studied the birds, wondering where they were going, whether they longed for freedom. And while she'd often longed to escape her small home town, right now, in this moment, she was glad to be here, to witness that, and enjoy the beauty of her surrounds. To enjoy this feeling, a feeling she hadn't known for a long time, but which felt a little like… peace.

Tom picked up his next slice. "I'm glad you came. I've got to admit after the way you avoided me in the nut shop, I wasn't sure you trusted me."

Oh, that. She winced. What a child she could be. "I figured there was safety in an open space."

"You figured right."

"I don't know you enough to know whether I shouldn't trust you yet," she countered, peeking across.

His half smile caused her stomach to loop the loop. Then she realized what she'd said. "Oh."

"Hey, I know what you mean." He gestured to her pizza. "That sure looks good."

"Want to trade?" she asked.

"Like we're in grade school? I'll swap my banana for your apple?"

"Sorry, I only have supreme and meatlovers, no banana or apple here. But that's okay."

"No, that's not okay. You can't say something like that and then take it back."

"Is that against the law?"

"One hundred percent."

She picked up another slice of supreme then pushed the box nearer him. "Save me a piece of meatlovers."

"Are you sure?"

She nodded, then said around another mouthful of cheese-draped olives and anchovies, "I love meatlovers."

Tom hesitated, his hands hovering over a piece. "I meant…"

She snickered. Oh, she knew what he had meant, but took great delight in confounding him again. It had been so long since she'd bantered with any man, this experience was making her feel almost giddy.

He glanced at her, and she felt the weight of his gaze on her skin, but concentrated on eating like a lady, and not like the hippopotamus she tended to become when she ate on her own.

Around them, the park was pretty empty. The heavens didn't seem to care though, now arrayed in streaks of rose and gold. She swallowed her last mouthful and tipped her head backwards as she studied the sky. So beautiful. She totally understood why he had come. It was the exact same reason she had. A time to savor a rare moment of beauty in this world.

"It's so beautiful," she murmured.

"You know the heavens declare the glory of the Lord," he murmured.

She froze. Was Tom a believer?

She shifted her gaze to the lake, soft with its gentle swell, the slightest undulations evidence of the wake from a faraway boat likely heading home.

"Hey." He nudged his box closer to her. "Have at it."

She glanced at his remaining slices. Chicken supreme and the vegetable one. Her mouth salivated. "Are you sure?"

"I don't say things I don't mean." He offered a crooked smile. "Besides, I'm fully planning to relieve you of that piece of supreme, so go for it."

Very well, then. She scooped up the slice. It wasn't as hot as hers was, but that wasn't surprising. But despite the temperature, it still tasted as it should: creamy, cheesy chicken goodness. "So good."

Tom smiled, raised his eyebrows at her, and touched the side of his mouth.

She touched the side of hers, and picked at a string of that cheesy goodness. Fantastic. Way to go with any attempt to impress. She was *so* classy. Not. Mom would be disappointed in her.

"Were you saving that for Ron?"

"For who?"

"Ron." He shrugged. "Sorry, it's a dumb joke my dad always likes to say. Like food crumbs are being saved for later on, Ron."

"Are you a dad?" she asked. Weirdly, with this almost-stranger, she felt no compunction to behave like she might normally would.

Tom choked. "No. I'm not married either, if that was your next question."

"It wasn't." But still, good to know.

"Then why?"

"Because dad jokes should really only be said by dads. You look too young to be telling them."

"How old do you think I am?"

This was a game that never ended well. "I don't know. Mid-thirties?"

"So not too young to be a dad."

She guessed not.

The silence stretching between them was filled with the next question, one she'd never ask anyone to ask her. But she might as well say it, just to snap the tension. "I'm thirty-one."

"I know."

"You do? How—oh." She exhaled. "It really seems unfair you know all this stuff about me just because you looked me up."

"Hey, I can't help it if I have a good memory."

"So that's how you knew where I lived."

"Actually, confession time: I remembered the street name but not the house number of your address. But then I recognized your car and figured you'd likely be home, so it seemed rude to not call in with your food."

"It would've been really rude," she agreed, swallowing a smile.

Huh. He'd actually tried to find her, even if his defensiveness suggested he didn't want her to think him a stalker.

"So, is this even allowed?" she asked.

"What?"

She gestured between them. "You know, you and me eating together." Like on a date.

"It's not like you're a criminal." He arched a brow. "Unless there's something that isn't on your background check."

"No!"

He smirked. "That's what they all say."

She swatted him, and he chuckled.

"Obviously nobody has picked up on your propensity to violence."

She snapped the lid closed on her pizza. "I think I've had enough."

"Aw, don't go. This has been nice. And back to your question from before, it's fine to eat at a park, and share a table with a fellow human—"

She rated as a fellow human? Wow.

"—and make the most of a pretty night. It's not as if this is a date, now, is it?"

"No." Disappointment sang in her soul. Although why she was disappointed he was agreeing with her she didn't care to explore. Maybe it was simply because she was so starved for affection, she clung to any crumb that might possibly be regarded as more. But as he'd just made clear, she counted as a fellow human, nothing more. Which really set the bar high. And caused her heart to sting. And maybe the backs of her eyes to smart.

She took a swig of water. She wasn't going to rush out of here like she was upset about his acknowledging the lack of date-ness. But neither was she going to linger and give her senses time to further notice and appreciate things like his woodsy scent, or the muscles in his forearms. She pushed the box away. She had to get out of here.

He motioned to his remaining slice of vegetable pizza, and she shook her head. "Thanks, but I should go soon."

"But the sky is at peak loveliness."

Now that was a phrase she'd never thought to hear a police detective say. She smiled.

"What's that look for?"

Anna's shoulders lifted, dropped. "I don't know."

"Yes, you do."

She peered at him. "Is that how you interrogate suspects?"

"Only if they're suspect."

She rolled her eyes at that one, while amusement bubbled like fizzing water inside. From their first few interactions she never would've suspected the man to have a sense of humor, and yet he did. And even with the corny dad jokes it wasn't terrible. But what was terrible was that she could feel herself on that slippery slope where she could start to really like a guy, only to fall headlong into disappointment again. Which she so wasn't going to do.

So she moved, inched away, then stood. "Well, thanks."

"You're welcome. Thank you for trusting me enough to watch a sunset with me."

She nodded, the words "any time" begging to trip off her tongue. She bit them back. Found a small smile.

"You know, we could do this again some time," he said.

"Arrange to meet at a park and share pizza?"

"Or arrange to meet somewhere else and have a meal."

She bit her lip. They could, but it probably wasn't wise. Not for her needy heart.

"But you don't want to. I get it. And hey, I suppose I should have led with this, but I got distracted before."

"Got distracted from what?"

"About my comment about the heavens. Only, I'm curious about whether you believe in God."

God? "Why?"

"Because it's um, important to me that my, uh, friends share in that experience."

"You only want Christian friends?"

"No. But maybe I only want Christian female friends."

"Are you saying you don't have any male Christian friends?"

"No, I'm not saying that." He half-smiled. "You're pretty sharp, huh?"

"Sometimes." Other times she could be as clueless as a baby raccoon in the Sahara. "See you around, detective."

"Wait. You didn't answer my question."

"Which one?"

"The one about God. Are you a Christian?"

His question slammed into her chest with the force of a meteor. Yes, she was. Or she had been. But God had felt so far away for months now, she barely knew if that counted. Still, she'd learned over years of church attendance and Bible study that faith wasn't based on a feeling. And the Bible did say nothing could separate her from God's love, so she guessed that meant she still was. So she nodded.

Tom smiled, and her heart shivered.

No, we're not doing that again. Just because he has a nice smile it doesn't mean anything. Stop getting carried away. She was going to have to play it cooler than ice.

"So, in that case, how about the second one."

"The second what?"

"The second question. About doing something like this again sometime."

She shrugged, picking up her near-empty pizza box. "You're the detective. I guess you're going to have to detect."

She could've fist-pumped herself as she strode away, her movie-worthy exit only hampered by the near empty pizza box she held. Still, that had been one of her finer moments.

A shriek of laughter drew her attention to a couple of benches on the opposite side of the rotunda. Her steps slowed, and then quickly picked up pace as she recognized those picnickers.

What was happening? Why had they decided to come here? Oh, she hoped they hadn't seen her with the nice detective. She hurried to her car, placed the pizza box on the passenger seat, then prayed for her car to start the first time. No way did she want to be seen by any of them.

The good vibes from earlier dissipated, the familiar disgruntlement spreading across her chest. How dare they abandon her, then go on leaving her out of things, like she was no longer somebody they needed to include? That hurt as much as anything else. Oh, she was so tired of this.

As she drove away, her phone rang. She checked the dash's screen and recognized the number. Her mom. Well, she'd likely leave a message, probably about the two of them having dinner tomorrow night, even though Anna always had dinner there on

Thursday nights, and her mom always called to remind her. The call ended, and a voicemail was left, and she tapped the screen for the message which the car's stereo spoke aloud to her.

"Anna darling, it's your mother speaking. I trust you are happy and keeping well."

Her mother could trust all she liked. It didn't mean it was true.

"I'm just calling to remind you that we are due to have dinner tomorrow night. I'm looking forward to catching up and hearing all your news."

That made one of them.

"So I'll see you at six. And if you have a special friend you might want to bring, or if you'd like me to find one for you, let me know. Oh, and while I'm thinking of it, I was talking today with some of my friends at the country club, so if you're needing a date for the Summer Ball, please let me know. See you tomorrow, sweetie."

The message clicked off, and she steered onto Maple Street, her nose wrinkling at her mom's reminder.

Bless her mother. Her mom's world had basically shrunk to seeing Anna married with a tribe of children. Which did not fit Anna's plans at all. Not the tribe of children, anyway. One or two would be nice. Maybe. Not that she liked children overly. Rachel's little girl, Jemima, was sweet, and she imagined Serena's children would be perfect little angels. And yes, Toni's son was gorgeous. But on the whole, she didn't really like kids, and they didn't really seem to like her, which was okay.

Not every woman had to be maternal. Even if this particular woman sometimes wondered what it would be like to have her own kids, to have a man who not only loved her, but was good with children too. But that thought seemed as impossible as touching the evening star, now glittering high in the lilac sky.

And while she'd just eaten with a man who might believe in God, and by extension, perhaps believed in miracles, she knew she'd need something of atomic-levels of the miraculous to untangle the mess in her heart. Seeing her former friends had reminded her she wasn't in a good place, and could barely trust herself to make good decisions with her relationships these days. So while she'd had fun with Tom tonight, it was probably best to leave it in the too hard basket, and let hopes of anything more die. That way she'd save herself from the inevitability of heartbreak.

"Woodmore? We need you in the interview room."

Tom looked up from his computer. "I'll be there in two minutes." He saved the file he was working on, quickly checked his email, then grabbed his jacket, interview pad and pen, filled up his mug with the criminally bad brew they called coffee here, and headed through the rabbit warren of rooms to the interview room.

Inside sat the police constable who'd alerted him along with a man he vaguely recognized.

Jones glanced at him, then rose. "Here he is now. Detective Woodmore, this is Pastor Joel Wakefield, who has alerted us to a possible situation north of here."

"Thanks, Jones." Tom held out a hand which Joel gripped as Jones departed. "Detective Tom Woodmore. You're from the Muskoka Shores community church, right?"

"I've been assisting there for a few years now, yes." Joel squinted. "Now I think of it, I've seen you there before, haven't I? Was it a service or a wedding?"

Tom snapped his fingers. "A wedding. Toni and Matt."

"That's right. Toni is my sister. You helped put her stalker behind bars."

"Yes." Her ex had basically put himself behind bars, with his confessions. "That was a good result. How are they doing now?"

"Toni and Matt are doing very well, praise God."

"Amen," he said, without thinking.

Joel arched a brow.

Yeah, Tom didn't exactly hide his faith at work, but he didn't make a habit of Amen-ing either. "I attend your opposition," he confessed. The church where his folks had always attended.

Joel smiled. "It's good to meet another brother, no matter where he attends."

True. "So, I suppose we should get down to business." He motioned to the recording machine. "Is it okay if we record?" At Joel's nod he switched it on, gave the date and time, and his name and Joel's. "What is it that has brought you in today, Pastor Wakefield?"

Joel sighed. "I wish I had something more concrete, but perhaps you're similar to me, and you get a sense when something is not on the straight and narrow."

He nodded. One of the things that made him good at his job was a sixth sense about people and situations. He figured Joel might call it the gift of discernment. "I do." He leaned back in his chair, took a sip of bitter coffee. Hid his wince. "So what's got you concerned?"

Joel leaned forward, his elbows on the interview table, his fingers clasped like he could be praying. "So, yesterday I was called out to a property a little north of here to witness some documents. I get asked to do that sometimes."

Tom nodded, letting Joel tell his story his way. Too often people who were guided too closely tended to leave out details that later proved important. Letting people tell things at their own pace made them feel comfortable, which could lead to them spilling more. "Where was this?"

"The Muskoka Ferns Lodge."

Tom made a note of that.

"It's about ten miles north from here. It's a low-cost residential lodge for the disadvantaged."

He nodded, the facts slotting into recognition. He'd heard about it, but not in any official capacity before. "And what was it that raised alarm bells?"

A sigh escaped the pastor. "It was the fact I was asked to witness these signatures from some of the residents there, then when I arrived the documents were already signed."

Tom glanced up. Uh oh. "What were the documents for?" One guess…

"That it would give the owners permission to change the residents' bank accounts and have their welfare cheques deposited directly into their own account."

Bingo. His pulse increased. "Do you recall the name of the account they were supposed to be changed into?"

"Strong Hearts Inc. When I asked the property manager what that was, I was told it's a non-profit, and that this was being done to facilitate things more easily."

Tom wrote that down. "Did you ask why the documents were already signed?"

"The manager of the facility just laughed it off, saying it was an accident, but something about how he dismissed things so easily didn't sit right with me."

"Did you speak with any of the residents?"

"I tried, but the ones I was directed to talk to, well, they couldn't talk. From what I could gather they might be deaf, or mute. I don't know if some might even have certain psychiatric issues, but whatever it was, something wasn't right."

No, something definitely wasn't right. That same tingling awareness that had helped him in his job before was activated in full Spidey-sense mode now. Still, he had to do things by the book, collect the evidence, not just go with his gut. "Were you able to communicate with any of the residents and confirm this?"

Joel shook his head. "I ended up leaving without signing, and after praying about the situation, I felt I should come here and report it. I thought you should know, because I have a feeling the managers might try to do that with someone else, who may not be so…"

Tom waited, wanting but not daring to finish the man's sentence. This was where he had to stay patient, to not allow any accusations of bias to come into play.

A wince crossed Joel's face. "Scrupulous?"

Tom did his best to stay impassive. He'd been blessed with a face that gave little away, which made him good at his job, if not great at other things. Like smiling, or showing emotion too easily. "So, you're saying…?"

He let that sentence hang in the air, waiting for Joel to finish.

Joel sighed. "I'm saying I have concerns about that place, about the management there, that they might be coercing their residents to pay for substandard care."

"Substandard?"

The pastor wrinkled his nose. "I couldn't help but notice some of the facilities there looked poorly looked after."

"Such as?"

"Such as missing hand railings, and broken steps. For a facility that says it cares for the elderly those seemed like real hazards to me."

They seemed like red flags to Tom. "Did you say anything to anyone?"

"I asked John Vanderman, the property manager, about it and he assured me they had a local contractor come and deal with things on a regular basis."

"Did he give you a name?"

"Taylor Constructions. They're local, attend my church. Good people."

Tom nodded, writing that down too. "Do you have anything else to add?"

"No. But I am concerned, and happy to do whatever I can to

help. I hate to think that vulnerable members of our community might be getting taken advantage of in this way."

Tom studied him. "Have you had dealings with them at all before?"

"Never. But I only moved here a few years ago."

"You said you were an assistant pastor. Does that mean your head pastor might know more about this place?"

"I will ask him. John McPherson. He's the one who officiated Toni's wedding."

An older man. Tom remembered now. "I'll call him, and see what he might have to add. I don't suppose you remember the name of the legal firm these documents were filed with?"

Joel mentioned the name of a business based in the next town north, another Tom would have to investigate.

"Thank you. I'm afraid I'm going to have to ask you to write this all out and sign it." It might be early days, but getting a potential witness to write an affidavit would help in facilitating further investigations. Like convincing a judge to obtain a search warrant.

"No problem. Like I said, I'm happy to help."

"Thank you." Tom switched off the recording machine, retrieved several sheets of paper used for these purposes, then gave Joel two pens. There was no point in things taking longer with a pen that didn't work. "We really appreciate it. Now, would you like a coffee while you do that?"

Joel eyed Tom's mug. "I don't know if I'm willing to risk that. Call me weak, but I much prefer Suzy's from The Coffee Blend."

"So do I, but she's not exactly next door."

"I'll be fine." Joel motioned to the page.

"Please add anything else you think we should know. I'll be back in a few minutes."

Joel nodded, head already bent to the task as he began writing.

Tom slipped away, and found his boss, Gabe Doughty, then waited in the door of Gabe's office while he finished his call.

"What is it, Woodmore?" He gestured to the seat on the other side of his desk.

"I think we might have a situation at a residential care facility further north." He sat then briefly outlined what Joel had said, finishing with, "I'm going to talk with these people Joel mentioned, but I wanted to know if there were any other incidents reported to this place."

"Muskoka Ferns Lodge." Gabe's brow wrinkled. "I seem to recall something about that place, but can't place it. Have you checked the records?"

"Not yet. But I figured the person who'd been working here longer than anyone else might know more than what gets officially written up."

"I'll have to get back to you. I can't remember everything, but there were definitely some rumors once upon a time. See what you can find out in the records, and I'll do a deep dive into the recesses of my mind and see what I can remember."

"Thanks, boss."

Tom returned to check on Joel, who said he was about halfway there, so Tom returned to his desk and pulled up the files on Muskoka Ferns Lodge. Huh. An elderly man had been reported missing about a decade ago, but no trace had ever been found of him. He drummed his desk, frowning. It wasn't crazy uncommon for people to go missing, especially elderly people with dementia, who might wander off into the woods and meet with an accident. He'd worked on cases where despite the best tracking available, people could seem to literally disappear. But the fact this hadn't been followed up recently, and was connected to the same place, raised more of those internal warning signals.

He returned to the boss's office, popped his head in. "Missing person."

His boss's face cleared. "That's right. Hmm. Maybe it's time for you to revisit that one too."

Tom saluted and returned to find Joel was signing off his statement. "All good?"

"I hope so. I might've added a few more things, some names I remember, that I hope help."

"I really do appreciate this, Joel, and if it's what it sounds like, then I think there will be some very appreciative members of that community, too."

Joel stood, and stretched out his hand. "I'll be praying."

Tom gripped his hand. "So will I."

"Thank you. I don't know how you manage dealing with such things."

"It's all part of the job. I imagine your role isn't always easy either."

"That's the truth."

Hmm. Tom's family might be Christians, but finding others who understood the gritty underside of life and still chose to believe were few and far between. Some of his colleagues preferred numbing the reality of what they saw and had to deal with via alcohol or other means.

Joel smiled. "Maybe one day, if you don't think your church folk would mind, we should get a coffee. I promise, no poaching."

"That'd be good."

Tom waited as Joel got into his car, his gaze snagging on a red car that drove slowly past. His lips twitched, remembering last night's pizza non-date with the owner of a red vehicle, and he wondered how she was doing. Maybe it was stupid, but the persistent tug of appeal had made it hard to sleep last night, as for the first time in a long time he hadn't spent the night with his mind scrolling through his various cases. Whether it was the beauty of the peace-inducing night skies or the fun he'd had with Anna's sass and snark, he'd found himself thinking about her instead, and wondering just what she'd meant by that last comment. She'd wanted him to "detect" if she wanted a date, huh? Challenge accepted.

He moved back inside, his thoughts shooting back to his new case, to Joel, Toni, the wedding.

Then he blinked, remembering. He now knew exactly where he'd encountered Miss Anna Morely before.

CHAPTER 4

"*H*ey, Mom. Good to see you."

Anna exchanged a barely-there kiss with her mom, then her mother gestured down the hall from where delicious scents suggested the usual Thursday night meal was nearly ready. One guess: baked salmon and salad, just like Mom had started preparing ever since she'd first commented on Anna's more curvaceous size several months ago.

And while Anna didn't mind salmon, the fact her mom was obviously trying to "manage" her diet, at least on Thursday nights, made her feel like a little kid again. Her dad's lies and her mom's interference were part of why she'd moved out of their home as soon as she could afford a mortgage, into a home two doors down from where Staci Everton lived with her grandmother, Rose. Or had, until Staci had married James on New Year's Eve. She wasn't sure where they lived now.

Sure enough, a healthy-looking tossed salad awaited in the blue glass bowl that it was always served in. Beyond the dining room's windows, the waters of Lake Muskoka shimmered softly, pale peach in the late afternoon light.

"Want me to set the table?" she asked, as she always did.

"You know where everything is."

She sure did. Ever since her parents had divorced, her mom had insisted on these weekly dinners, as a way of "connecting as a family" again. And while at times she had chafed under the "little girl" mantle, in the past months of estrangement from her friends she had really appreciated the routine. Even if some of what her mom talked about felt foreign these days.

As her mom retrieved the salmon from the oven, Anna collected the knives and forks and set the table, with both place settings facing the view as per usual. One of the advantages in coming here was the gorgeous scenery to look out on. Mom's settlement in the divorce had seen her obtain this amazing house in a gated community along one of the more ritzy streets lining the lake. Of course, it wasn't anywhere near as fancy as those a little further away, like NHL player, Dan Walton, who owned a place next door to his wife's aunt and uncle, John and Angela McPherson. John just so happened to be the pastor of the church Anna no longer attended—yep, it was a small world. Rumor had it that Lincoln Cash had bought the house on the other side of the McPhersons. That area, known for its celebrity summer "cottages," had houses triple the size of her mom's. Well, she imagined they would be, having not been inside, apart from John and Angela's once or twice, and theirs was unpretentious and normal-sized, a real cottage, not a celebrity summer retreat.

"The lake looks so pretty at this time of day, doesn't it?" Anna said.

"Did you see the sunset yesterday? Simply stunning."

Anna nodded, conscious of whom she'd eaten with yesterday. Her smile flickered. She wondered if he'd thought of her again. Probably not.

Her mom soon served the meal, and placed the slice of salmon on Anna's plate, along with a healthy portion of salad. No bread, though. Her mom didn't believe in what she called unnecessary carbohydrates, which led to a sad lack of bread at every meal. Still, the knowledge Anna had plenty of bread stashed at home for a late-night snack, if necessary, would help her get this much lighter meal down. And while she enjoyed it, it didn't quite compare with last night's pizza.

"What's that look for, honey?" her mom asked.

Anna instantly flattened her lips. "Nothing." She forked a mouthful of lettuce in.

"Oh, come on. I can tell it was something. What have you been up to lately? Have you seen your friends at all?"

"No, Mom." Why her mother persisted in this erroneous belief that Anna was still friends with Serena, Jackie, and the others was another of those skin-crawling elements to having a meal here. Her mom seemed deaf to Anna's complaints about the injustice, and had said more than once that Anna should forgive them. Which seemed ironic from a woman who had chosen not to forgive her husband's betrayal, and had divorced instead, but such was life.

"Oh, that's such a shame. I really feel like—"

"Actually, Rachel came in to the doctor's yesterday. I spoke to her then." To tell her to sit down, and to take her money, but that counted, right? She hoped her mom would buy it, anyway.

"That's good." Her mom's worry lines eased. "And how is she?"

"Much the same." Although Rachel had seemed quieter, which was odd.

"You know, I heard a funny rumor about your friend Jackie."

Anna stiffened, and concentrated on lifting her fork to her mouth. She wouldn't ask or give her mom a moment of grist for the rumor mill.

"Apparently she's quit her job at Golden Elms."

Anna's attention snapped to her mom's face. She swallowed the lump of fish painfully. "Really?"

"You didn't know?"

"No." And she kind of hated not knowing things. Why had Jackie quit? She loved working with the elderly.

"They say it's because of her boyfriend, that she keeps jetting off to see him."

Anna pressed her lips together, as thoughts of Lincoln Cash mingled with the stew of resentment. How dare Jackie judge her, when she was having goodness-knew-what trysts with Lincoln? Talk about a hypocrite.

But she couldn't let her mom see how much she resented this, so she asked the question that she knew would shift the focus off her and result in an avalanche of her mother's no-need-to-respond chatter. "So, how goes the preparations for the Summer Ball?"

"Oh!" Her mother's eyes lit, as if she could finally share what she'd been secretly wanting Anna to enquire about. "I'm so glad you've asked."

Thus began a lengthy account of various issues that her mother, and various other women on the Muskoka Charity Fundraising committee—the Musko-cheers, they liked to call themselves—were facing, including a change of venue to the grand ballroom at the Muskoka Shores Resort.

Anna stilled. Serena Williamson—now Wakefield—worked there, as the events coordinator. Or she had, last time she'd heard. Did the change of venue now mean—

"Of course, this means I'm working with Serena, you know. She says hello, by the way."

Anna nodded, sipping her water, in an attempt to avoid replying.

Her mother continued, not needing Anna's answers, which was just as well. Regret gnarled heavy across her chest. This was not supposed to be how tonight went. It was supposed to be a simple meal, a quick catch up, not a dive into personal recriminations. For how could she keep blaming all her friends when they were obviously making attempts to reach out? Rachel had, and now Serena. They'd both kept trying, even making the effort to send flowers for her birthday last month, whereas she… She hadn't done anything.

"…which is why we are trying to finalize things so we can open the tickets next week."

"Tickets?"

"Oh my goodness, Anna, where is your head at these days? It's like you haven't been listening to a word I've said."

"Oh, I've been listening." Sort of.

"So, have you found a partner for the ball?"

"Mom, you know I don't have a boyfriend. And no," she cut her mother off. "I don't need you to try to find me someone."

"I was just going to say that Kyle is still single, and might appreciate a gentle nudge from Heather."

"I really don't need you interfering."

As soon as that last word escaped, she knew it was a mistake as her mother's face tightened. Mom preferred to call it caring, not interfering, and resented whenever Anna mislabeled her good intentions.

"Mom, I know you are looking out for me, but I'm not sure I even want to go. I don't have anything to wear, anyway."

"You would if you didn't keep eating junk food, my dear."

Anna winced. So complaining about a lack of appropriate formal attire was not the answer to getting out of things.

"Come on. It's always for a good cause."

"Remind me which good cause it is this year?"

"Oh, Anna, I can't believe you can't remember, especially as I've been talking about this all night." Her mom sighed. "This year's ball is raising money for the Strong Hearts Foundation."

"Which is? Sorry, Mom, I'm so tired."

"They do work you hard at the clinic, don't they?"

And she might've spent a little too long staying up watching a few old episodes of *Law & Order*. Something about Tom reminded her of a young Benjamin Bratt. Maybe it was his dark eyes.

"The Strong Hearts Foundation is a non-profit Heather started a few years ago. Remember? Heather asked me to be part of the board. It's designed to help those who are underprivileged find housing."

"That's right."

"Well, you know each year the Musko-cheers like to raise money for a different charity, and it's been a few years since we've supported Strong Hearts, so we're doing it again."

"Great." Although it had always seemed a little strange to her. If Heather cared so much about the poor, then why didn't she just sell one of her many houses? Surely that would be better than all the hard work involved in putting on a charity event. Not that she'd say that. The last time she had—five years ago—had made for a very frosty response from her mom, and given their relationship was so much better now, she had no intention to return to Siberia anytime soon.

Fine then. Mom won. Again. "Is there anything I can help you with for the ball?"

"Oh, you are a good daughter, aren't you?" her mother cooed. "Well, I'm so glad you asked, because actually there is quite a lot left to do…"

IT WAS late by the time she returned home, having agreed to help her mom with the tickets and organizing table seating among other things. She passed Rose Everton's house, then slowed, passing one more, then turned into her drive. Maybe she could've walked to her mother's and gotten more exercise which might help with fitting into one of her ballroom gowns again. Oh well. There was always tomorrow. She'd try to eat more healthily and exercise, at least for the next few weeks until the ball.

When she parked, she noticed a small package by her door. They didn't have a problem with parcel delivery thieves here in Muskoka Shores. Not that she knew of, anyway.

She locked her car then moved closer. The small flat brown box was written in black marker and addressed to Miss Anna Morely, which made her smile. She was so used to being Anna that to have had Detective Woodmore use her full name like this recently felt rather quaint and chivalrous.

She studied the handwriting. The block letters looked masculine. Was it from him? Nobody else called her that. But why would he be sending her something? Really, she had to get a grip, to tamp down the tickle of anticipation at the thought it might be from him.

Once inside, she opened it. And discovered a voucher to The Coffee Blend, and a flyer advertising an upcoming event, where dinner-type food would be served along with the usual pastries and light meals. This Friday night was circled, along with a question mark. But there was nothing else. Which made her smile, then wonder. Okay, so this had to be Tom, right? And it had to be his way of "detecting" whether she wanted to go out with him again.

The urge to call Serena to discuss this with her—to call an emergency "soiree" like in the past to find out what she should do—grew. Then slowly faded.

No. She'd better not. She'd bet Serena would only tell the others and they'd all gossip about her behind her back like they probably already were doing. No, Anna would do better to keep this a secret. And enjoy the fact that a man like Tom might actually want to spend time with her at all.

TOM NODDED to Gabe as his boss drew near Tom's desk. Files and pictures lay across the desk surface, an organized mess some might call it, but he knew where everything was. It wasn't his preferred method of research, but when he was forced to work in such a limited space, and the case seemed to be fast moving, peeling away layers like an onion, it was the best he had.

Gabe sank into the nearby spare chair belonging to a colleague who was currently on leave. "Looks like you've been busy with the Muskoka Ferns Lodge case." He nodded to the portable whiteboard Tom had set up nearby. "Hit me."

Tom pointed to the whiteboard, where a range of names were listed. "I've gone through the statements from Joel, the pastor who first mentioned the signed documents. From the names he gave me I've called the others, including Joel's boss, John McPherson, and the contractor they've used, Damian Taylor. Neither John nor Damian have gone there, but Damian did mention that his father, who used to run the company, might know something. So I've been on the phone with him this morning, and learned that he last visited the Lodge a number of years ago."

"And?"

"When I asked, he said, quote, 'my dogs have a better place to stay in than those poor people' unquote." Tom's fingers clenched. "It seems there were problems with the lack of bath-rooms, and a lack of insulation, but he wasn't told to fix those problems, only the more pressing ones."

"He didn't report it?"

"He said he did, but I haven't had a chance to follow up with community services yet."

"Do it." Gabe frowned. "It sounds like we're getting closer to having something to put to a judge for an ITO."

Tom nodded. The Information To Obtain search warrants presented to a judge could include everything from hearsay evidence to concrete facts. "I worked on a similar sounding case in the city, along with the drug squad and money laundering unit. I've checked some of those reports and a colleague from the fraud squad mentioned a discrepancy concerning John Vanderman, the property manager, whose name also appeared on a property infraction, something about a tax infringement."

"So that's two strikes. Anything else?"

"Well, as we mentioned yesterday, there is also the case of the missing resident. A Mister…" Tom checked his notes. "A Mr. Carl Lethbridge, aged 72, who went missing ten years ago. I checked the notes, sir, and it seems the case was left unsolved."

His boss sighed. "We didn't have the resources back then that we do now."

"Well, I took a look into it, and checked his name against the social security database, and it seems his cheques were still being mailed to the address even after his sister reported him missing."

"Which address was that? No, let me guess: the Muskoka Ferns Lodge."

Tom's chin dipped. "I know it was ten years ago, but coupled with what Joel has said, and what else we know, I wonder if that's enough for us to present to a judge."

"You want a search warrant?"

"I do, but first I'd like to see the place, and get the lay of the land myself."

"You can visit. You don't need a search warrant for that."

"Yeah, but if there is something shady going on, I don't want to give them a heads up that there is something they need to hide."

"But a search warrant requires a lot of resource, and I'm sorry, after the failed attempt of ten years ago, I don't see an easy way of getting the higher ups to sign off on that."

Tom chewed his lip. Executing a search warrant was a big deal, so he understood the concerns. Especially if there was no result. *Lord? What do I do?*

Tom paused, as an idea took on substance. "I wonder…"

"Wonder what?"

"How would you feel if I volunteered myself to work undercover as an offsider to Damien Taylor? Joel believes that they will ask Taylor Constructions to do some more building work. If they do, this could be a good way to sniff around and get a sense of things before going in with the big guns."

"It could, if they ask them." Gabe's head tilted. "You've done a little undercover work before, haven't you?"

"A little. Not too much. But this is more of a one-day job. Get in, get out, get it done. They'd barely notice me, so don't need to be any the wiser."

"And you think this Damian Taylor person would be open to that?"

"I think from what Joel has said that Damian, who attends his church, would be horrified to know what his father has said about the state of the place and would be willing to help."

Gabe lifted a brow. "Could you pull this off? Do you have any experience in construction?"

"I can hammer a nail and I've put up a sheet or two of drywall."

"Then see what you can find out. Of course, that's dependent on them using Taylor Constructions again."

"Which they might do if Joel was to call and say he's of a mind to report their premises as unsafe."

Gabe's eyebrows shot up. "He'd do that?"

"I get the feeling he'd be happy to."

"Well." Gabe nodded, his gaze thoughtful as he studied the whiteboard. "That still isn't a guarantee they'll use Taylor for the work—"

"It does mean they will be scared into fixing the premises, which I guess is a win for those residents, either way."

"You seem to really care about this," Gabe said, eyeing him thoughtfully.

"Absolutely. I hate to see injustice."

"Hmm. Well, tread carefully. Those names up there," Gabe pointed to the top of the whiteboard, "are not without money or influence."

Tom was aware of that too. "Which is why I'd prefer to investigate without alerting their suspicions."

Gabe's phone buzzed, and he glanced at the screen then sighed, pushing to his feet. "Okay, well keep me informed." He pointed to Tom. "And good work."

"It'll be good if we get to the bottom of this," Tom said.

"Always. Now don't forget, you don't have to work the weekend, so make sure you take a break, do something fun."

"Yes, sir."

"And I don't mean going to the gym or visiting the shooting range." He cocked his head at him. "I might've heard a rumor about a certain detective having a date at the lake with a lady friend."

Tom's cheeks heated. "That wasn't really a date."

"You are allowed to have a social life though, son." He paused, considering. "Just be careful who you're seen with, especially if you want to get involved in this undercover business."

He nodded, as Gabe left, and wondered what he meant. For all Tom didn't know Anna Morely well, he knew the most important basics. She was a Christian. She was single. She had a great smile. And a snarky, fun sense of humor.

Anything else he hoped to find out on tomorrow night, when he hoped, if she chose to come, that he could detect enough interest to take this further.

CHAPTER 5

Friday. End of the week. Anna glanced at the clinic's clock, counting down the hours. She wasn't rostered on for the clinic's Saturday morning shift tomorrow, which left her free to help her mom with organizing for the ball. Already she could feel how important this would be to her mom, and given the fact her lack of a social life these days meant she was a lot more free and available, she didn't have the ready excuse of previous years. Ah, well.

The phone rang, and she answered automatically, only realizing partway through that the voice sounded familiar. Mrs. Trudy Peterson, the church secretary.

"Anna?" Trudy asked. "Is that you?"

Anna swallowed. It was amazing how she'd been able to avoid so many people from church these past months, and now it seemed she'd been hit by the ghosts of Christmas past wherever she went. "Yes."

"Oh, honey, how are you?"

Emotion balled in her throat, refusing her reply.

"I'm sorry. I know you're very busy. I just wanted you to know we've missed you."

Anna cleared her throat. Tried for a "thank you" but it sounded more like a sniffle-grunt.

A flashing light indicated another call was coming through, so she coughed, managed a more clear-sounding "thanks" and "see you on the seventeenth at ten with Dr. Morgan," and hung up, then took the next call. Christians. Honestly. What was with the caring all the time?

This next caller was not so easy to deal with, however, complaining when Anna told him that Dr. Wells didn't have availability for two more weeks.

"But I need to see him today."

"I'm sorry, he's very popular, and only works here part time. You could see another of our doctors—"

"I don't want another one. I want him."

"Well, sometimes we have cancellations, so I can add you to the waiting list if you like."

"How long is that list?"

She checked. "You'd be number five."

"Are you serious?"

"As I said, he's a very popular doctor. So would you like me to add you or not?"

The man gave her a very pithy and highly personal response about exactly what she could do with herself, which made her end the call in a hurry, feeling shaky.

"Are you okay?" Gabby asked.

Anna told her what the man had said, adding, "I'm not adding him to any waiting list."

"I should think not. In fact, I think you should mention this to Dr. Lewisham and see if we can get him off the books if he treats you like that."

Anna nodded, nerves roiling through her stomach. She didn't recall encountering the man before, and probably he was having a very bad day, but still. She'd dealt with plenty of impatient and traumatized people, but never received such vitriol before.

"Anna?" Gabby's eyes held compassion. "Go have your break early. I can cover you for fifteen minutes."

Anna nodded again. Collected her bag. Exited out the staff door. She really didn't want to bump into anyone she knew right now. And a coffee—actually, something with some solid carbs attached to it, laden with sugar and fat—would help. A lot.

She turned the corner, and nearly slammed into a figure she recognized.

"Anna!" Serena Wakefield's eyes widened, as she pivoted the baby stroller to the other side of the pavement. "I'm so sorry, I didn't see you there."

Anna shook her head, her gaze lowered. *Seriously, God? Another encounter?* Honestly, it was like He was trying to say something.

"Anna?" Serena's voice was soft. "Are you okay?"

Her chest pulled tight as the emotions from the earlier incident massed within, begging escape.

Serena tentatively placed a hand on Anna's upper arm, the action so similar to what she remembered a tear escaped.

Anna swiped it away, then the next, as she slowly shook her head.

"Oh, Anna."

Anna peeked up, saw Serena's eyes were glistening with unshed tears, which only propelled hers to escape.

Before she knew it, she was being wrapped in Serena's arms, being called "Honey," and feeling the warm comfort of a friend who had known her most of her life.

Serena murmured soothing words, rubbing her back slowly, as if unaware of her own baby's vocal protests from the stroller. A baby Anna had never seen. A baby she should've met by now, and would have, if she wasn't such a bad friend, and such a horrible person, and—

"Hey, it's okay."

No, it wasn't. Her chest heaved with silent sobs. How could she deal with such kindness? She didn't deserve it. Not one bit.

After what seemed a waterfall of tears, Anna pulled back, swiping under her eyes with one hand as she accepted a tissue with the other. She blew her nose. "I don't know why I did that."

"Hey," Serena was rubbing Anna's upper arm. "It's okay. Whatever it is, it'll be okay."

Anna drew in a deep breath, air sliding past her clogged nose. "Sorry. I just got a phone call and—"

"Is your mom alright?"

"Yes, she's fine. No, it was an abusive phone call at the clinic and it kind of shocked me."

"I'm so sorry that happened," Serena said, in a manner Anna could feel the genuine sympathy.

"I was just going to get a coffee, but now, I don't know…"

"Have you got time to talk now, or can we do it soon? I've really missed you, Anna."

Anna swallowed, met Serena's pleading eyes, and nodded.

As Serena's face lit, Anna realized what her nod had implied. "I mean, yes, soon, but I can't talk now. But… but I'd like to."

"Oh, I'd *love* that. I have missed you so much. We all have." Serena jiggled the stroller and the baby's protest died. "I'm having another soiree tonight and I'd love for you to come."

Tonight? "I… I can't. Not tonight." She was meeting Tom. Besides, meeting the others felt way too soon, fraught with too many landmines. Some people, Rachel perhaps, might be okay, but she still hadn't reconciled in her heart how she felt about Jackie. Okay, to be blunt: Anna still hadn't forgiven her former friend for saying what she had, and knew she needed more time to sort that out before seeing her again.

"Then you just tell me when. I'll drop whatever for you." Serena's face softened. "You don't know how long I've been praying for this."

Anna's throat tightened again, and she could only nod,

which Serena probably thought meant she'd been praying too, when she hadn't. Not really. She'd been too busy living in regrets, denials, and offense to really allow God to speak to her. Not that she'd really been paying much attention to Him lately.

"I… I should go. I've only got a few minutes before I need to get back." And probably didn't have time for the coffee and pastry now. Fixing her makeup so she didn't look like she'd just experienced a crying jag was probably the more important priority. And if she skipped the pastry, it might help with that fitting-back-in-a-dress plan.

"But you haven't got your coffee yet," Serena said.

Anna shrugged. "It doesn't matter. It wasn't like I had time to get to The Coffee Blend anyway."

"Yeah, Suzy makes the best. So maybe we should go there when you're free. Are you free at all tomorrow?"

"I'm kind of helping my mom with the Summer Ball, but maybe I could do something."

"I'll message you, and we'll make a time, okay?"

Anna nodded. And this time she might even reply.

Anna's head throbbed with a slight headache for the rest of the day. Crying always did that to her. But Tom's cryptic message about dinner had her too curious to cancel. If she didn't show, he'd probably think she wasn't interested and not ask again. And while she wasn't sure she should be interested, the fact he kept cropping up in her thoughts meant she didn't want to do anything to put him off, and potentially lose the chance to explore something more.

So after work she showered, and took care with her hair and makeup and found clothes that didn't scream date, but still looked like she was making an effort. Walking in heels long distances had never been her scene, so she'd have to drive. But she could squeeze in some extra exercise by parking a little way from the store and walking that much easier distance. Her fitting-back-into-a-ballgown plans might thank her.

She parked behind Brandi's Bookstore and Gifts, knowing the small parking lot was usually free even when peak tourist season hit. After collecting her bag and a jacket in case it turned cool, she locked her car, then paused, eyeing the paint splatter she still hadn't dealt with. She really should do something about the paint. Maybe she should ask Tom for his brother's business number so she could get that sorted. Although by now it was probably settled into the paint and would be stuck there forever. Oh well.

A long exhale helped keep the nerves at bay. Why she felt nervous she wasn't really sure, especially after her encounter with Serena earlier seemed to have tipped her world on its side. Regret renewed that she had taken so long to do so, as there had been something so right about reconnecting with her, like a jigsaw piece of her heart had snapped back into where it belonged, giving a fuller picture once again. Like things were finally going as they should.

Tonight also held a similar tantalizing possibility. Even though Tom had been quite cautious in his approach, it made her wonder if maybe things could work out in that regard too. Except she'd always been so bad in finding and maintaining relationships, that she had close to zero trust that she could make this one work either.

"You're being stupid," she muttered to herself. She was doing that thing again, getting carried away, when really, Tom hadn't even truly asked her for a date, just simply mentioned that Suzy was serving dinner. It wasn't exactly candles and roses. It was only food. A meal. Like she'd have to have, anyway.

She lifted her chin. A girl had to eat, which meant she could be here, casually, for the food, if nothing else. So what if she was wearing red lipstick and heels? It didn't have to mean anything, did it? Her stomach tensed. Although maybe it would be better if she wiped the lipstick off. Or just went home.

But by now The Coffee Blend was only a few feet away, and through the large windows she could see most of the tables had filled. She had attended a few of these Friday night suppers before, but this was the first time she was supposed to be eating alone with a man. What would Suzy think? She wiped damp hands down her jeans. Was he here? She peered through the window but couldn't see him. Her heart dipped.

He hadn't said what time. Maybe that was what the voucher was for. She could fill up on coffee while she waited for him to show. That was, if he showed.

Ignoring the new knot of tension that last thought provoked, she went inside, and Suzy welcomed her with a smile.

"It's looking busy." Anna glanced around.

"Sit anywhere that's free," Suzy said. "Apart from the reserved tables."

Anna nodded, scanning the room. Would Tom have reserved a table? Her heart fell. He definitely wasn't here. Although plenty of others were, including Brandi and her new man friend. Anna waved, but didn't go near, her lipstick making her feel like she was on show, like everyone here could tell she was supposed to be on a date, but the guy hadn't shown. Awkwardness rushed her to the nearest open table, and she sat, relieved to snatch up a menu to hide behind as disappointment rolled in like waves against the shore.

"Anna?" a voice came from above.

She peeked up, saw Kyle Crayling, the man who her mom had not been shy about saying she hoped would marry Anna one day. This, despite the fact they'd only ever been sort-of friends and possessed zero real connection let alone chemistry. Honestly, moms could be so delusional. "Um, hi."

He smiled. "You've got skills."

"How so?"

He tapped her menu. "Not everyone can read upside down."

She quickly righted it, and ducked her head. Great.

"Good to see you out and about," he continued.

She peeked up, saw his face held gladness not pity, and nodded. "Thanks."

He slid into the seat opposite, and she froze, wanting to protest, but not sure how. Who knew what time Tom was coming, if he came at all. Surely that would be time enough to briefly pretend to be sociable with Kyle before getting rid of him. She lowered the menu past her chin, hating how his eyes rounded. Yes, she knew her lipstick screamed date-worthy.

He whistled. "Well, hello Miss Morely."

Her cheeks grew hot. "I was supposed to meet someone here. At least, I think I was."

"Well, I'm happy to keep you company until he shows. Who is he, anyway?"

She shrugged. "Just… someone."

"Man of mystery, huh?"

Considering Tom dealt with solving mysteries, that was probably a fairly accurate description. "Yes."

"Okay." He settled back in the seat, and smiled. "Now I'm intrigued."

Her heart sank. Now, if Tom was to appear, she was in a pickle.

ANTICIPATION WAS RIDING HIGH as Tom parked next to her car. He smiled, recognizing the paint spatter. He'd have to convince Drew to give her a discount so she could finally get it cleaned off. But at least she'd come. He was so glad. And relieved. He really needed the break, to not think about the case which was fast consuming his world. Who knew just what was going on at the Lodge? Recent research and phone calls and rereading old interviews had made for some long, exhausting days. Having this to look forward to had provided enough motivation to finish, and be glad to follow his boss's advice for once and enjoy his night. Which he fully planned to do.

He rounded the corner, wondering what Anna was wearing, whether she'd dressed up like he had. Well, he'd exchanged his shirt for a fresh one, even if he no longer wore a tie. He had managed to spray on some cologne, which had earned him some tease from some of the other guys at the station. But he didn't care. She'd wanted him to detect whether she was interested? He'd consider it a win that she was here.

A delicious aroma wafted in the air as the door to The Coffee Blend opened. He peeked through the windows, hungry for a glimpse of her, to see her relaxed, before she saw him. But wait. His steps halted outside the window. What was she doing talking to that guy? He squinted. That guy who looked a little like the photo he'd dug up on the internet regarding his new case.

His stomach tensed. Should he go there, and potentially reveal himself as police? Who knew if Anna had already admitted who he was and what he did for a living? Maybe he should hang back, watch and wait, then decide if this thing with Anna was something he could afford to pursue.

Traffic passed on the main street as he exhaled. He didn't like waiting, or second guessing. And he especially didn't love feeling like there was a part of him second guessing whether she was worth this, and whether he should back off now. He didn't do wuss like in those Christmas movies his mom always liked to watch, where the guy backed off from the girl he liked, just because he saw her talk with another guy. He didn't get paid to jump to wrong conclusions, even if the two of them sitting inside seemed to share an easy familiarity. But was this hesitation due to fear that she might reject him, or was it more he didn't want to jeopardize the case? *Lord? Is it safe to go in there?*

He didn't sense a "no", so he went inside, nodding to Suzy behind the counter, who was looking a little frazzled and over-whelmed at the numbers here, then moved to the table where the dude looked up.

Tom nodded, but immediately switched his gaze to Anna, whose face brightened in a way it hadn't with the guy before. He smiled. He didn't need to be a detective to work that one out. "You came."

Her lips lifted higher. "So did you."

Okay, he was officially a fan of bantering with her. "I'm really glad."

"Me too."

At the cleared throat from the other man, Anna's lips pulled out into the tiniest grimace, then she gestured, "Tom, this is Kyle, an old friend. Kyle, this is Tom—"

Please don't say I'm a detective.

"—a new one."

Relief gushed and he gripped the man's hand. "Hey."

He used the moment to size him up. Unlike the hilariously inaccurate things he'd read in some novels, the man didn't possess shifty eyes or anything suspicious. He just looked normal. Although probably more handsome than Tom would've preferred. But his handshake was definitely weaker than Tom's.

Tom swiveled back to face Anna. There was no reason to give the man the chance to study him, especially if he was at all involved with his case. Just because he shared the same last name as those listed as trustees of the Strong Hearts Foundation didn't mean he shared a propensity for potentially criminal activity. Even if statistically it was far more likely. He inwardly rolled his eyes at himself. Look at him being generously-minded. Still, he needed to act fast and get the guy out of here, then somehow explain to Anna that he didn't really want her mentioning his occupation.

"So." He directed all his attention on her, ignoring Kyle. "Did you want to stay here, or would you like to go somewhere else?"

Her mouth parted slightly, her gaze shifting to Kyle then returning to Tom.

That's right, he silently agreed. Buddy old pal over there is trespassing.

Kyle sighed. "I guess that's my cue."

Tom nodded. He guessed right. "Good to meet you." To scope out the competition.

"You too." Kyle pointed a finger at him. "Don't do anything I wouldn't do."

"You betcha." That was highly unlikely, seeing Tom believed in following the law.

He kept his smile fixed as he waited for Kyle to say his good-byes and leave, then sat opposite her.

Anna's eyebrow rose. "You didn't like him."

This had the potential to go south. He couldn't admit the truth, but neither did he want to appear jealous. Still, option two was better than the first. "Look, can I help it if I was looking forward to seeing you all day, then felt disappointed when I saw some dude chatting you up when I want to?"

"You don't have to worry about him." Her lips curved, obviously pleased he'd gone the jealous route.

"So how do you know him?" Maybe this would be helpful for his case.

"His mom is best friends with my mom, so I feel like I've known him forever. But despite his mom and mine wanting us to get together, there's never been anything like that between us."

Phew. "Do you know him well?"

"Well enough, I suppose. It's not like we hang out much."

"Good." The further she kept away from Kyle the better. Tom couldn't afford to get involved with someone who could possibly be seen as having connections with a criminal family.

She smiled. "I didn't figure you to be the possessive type."

"I'm not possessive. But I don't want some other guy hanging around when I'm trying to get to know you."

Her smile took on an extra edge of sweetness, which made his chest squeeze. This felt like a dangerous game. In the past, he'd not dated people in the locations where he'd worked. Toronto had been large enough he could get to know Meghan and not have their social circles meet too often, or for anyone in her world to know when he'd graduated to detective status. But here in this small town, where people knew people, where people talked, it seemed only a matter of time before the proverbial hit the fan and he was exposed. Which reminded him…

"I, um, wanted to ask you something."

"Ask away."

"Did you, uh, have you mentioned to anyone about what I do for a living?"

"That you're a police detective?"

He nodded.

"No."

Thank goodness. "Okay, it might sound weird, but I'd really appreciate it if you don't mention anything to anyone. At least for a little while."

"Why?'

Man, she was so direct. He liked it, but it also scared him a little. "Because I still feel new at working as a detective in a small town, and it's weird being in a place where people might know me in one context but treat me differently in another."

She studied him a moment then nodded. "I can understand that."

He exhaled. "Thanks."

"I know this is not the same, but I guess it's similar to when a patient presents at the doctor's and you know they have cancer because of the questions they ask or the tests you're asked to organize for them. Then you see them at church or down the street and it's like they're not defined by their illness anymore, and because it's out of context, you have to treat them as if you didn't know."

Huh. "It's exactly like that."

She shrugged. "I can imagine it's especially tricky when your work means you have to keep things on the down low, too."

He appreciated the fact she understood, that she could see his reasons for keeping quiet. There was a lot he liked about this woman. Not least of which was her natural good looks, enhanced tonight with a swipe of lipstick that drew attention to her lips.

The waiter came, and rather than make Anna wait longer, he snatched a quick look at the menu and followed her lead and ordered the pasta special. Two drink orders later, they were alone again. Well, except for all the others seated in tables not too far away.

Anna smiled, then ducked her head, and he studied her. At times she seemed so sassy, at others, she seemed almost shy. Who was the real Anna Morely?

He leaned forward. "You know, I should've led tonight with the fact I think you look really pretty."

Her smile quirked. "Yes, you should have."

Amusement rumbled through his chest, and she peeked up again. "So how was your day? Were you working on a case?"

"I'm always working on a case. Or ten cases. They don't tend to get resolved quickly, so a lot of what we do gets termed as an ongoing investigation."

"You sound like you're overworked."

He shrugged. "Even if people always obeyed the law, we'd still have things to solve."

"Like what?"

"Car crashes. House fires. You name it. Sure there might be

other agencies involved, but it's funny how often we get called in."

"It must be hard sometimes."

Yeah, it was. Sometimes. Other days it was tragic. "Let's just say there are good days and not so good days."

"So, did you have a good day today?"

"Define a good day."

"Did you feel like you accomplished things?"

That he most certainly had. "It's been productive, let's say that."

"And are you working again tomorrow?"

Was that an angling to find out if he was free to spend time with her? "The boss has banned me from setting foot inside the station. How about you?"

"I have the weekend free, too."

"That's good to know." He smiled.

She matched it. "It *is* good to know."

He exhaled heavily. "I wonder how long until our food arrives?"

As if summoned by his thoughts, their waiter arrived with their drinks, apologizing for the delay. "There's a bit of a delay in the kitchen, thanks to all the customers tonight."

"That's not a bad problem to have," Tom said.

"Except if you're hungry," Anna said, with a wink.

The waiter winced. "Which is why Suzy wanted to give everyone complimentary garlic bread while they waited."

"I was joking before," Anna said. "I don't need garlic bread. I don't plan on kissing any vampires tonight."

"Promise?" The question shot out before Tom could stop it.

She glanced at him. Smirked. "Depends."

Oh, he knew what that look meant. And no, he wasn't a kiss-on-the-first-date kind of guy. Even if she seemed okay with that. Forget a glass of coke. He needed a pitcher of ice water. Stat.

"So, is that a yes to the garlic bread?"

"Sure. Thanks," Tom said, before Anna's tease could cause the poor guy a moment's longer delay. She might not need garlic bread, but he was rapidly approaching hunger levels that meant he'd be happy to join a chili eating contest just so he could get a few calories in. And after that last comment-of-a-look, he'd be making sure she ate garlic bread too, just in case their lips were to get a little closer than he might normally allow for.

Not that there was anything normal about this situation. It felt so long since he gone on a date, and even that first date had been the last first date he'd ever thought he'd go on. But now Meghan was gone, and Anna was here, it was a lot of relearning to remember how to play the dating game. And while he might consider himself a good judge of character, he still wasn't sure if he could understand what signals this woman was putting out. Or if he ever would.

The basket of garlic bread arrived, and he offered it to her then took a wedge himself, glad it gave him something to do rather than focus on the confusion within.

"So, tell me about your day." There. That was safe, wasn't it?

Then she sighed. Okay, maybe not so safe.

"What happened?"

She shook her head. "Oh, it was nothing."

"Doesn't sound like nothing. I'm all ears."

"Fine then." She told him about an abusive phone call she received which drew his indignation. How did people think it was okay to abuse somebody who was simply trying to do their job? "What steps have been done about it?"

"Gabby, my fellow receptionist, told me I should make a complaint about him, so I did that. We have a two strikes out policy at the clinic, so if it happens again, then he'll be taken off the books."

"Sounds wise."

"I don't like the thought of somebody else having to go through that, but I don't want to be put in that position again. Anyway, that wasn't great, but then…"

"Then what?"

She gave a kind of half-shrug. "Then I bumped into a friend I haven't spoken to for a long time. It was actually just what I needed." She sighed. "I don't know what's happening, but I keep bumping into these friends, almost like God wants me to move on and forgive them."

"No. God wouldn't want you to forgive someone, would He?" he teased.

She wrinkled her nose at him. "Anyway, it was really good to see her. I… I hope to see her again soon."

"We all need friends in our lives."

"Yeah." Her gaze fell to the bread basket. "I know I haven't been the best in that regard lately. But I guess it's never too late to change, right?"

He nodded, and after offering the basket to her again, which she refused, he retrieved another slice of bread. It was really good, buttery, delicious. "You sure you don't want some more?"

She sighed. "I might want it, but my mom reminded me this week that I'm supposed to attend a ball next month and I need to fit into my dress."

He had a vision of what Anna in a pretty ballgown might look like, and had to sip his coke. This woman was not good for his imagination. "Tell me about the ball."

"It's a fundraiser for a local charity. The Strong Hearts Foundation?"

Her voice pitched up, like it was a question. He blanked his face even as his heart prickled with interest. "Tell me more."

"It's an organization that helps the poor find low-cost housing. It's run by the mom of the man you didn't like before."

"You mean…?"

"Kyle Crayling, yes. Why?" Her look turned teasing. "How many men do you not like?"

Plenty, if the truth was told. But as most of them were now behind bars he didn't dwell there. "I'd rather talk about the ball." Would she need a date? Could he offer? What would this mean for any undercover work he tried to do? Or was all of this getting way ahead of himself? Regardless, he wanted to know more. About Anna, the Craylings, and about this ball.

CHAPTER 6

"I'm so glad you came," Serena said the next day, when Anna met her at the Wakefields' home. She'd been hesitant at first, but then when Serena had assured that it would only be her and the new baby, she had agreed. So she had arrived, with apology flowers from Annette's Florist, and a beautiful soft toy bear as a belated gift for the newborn.

And looking around their cozy nest, seeing the love here, evident in everything from Caleb's baby room to photos of the new family of three, her heart was filled with fresh regret that she hadn't been here along the way, excited for her friend. How selfish had Anna been, focused on her disappointment and pain, that she'd missed out on supporting her friend through such momentous life changes? Her chin wobbled, as emotion fought to escape.

"Anna, what is it?" Serena asked.

"I… I can't believe I missed so much. That I wasn't the friend I should've been. I'm so sorry."

"Hey, it's okay. You're here now, and that's the main thing."

Serena was too gracious. Especially when Anna knew it was

all Anna's own offense and pride that had imprisoned her in bars of selfishness. "I… I haven't really been okay."

Serena studied her, her expression soft. "But admitting that means you want to change, right?"

She supposed. She mostly did, but some aspects held her back. Wanting to change didn't mean any of the things she faced had altered. And while she still sensed frustration about her lack of a boyfriend, even though she'd had a great date last night, she knew the muck inside had to go. But trying to express that felt awkward and exposed just how bad a person she really was.

Serena gestured for Anna to take the comfortable lounge opposite where she began breastfeeding her baby, covering up, but nonchalant all the same. Even that action seemed so awkwardly personal, yet also intriguing. Didn't it hurt? Once upon a time she'd simply have asked such a question. Now, it felt like such personal exchanges weren't allowed, that it was something the couples of her group could share but she, on the outer, could not.

"Is this bothering you?" Serena asked, gesturing to the cloth-draped baby's head.

"No. It's just I haven't really seen it."

"Rachel breastfed her children."

"That feels a lifetime ago. And I guess I was too busy with studying and starting work to notice."

"Joel has been so supportive. He gets little Caleb up at night and brings him into our bed. He's also told some of the more conservative members of the congregation to mind their own business, when they've felt to share their opinion about me breastfeeding in public."

"Good for him."

"That's what Rachel said last night when she and the girls were here."

When Anna had been out on the best date of her life. She'd seemed to connect with Tom on so many levels, their conversation easy, the sparks just waiting to fan into flame. But still she hesitated. Her hungry heart was always too ready to believe for more.

"We missed you," Serena said softly.

"I… it's… Oh." Anna sighed.

"A little awkward?"

Anna nodded, wrinkling her nose. "I feel like I don't fit in. All of you are paired up and playing happy families, and I'm still me. But if I was to say that to anyone, then I'd get judged for feeling sorry for myself when really, I'm just expressing a fact."

"You can express a fact without feeling sorry for yourself. But you can't know what others might be thinking."

Others. Like Jackie.

"We've all been on our own journeys in recent months." Serena's voice was gentle.

Anna nodded slowly. "I know that Rachel seemed different the last time I saw her. Softer somehow."

Serena nodded. "She and Damian are doing much better. I think she felt a little intimidated by some of the recent relationships."

Too. Serena didn't have to add that word. It was obvious.

Anna glanced away, out the window. This house which Joel had bought when he and his sister had first moved to Muskoka Shores had been a bit of a fixer upper, although blessed with a great view as it was positioned on the shores of Lake Muskoka. Toni rented Serena's old house now, and lived there with Matt and Ethan when they weren't in the city.

Suddenly she could understand some of Rachel's envy. Toni had married Matt, a big-time financial investment guru from the city, who was loaded. Staci Everton, a famous author, had waltzed in and married ex-missionary Dr. James Wells. Then Jackie had scored the largest catch of all with a Hollywood heartthrob as a boyfriend. How was an ordinary girl from a small town ever supposed to compete with all that?

But still. "Rachel is already married, got kids, a great business."

"A wedding ring and a baby or two doesn't mean comparison stops." Serena's mouth twisted wryly. "Would it surprise you to learn that I might've been envious of you a few times in recent weeks?"

"You're kidding. Why would you envy me?"

"Because you're single, able to do what you want when you want, and don't have this tiny creature who is dependent on you, twenty-four seven."

"Yep. Well, I've sure been living the dream, living it up every night." She scoffed. "Come on. My life isn't a fairytale. That's Jackie, isn't it?"

Serena shook her head. "I don't think her life is a fairytale. She might've met her handsome prince, but there have been plenty of trolls out there trying to make her pay for Lincoln falling in love with her."

Oh. She'd heard some of that, but hadn't realized it was still going on.

"She misses you too, you know."

Sure she did. Like someone with a Hollywood hunk of a man paying attention to her could miss plain old boring Anna. "Well, she should make more of an effort then."

"I thought she had tried."

Ouch. Anna's gaze dropped to the floor. Okay, the truth was Jackie had tried last year. And Anna had rejected her. But she couldn't admit that to Serena. Not yet, anyway.

"Don't shut her out," Serena pleaded. "She's got her own battles, and I know it would mean the world to her if she knew she had your support too."

"I… I'll see." Maybe.

Serena's face relaxed, and Caleb's head bucked away. Anna was half tempted to watch, not from some pervy reason, but because it looked difficult to juggle all the things and she wondered how Serena managed it. Instead, she rose and offered to make Serena tea.

"That'd be lovely, thank you."

As Serena did her new mom thing, Anna moved to the kitchen, admiring the olde-worlde white-and-blue canisters of coffee, tea, and sugar, and studied the news about the Naioth Children's Home on the fridge. "Is this orphanage connected to your parents?" she asked.

Serena nodded. "They signed up for another five years, and have been working there a bit."

"Wow." She couldn't imagine her mother moving to India, and staying there for years on end in the heat and deprivation.

Anna made the tea, then returned with two cups as Serena burped the baby then laid him down on a bunny rug. "Here you go."

"I feel so bad you doing this for me," Serena protested.

"Well, too bad, queen of hospitality."

Serena smiled. "Oh, you have no idea how good it is to have you here again."

Oh, she had some idea. It was nice to be back. To *feel* back, within her spirit, too, and more like the old Anna again.

"So tell me, what else has been happening with you?" Serena asked.

Something within hesitated to share about last night. Not because she was embarrassed, and definitely not because she had anything to be embarrassed about, but because it still felt so special and new that to talk about going out with Tom might make it lose it golden shimmery dreamlike quality. Plenty of people had seen them, so it wasn't exactly a secret, and she knew that Serena might be hurt if she didn't share. But considering their strained relationship of the past however many months, she probably would understand why Anna hadn't instantly spilled every detail about her life.

"I'm helping Mom with the Summer Ball."

"That's right. I spoke with your mom about it, and Cherry and I are working on making it a beautiful event. It's good to see it's happening again."

"It's been a few years, but yes."

Serena picked up her tea then made herself more comfortable on the lounge. "Remind me, what charity is it in aid of this time?"

Anna told her, then paused. Why was she talking about the ball when she really wanted to talk to Serena about something far more important? And maybe it was still sparkly new, but the urge to tell Serena was growing stronger. She'd really value a different perspective on it, from someone she knew would pray for her, and not just express disappointment that he wasn't Kyle Crayling.

"What is it?"

Her eyes pricked with moisture. She'd missed this, this closeness with a friend who knew her well enough to know why she hesitated. "Okay, so don't get all thingy about this, but I… I may have met someone."

"What?" Serena's face lit.

"I know. It's all new, like *really* new, and I don't think it will go anywhere, but maybe it will. Who knows?"

"God knows," Serena said softly.

Huh. She supposed He did.

"What's his name?" Serena asked.

"Tom."

"What does he do?"

"Um, he works in local law enforcement."

Serena's eyes widened. "Not Tom the detective?"

"What? How did you know?" She winced. Man, she wasn't good at keeping secrets.

"Do you mean the guy who helped Toni with her stalker ex, that Tom?"

No. She blinked. No way. No *way*. "Oh my gosh. I can't

believe I didn't realize it until now." How could she not have known? Did he know? He mustn't have, otherwise why hadn't he said anything?

"Is he a Christian?"

Anna nodded. "He, uh, goes to Joel's competition."

"Oh! He must be…" Serena bit her lip.

"He must be what?"

"Oh, just something Joel had to do the other day. It doesn't matter. What *does* matter is you and Tom. Tell me more. I want to know everything."

So Anna did, not leaving out a detail. Not even sparing Serena the hope that she'd sort-of wanted a kiss, but when he'd walked her back to her car—the car he'd said he'd get his brother to give her a quote on fixing—he'd simply asked if they could meet on Sunday afternoon, before quickly hugging her goodbye.

"And how was that?" Serena asked, smiling.

"Oh my gosh." His hug had been wonderful. Every pore tingled afresh at the memory. Tom was so strong, his muscles evident, his scent tantalizing. It was the perfect hug. Except for her wanting more.

But he'd leaned away before there could be any question of that, which had left her wondering if maybe he wasn't into it as much as she was. Then he'd smiled, and waited for her to get in the car, like a true gentlemen, before reminding her of their date on Sunday. Then the butterflies in her stomach had been given full permission to soar.

"I'm going to guess that you enjoyed it." Serena chuckled.

"Yes," she admitted shyly. "But look, I know I have a tendency to get carried away so I'm trying really hard to not get carried away. But it's *really* hard."

"Because he's easy to get carried away over, huh?"

"Yes." Her nose wrinkled. "And I just know that some people will think that about me."

"Some people meaning Jackie," Serena guessed.

She nodded. "I guess I'm just not ready to feel judged some more."

"Anna, remember what I said earlier? You don't know how others feel about you and you won't if you keep this distance. But it is interesting that you keep mentioning Jackie as if you really are concerned about what she thinks of you. And I know this may not be what you want to hear, but I've found in my life that if I don't really care about someone then I don't think about them or talk about them very much. And the opposite is true, too."

Anna exhaled, her gaze dropping to baby Caleb. "I think that's what has been so hard. I thought Jackie was my friend and so for her to say what she did felt so insulting."

"Remind me what she said?"

"She basically told me to grow up and stop feeling sorry for myself."

Serena nodded, but didn't say anything.

And suddenly the air between them felt shaky. Is that what Serena had thought too? She couldn't stay here if that was the case. She put her tea down. Shifted up from her seat.

"Anna? Where are you going?"

"I just remembered I have to help my mom with some things for the ball."

"Oh. I hope you're not going because of what I just said."

Why did Serena have to be like that? She'd always been too discerning. "I'm not," she lied, faking a smile. Clearly any thought of a restored relationship was premature.

She blinked back tears, knowing she was being childish, but feeling helpless against the forceful habit of so many recent months.

So with a caress on the head for baby Caleb and a rushed kiss on the cheek for Serena, she exited.

TOM SLOUCHED in his desk chair and studied the computer screen, his promise to Gabe to take a break this weekend now far away. He'd been tempted to spend more time with Anna, to see if their perfect date could translate into another on Saturday, before feeling a prompting to go slower, and leave it until Sunday afternoon. So he'd done that, wondering whether she'd be okay, before realizing that of course she would be. Besides, if God was the one prompting Tom to go slower, then who was he to question Him? He realized now that he still didn't know her too well, or her dating history. Neither did she know about his fiancée and what had happened there. And those were some big questions to discuss before getting any more emotionally involved like what a kiss might do. So instead of wondering about whether he'd done the right thing, and second-guessing himself yet again, he ignored the usual Saturday clean-the-house routine and decided to revisit the station and see if he could find out more about this family that Anna knew.

He clicked on an opened tab and read about the Crayling family. Long time members of the township north of Muskoka Shores, Spencer and Heather Crayling seemed to have a finger in every pie. Business. Community organizations. Charities. And their son Kyle seemed to have a thumb too.

His chest tensed as he read the long list of accomplishments. So-called accomplishments, because who knew how much Kyle had actually earned the hard way and how much had been paid for by his family? Which was uncharitable of him. Which wasn't very Christian. But something about that family bugged him. And no, it wasn't just that Kyle and Anna seemed to share a history, even if it was completely innocent.

He folded his arms, squinting at the screen.

"Woodmore?"

Uh oh.

Gabe frowned at him. "I thought I told you to take the weekend off. What's more, I thought you agreed."

"Sorry, sir. There's just something about this case that's really bothering me."

His boss glanced at the screen. "You suspect he's involved, too?"

"I've got nothing but a gut feeling."

"Gut feelings don't tend to fly too well with the judge. You're gonna need something a little more concrete than a hunch."

"I know."

"What have you got so far?"

Tom outlined the ITOs he could include in his application for the judge to consider a search warrant: hearsay, a missing person, and broken buildings that suggested potential neglect. "It's not that much to go on."

"What about the missing person? Have you contacted any of their relatives?"

"Not yet," he admitted. "I've read their statements, and the reports from that time, but it seems there was a lot that was held up in the courts."

His boss nodded. "The Craylings are a powerful family. Which is why we need every T crossed and every I dotted."

Which maybe meant that go-slow with Anna was important for lots of reasons. He didn't want to do anything to compromise the case, and if she knew he was investigating her childhood friend, that might not go well.

"What's that look for?"

He sighed. He really didn't want to mention this, but sensed if he didn't say it now, it might come back and bite him later. "Look, in the interest of full disclosure, I think you should know that I went out with Anna Morely last night."

"Good for you."

"Except, she's friends with this guy." He pointed to the screen.

"Ah." His boss eyed him. "And you're telling me because you don't want there to be a conflict of interest, right?"

"Pretty much."

"I don't think I need to tell you what to do."

He exhaled silently. Which was exactly why he hadn't wanted to tell his boss. "Is there anything I need to know about the Morely family?"

"Regarding this girl you're about to dump?"

"It's not exactly dumping. We've only been getting to know each other which means I can step away and it shouldn't matter too much."

"Yeah, but we know women always get the wrong end of the stick."

Hmm. That attitude might explain why his boss was divorced.

"Look, I can understand that you might want to keep seeing this woman, but I would advise you to tread slowly and lightly, indeed. As for her, there's nothing on her record is there?"

"No, she's clean."

"In that case, from what I remember, the family is not unlike the Craylings in that they've always had money and been used to the finer thing of life."

Hmm. Anna hadn't presented like that, with her older make car and humble house.

"I think the parents are divorced. From what I remember he's some hotshot property developer down Miami way, while the mother is involved in all kinds of committees around here."

"Anna said her mom is involved in the fundraising Summer Ball. Guess who the lucky charity is this year's recipient?"

Gabe shrugged.

"The Strong Hearts Foundation." He clicked open another tab. "Which is administered by..." He pointed to the smiling faces on the screen.

"Oh! Now that's interesting."

"Isn't it?"

Gabe frowned, then peered at Tom. "Are you still planning to go undercover?"

"If I can. Just to scout around. Of course, it's a little trickier now if Kyle is out there as he may recognize me."

"Does he know you're a cop?"

"Only if he looks me up."

Gabe winced. "It's not that hard to do. But only if he's suspicious, or jealous. Did either of those seem likely?"

"Not really."

"Hmm. Maybe you shouldn't pull the pin on your girlfriend just yet."

"What do you mean?"

"I mean, it might be advantageous to maintain a connection and see if you can get invited to this ball."

"I'm sorry but I'm not really comfortable with exploiting a relationship to solve a case."

"Isn't that what undercover work involves?"

"Yeah, but going to the Lodge is just for one day. It's not going deep undercover. Just long enough to learn if there's anything problematic there."

"Exactly. So if that succeeds then perhaps we can see whether it's worth pursuing things further."

He nodded. But already knew he didn't want to stop. God might have told him to go slow, but He hadn't said stop, which had to mean He wasn't against Tom exploring a potential relationship with Anna.

There was just a lot of clutter that needed to get sorted out first.

Like this case.

"We can't afford to keep paying you overtime, so you better not be here tomorrow."

"No problem. I've got plans." Like he did every Sunday. Church. Lunch with his family. And later, he now had a date.

What he'd do for that he still didn't know. Especially now. He needed something that was fun, that didn't give intense vibes, or suggest they were at a place that was more serious than it could afford to be just yet. He might have his boss's blessing, but he wouldn't use Anna. Things felt so tentative between them, that he didn't want to risk doing something that might make her cut off all ties with him once this case was solved. He'd just need to continue to follow God's promptings and trust Him to lead them on.

CHAPTER 7

Sunday morning light peeked around the curtains. While she thanked God for summer arriving soon, she did not appreciate the way the sun seemed extra perky these days, forcing the unwilling to get up far earlier than a human body was supposed to. She groaned, pulled a pillow over her face, and rolled away from the light, as the thoughts of what to do today flitted through her head.

Church? No. If she went, she'd be inundated with the well-meaning and good-intentioned who would in one breath welcome her back and in the next ask her where she had been, their judgement as palpable as their interest. And while she had thought she might be glad to see some friends, hurt from Serena's comment—or lack thereof—concerning Anna's immaturity only made her want to stay home. Good thing one didn't have to go to church to be a Christian. Even if she always felt better about her walk with God when she was hanging out with fellow believers. She and Tom had talked a bit about church on Friday night, which made her wonder what Tom's church was like...

At least she had this afternoon's date to look forward to. She'd been surprised when he did not suggest doing something yesterday, but the fact he hadn't meant that she'd got a lot done with her mom. When she had returned home from her mom's she had listened to a true crime podcast while she cleaned her house and did a week's worth of laundry, so Saturday had ended up being productive. Leaving her with this Sunday morning with nothing much to do.

A bird's persistent twitter stole beneath the pillow, insisting she wake. "Nope," she mumbled. "Not playing."

It kept chirping, like it hadn't heard her, the insistent perky chirrups and cheeps rousing her as thoroughly as the scent of the morning's first coffee.

"Fine," she grumbled, opening her eyes. Had God sent that bird to plant itself outside her window so she could get up and feel convicted about not going to church? Was that it?

She groaned, rolled to the other side, and peered through eyelids that wanted to close as the sunlight shafted through her room, tracking a path of brightness to alight on the pile of books in front of her bedside table. She peered at the top book, moved to touch it, then it toppled from the pile, sliding to reveal the one below. The one she hadn't touched in months. Her Bible.

Nope. She refused to believe that God had sent a bird to twitter her awake just so she could read her Bible. He loved His children, which meant He'd want them to sleep, right? She rolled her eyes at her silliness, as conviction grew to pick it up and read like she used to.

"Ugh." She reached across and grasped it, then pushed herself up in her bed so she could read. Then wished for a maid to make her a cup of tea. Or a husband. Then wondered if Tom liked to sleep in and if he knew how to make hot tea and—

"No!" She couldn't afford to think like that. She wasn't getting ahead of things. Not anymore. Slow and steady had to be the case. She couldn't afford to do anything to mess this up. Not again.

She flicked open the cracked, worn black leather cover, and the pages fell open into the middle, into Psalms, where she had hastily placed a book mark the last time she had opened it. At a gathering with the girls. Back at Jackie's, when their Bible study about an Old Testament tough chick named Jael had led to Deborah's song in the next chapter, the ending about those who loved the Lord being like the sun leading her to a cross-reference Psalm Nineteen. The very Psalm that Tom had mentioned during their sunset and pizza non-date.

She read it now. "The heavens declare the glory of God; the skies proclaim the work of His hands."

Her lips twitched. Well, the birds certainly proclaimed.

She read on about the description of the sun, a metaphor for God, who was consistent, ever faithful, with nothing hidden from Him. Her heart shriveled. Nothing was hidden: not her bad attitudes, not her faithlessness.

Then she read verse seven. "The law of the Lord is perfect, reviving the soul." She winced. Her soul could do with some reviving. And some joy. And wisdom. And all the other good things listed here. Maybe not reading her Bible in months had contributed to the dead feeling inside. Already, just by reading this tiny portion of the Bible again, she could feel her soul prickling to awareness again. Imagine how alive she could feel if she really jumped boots and all back into believing like she used to.

But if she did so, if she hopped back on the trusting God train, then wouldn't that mean she'd have to forgive Jackie and swallow a whole lot of pride? Just the thought of that seemed so overwhelming that she closed the Bible so the words wouldn't convict her any longer. Although it was too late. She'd become a Christian years ago and had read through the entire Bible many times and had done her best to follow what it said. And she knew what God wanted her to do.

The last verse of Psalm Nineteen had been underlined, and

she could see it now, its truth blazing through the closed covers. "May the words of my mouth and the meditation of my heart be pleasing in Your sight O Lord, my Rock and my Redeemer."

Yeah, that wasn't her. She knew her words and meditations wouldn't have pleased God. She'd been selfish and self-centered for so long now that trying to change seemed to require strength she didn't have.

"I can't do this, God." She swallowed. "I don't want to forgive."

And as those words escaped, the Bible slid from her hands, falling open to the book of Judges, chapter five, where the conclusion of Deborah's song taunted. "May all who love You be like the sun when it rises in its strength."

She shivered. She might still love God, but she had no strength. And definitely had no strength to face His people in church today.

So she pushed it off the bed, rolled over, and closed her eyes and prayed to go back to sleep.

Tom GLANCED AT HIS WATCH, then forced his legs to keep pumping. It was a glorious morning, the sky was blue, and it was great to be alive. And nothing beat making the most of the morning coolness than taking a jog around his neighborhood.

"Dude, you're slacking."

He glanced at Marc, whose competitiveness knew no bounds, as they completed their usual Sunday morning circuit. Having a firefighter brother who had to keep fit like he did had some benefits. And doing these Sunday sprints—because with Marc it could never be a simple jog—was helpful. It meant that after they'd return to their respective homes and go to church then he'd have time to repent of the attitudes his brother's pushiness always stirred in him. By the time he showed up at

Mom and Dad's for lunch he'd love—and like—his brother again.

The flagpole at the high school appeared, always the sign that their run was almost at an end.

"Race you!"

Marc took off, which forced Tom to push harder. His brother might be two years younger but there was no need to let him think Tom was an old man yet.

He dragged in another breath and ran faster, faster, and tapped the white pole a second after Marc did.

Marc turned, panting, hands on hips, then smirked. "Got you again."

"You almost didn't."

"But I still did."

Tom swung his arms in an effort to disguise his need to drag in oxygen. "I think you're slowing down."

"I think you're wrong. I'm still faster."

"So you should be. If you lost then all that gym work you do is for nothing."

Marc's brow furrowed as Tom knew it would, and he bit back a laugh. Yeah, he might not be able to beat his brother in a race, but he still knew how to press his buttons.

With his hands on his hips, he moved to his bike and grabbed the water bottle strapped there, sucking down blessedly cool water.

"You triathlon-ing again?" Marc asked, nodding to the bike.

"It's still too cold to swim, so no. But I figured it wouldn't hurt to ride home."

"And keep working at that fitness, huh?"

"You know it."

Marc smirked, then nodded. "Catch you later."

Tom lifted a hand, then exhaled, glad for the chance to finally escape his brother's high intensity. Marc seemed to live at high speed, with adrenaline junkie tendencies that lived for fighting fires and anything that held an element of risk and danger. Having seen far too many of the consequences of danger, Tom was far happier to balance high intensity with necessary moments of physical and mental relaxation. And running with Marc was good for keeping up brotherly relations as much as it was maintaining his fitness.

As he rode home, his thoughts tracked through his plans for the rest of the day. Shower. Church. Lunch. Then his date with Anna.

He smiled, the cool morning air whipping his skin as he curved into Poplar. Was it creepy that he wanted to pass her house now? Probably. So he avoided going down her street, and took the next cross-street that led nearer his house. Well, his condo, really. When he'd first moved back, he'd realized he didn't need all the stuff he'd once thought he did, so he kept to a fairly minimalistic aesthetic these days. Even the engagement presents he and Meghan had received he'd either given back to the givers, or donated to charity. He didn't need stuff. He didn't need clutter. He did need God. He needed his family. And while he loved his work, he didn't define his life by that, even though it was a hugely important part of his life, and something that gave meaning to his time here on the planet. But one day, he wouldn't mind moving from this place to something larger, like on those days he dreamed about a future with a wife, a family of his own. One day. With someone who wanted that kind of thing too.

Which was yet another thing to talk about on his date with Anna this afternoon. There was no point pursuing a relationship, especially one that had the potential to be a little complicated, considering who her family was friends with, if they did not share the same hopes. But he didn't really know how to discuss something like that without the date taking on an intensity he'd really rather avoid. *Lord, you're going to have to give me some wisdom about that.* And about what to do for a date that didn't scream too casual, but neither gave rise to expectations beyond what he could manage.

He blew out a breath as he drew into his drive. Good thing God was into giving wisdom.

HE SLID damp palms down his shorts as he waited outside her door. Five seconds, then he'd knock again. One, two, three, four—

The door swung open, and Anna met him with a wide smile. "Hello, Mr. Right On Time."

"That's me." He surveyed her outfit. A green top and jeans and sandal-slide type shoes, perfect for what he had planned. "You look good."

"So do you." Her eyebrow arched. "A little more casual than I've seen before."

He shrugged. "It's nice to take a day off from the suit."

"You didn't yesterday?"

"I ended up working."

"I thought you had the weekend off. A workaholic, huh?"

"I try not to be, but it's the nature of the job. Sometimes you've just gotta pull the extra hours until it's done."

She nodded. "It sounds a bit like my friend, Staci Everton. She's an author?" She said that with an upward lilt, like a question, as if he might recognize the name.

He shrugged. He didn't.

"Anyway, she's often said she has to finish a story regardless of what else is going on, that it's like this living thing inside of her that needs to get out. I've thought it makes it sound like she's possessed, but I've never said that to her."

He chuckled. "That might be why she's still your friend."

The light in her face faded. "Maybe."

Okay, so there was a mystery there about her friend which

made him wonder. But today he had bigger things to deal with. "So, are you ready?"

"Let me grab my bag."

He waited outside as she left the front door open. From here he could see inside, and the fact it was so opposite to his made him smile. Every wall held art or crafts like what his mom loved, and a scent of vanilla and honey lingered in the air. It felt homey, almost quaintly old-fashioned, and gave plenty of clues about who this woman was.

"You can come in you know," she called.

"Depends on how long you're going to be." Punctuality might be his middle name, but it seemed it wasn't hers.

She reappeared, bag in one hand, and a jacket in the other. "Okay, I think I'm good to go."

"Now, I hope you don't mind, but I thought we could go in separate cars."

She blinked. "Uh, okay. Are we going far?"

"Not even five minutes."

She nodded. "We could've just met there."

But then he wouldn't have gotten this glimpse into this part of her life. And, "I might have a surprise in store."

"You are a man of mystery, aren't you?"

"I guess it goes with being a detective."

She smiled, pulled the door closed, and moved to the drive where her Mazda sat, still wearing its bonus paint. But not for much longer.

He held up his car keys. "Happy to follow me?"

"As long as you're not leading me to the woods to murder me, then sure."

His brows rose.

"Oh." Her nose wrinkled. "I suppose I shouldn't joke like that with a detective. Sorry."

He shook his head. "I know you were joking."

She winced. "But still, I bet you've had to deal with that kind of stuff in the past, and obviously I don't think you would murder me, but yeah. Sorry. Put it down to watching too many true crime podcasts."

Uncertainty hit him. She wasn't going out with him because of his job, was she? He'd had some colleagues in the city who'd shared about women they'd dated who seemed more fascinated by their job than themselves. And he didn't want Anna going out with him because she thought she might get an insider look to "true crime."

The question chased him as he drove to their first location, his heart swirling with fresh concerns. For just as he knew his job wasn't suited to every personality type, so being married—or in a relationship at least—with a police detective took a certain kind of personality type, too. So if she was inclined to be fearful every time he stepped out the door, and reached the point where she begged him to quit—as had happened to some married colleagues—it was better to know that now too. Before their lives grew any more entwined, and hearts got hurt. He was about serving and protecting, not dumping and breaking, after all.

He pulled up outside a warehouse complex, and got out, waiting as she pulled in beside him. She got out, took off her sunglasses, then glanced at him dubiously.

"Hey, don't worry. I'm not going to murder you and stash you in a shipping container."

"Good to know." She shifted her bag, as if nervous.

Man. He really shouldn't have said that. He held up his hands. "Look, I know that you might think this is presumptuous, but I was talking with my brother at lunch today and I might've mentioned something about your car. He said he had some time and could fit it in. But only if you want."

"What do you mean fit it in?"

He pointed to the sign above. Drew's Car Repairs & Detailing. "He said he can clean off the paint, and have it ready for you tomorrow afternoon, which means leaving it here tonight so it's ready to be dealt with first thing tomorrow. He gave me the key so I can drive it into the yard, so it'll be safe overnight. But only if you want."

"Of course I want. But..." She licked her lower lip. "How much will it cost?"

"Well, considering he's my brother, and you're my friend—"

Her eyebrows arched at that last word.

"—I might've convinced him to do it for free."

Her eyes rounded. "No. He can't do that."

No, he wasn't really doing that. But Drew had agreed to drop the price to the family special, which meant covering the costs of parts, but not labor. Tom had agreed to pay the difference. Not that he was telling her that.

"He doesn't even know me."

"But he knows me. And he loves to help out family and friends." An exaggeration. Drew tolerated the constant erosion of his income, but did it anyway. Sign of a good brother, that one.

She shook her head. "I can't accept a freebie."

"What about the family rate, then?"

"I'm not family."

"But you are my friend, right?"

He hoped she'd say yes. To agreeing to the status of friends, if not to accepting the offer of free help.

"I... I would like to be your friend," she said softly.

"Good. Because I have to admit I don't make this offer to just anyone."

Her smile was tentative. "No?"

"No, ma'am. In fact, I don't think I've made this offer to anyone else before."

"I'm one of the privileged few, huh?"

"Very privileged."

She chuckled. "Okay, I get the feeling you're going to try to twist my arm if I protest too hard. But I'm not doing free. So tell me what the family rate is and I'll pay that."

He told her, and she nodded. "So I'll definitely have my car back tomorrow afternoon?"

"I know it means you're without one to get to work tomorrow morning, but I could pick you up on my way, if you like."

She studied him. "You're really going out of your way to help me, aren't you?"

He really was. But he didn't mind if it meant he got to spend more time with her and figure out if this tentative friendship had enough potential to be something more. "So that's a yes, then?"

"That's a yes."

He inwardly fist-pumped, then moved to the security pad, punched in the code, and then unlocked the garage door. She retrieved her jacket then tossed him her car keys, and after adjusting her seat, he carefully drove her car into the bay where Drew had said to park it. Then he locked up, set the code, and returned to where she waited beside his vehicle.

"So do I get to sit in front, or do I have to sit in the back?"

"Depends on whether you're a felon or not."

"The front it is." She opened the door, and sat in the passenger seat.

He got in, glanced across, his heart hitching. The last time a woman sat there who he wasn't related to had been Meghan. And while it had been a number of years since her death it still took him by surprise to see someone else sitting there.

"What are you looking at?" she asked.

"You."

Anna's tentative smile grew crooked. "I know, but you seem to be thinking."

"I am."

She huffed. "You really have that mystery thing going on, don't you?"

His lips tweaked up, then he reversed, one hand on the back of her seat's headrest.

"So where are we going?"

Great question. He'd been tempted to ask his mom at lunch before realizing that asking in front of the others was a solid invitation to inviting all his male relatives to offer their opinion. So he didn't do that, instead finding inspiration via a bottle on top of his mother's kitchen counter.

"Would you be okay if I kept it a surprise?" he asked.

"You really do like to keep a girl guessing, don't you?"

"I thought this would be fun, and it'd give us a chance to get to know each other more, so I hope you like it."

They made small talk on the road to Bala, and he knew they were cutting it fine for their appointment at two, but when he'd called earlier, he was told they just needed to be seated in that time-frame. He hoped that person knew what they were talking about.

He turned into the drive for the cranberry farm and noticed how she sat up straight. "Have you been here before?"

"A million years ago on a school trip. But I have friends who came here and enjoyed the wine and cheese. Is that what we're doing?"

"If that's okay with you."

"It sounds perfect." Her smile faded. "We're not going to have to climb into a bog though, are we? Serena said she and Joel had to, and I don't know that I really want to do that."

"Joel?"

"Joel Wakefield. The assistant pastor at my church. He took Serena here on a date, and now they're married."

He peeked across, saw her cheeks had pinked and she was glancing out the window, like she was embarrassed. But he wasn't about to get side-tracked into questions of dates at cranberry farms leading to marriage, not when she'd just said something similarly interesting. "You've mentioned Serena before. She's the friend you met yesterday?"

She nodded, and new tension filled the car.

"How did that go?" It was obvious, but he didn't like to make assumptions.

Still, her sigh gave it away. "Not as good as I hoped."

When it became obvious she wasn't going to say any more, he finally said, "I'm sorry."

"Yeah. Me too. Serena's nice, don't get me wrong, but now she's a mom and she's so busy with the church, well, I don't feel like things are the same as before."

"It's hard when those kinds of dynamics change," he said, steering into a parking spot.

She bit her lip, and he sensed she probably didn't want him pursuing this, but it was important for him to get the facts. And part of getting to know a person was knowing their relationships with others and what that might mean down the track. A person who isolated themselves from others could lead to a very different life compared to somebody who was life of the party and needed people around all the time. He was more inclined to preferring alone time, which was why it was interesting to see which way Anna veered.

They got out, and she peeked at him. "I've had some challenges with some of my friends in the past year, which is why seeing Serena was a little confronting."

"What kinds of challenges?"

She shrugged, her gaze falling to her painted toenails. "Just girl stuff. It wouldn't interest you."

But it did. Although he sensed pushing her any more would only make her close down. Still, he was getting more of a fuller picture of who Miss Anna Morely might be.

· · ·

OVER A PLATE OF LOCAL CHEESE, artisanal crackers, preserves and cranberries, they drank cranberry cider, and he learned more about this woman. She'd worked as a medical receptionist for nine years, had lived in Muskoka Shores for all her life, was an only child, her parents divorced.

She in turn seemed fascinated to hear about his family, his brothers, what had led him into police work, then she asked about his cases.

"Have you ever had a case you couldn't solve?"

"Are you asking because you like those true crime shows?" He smiled so it looked like tease.

Her nose wrinkled. "I only got into it more recently. It's not like something I've loved all my life."

"Just checking. Because I don't really want to spend too much time talking about my cases on my day off."

She winced. "Sorry."

"Hey, it's okay. But I just try to keep work at work and it's nice to switch off when I can."

"I can understand that."

"So, tell me more about you. How did you become a Christian?"

"Wow. Going in with the big questions, huh?"

"It's pretty important to me, so yeah."

"Okay then." Her forehead wrinkled a little. "I can't actually remember when I first prayed the prayer. I was pretty young, but then it became a lot more real when my parents got divorced. We'd always gone to church, and then things got tense between them, and I found that God was my comfort when everything else was going wrong. That, and my friends."

"Like Serena?"

She nodded. "And Jackie." She froze.

Okay. There was more here. "Jackie?"

Her gaze slipped away as she shrugged. "She used to be my friend. Then she got together with—get this, Lincoln Cash, you know the famous Hollywood actor?—and since going out with him she basically hasn't talked to me since."

"Wow." And… awkward. Didn't she know that Jackie and Lincoln were married?

When Lincoln had bought his "cottage" late last year he—or his "people"—had advised the police who had official permission to access the site, just like most celebrities informed the local authorities about regular approved visitors in case of security breaches. Lincoln's place was only a few doors down from Dan Walton's, the Leafs' top defenseman, who also owned a summer cottage on that stretch of lake. And while they might enjoy their privacy, and he gathered that Lincoln had wanted to keep his marriage a secret in order to protect his wife, he hadn't figured that his wife's former friend might not know. Still, that was not his news to share. He wondered if Joel and Serena Wakefield knew.

"I'm sorry that's been difficult for you," he finally said.

"Stuff happens."

Sure did.

"So what else do you want to know, Detective?"

"Have you traveled much?"

"Not as much as I'd like. You?"

"I visited Italy a few years ago." On the non-refundable trip he'd booked for his honeymoon with Meghan. Visiting with Marc just wasn't the same.

"Italy? Oh, that must've been amazing."

"It was." He'd amazed himself at keeping it together. At not breaking down at every place he and Meghan had talked about seeing together. Having Marc there had proved diverting enough, his insistence at trying pizza and gelato at every place they stopped to find the best had meant he'd clocked up plenty of miles in running it off.

He cleared his throat. Time to push this into something real.

"I was supposed to go there on my honeymoon, but my fiancée died before the wedding."

Her mouth fell open, her hand dropping to cover his. "Oh, Tom. I'm so sorry."

Her compassion—or maybe it was her touch—forced him to clear his throat. "It's a while ago now, but yeah. You were right before. Sometimes stuff does happen."

"That's so awful." She shook her head. "That's not stuff. That's heartbreaking."

"Which is why I was so glad I had God to help me through it all. I don't think I would've coped if I didn't have faith that God still held me in His hand."

Her gaze fell to his hand, and he turned his palm to hold hers more securely.

She glanced back up. "You seem so calm about it."

"I wasn't at the time. But like I said, it's been a few years now, and I guess I'm more reconciled to things. If it wasn't for God and for my family and friends who kept encouraging me to trust Him and His plans for my life, then I probably would've been more of a mess than I am."

She squeezed his hand then let go.

He missed her warmth, her touch. But he wouldn't push her. "So, how about you? Any great or tragic love story?"

She shook her head. "No. I've always been the one overlooked."

He heard the bitterness in that statement. Felt an urge to reassure her by holding her hand again. But then realized she was probably on her journey to finding acceptance in God, and needing to find security in being alone, just like he'd needed to after Meghan had died.

He drank the last of his cider, noticing the venue had almost cleared out and the wait staff were cleaning up. "I... I felt like I had to learn who I was again without Meghan in my life. And maybe this will sound weird to say, but I felt like it was a good chance to find my identity and security in God rather than feeling defined in a relationship."

Her gaze swerved to meet his. "That's the thing. I don't think I know how to do that. I thought I did, but in the last couple of years I've seen every single one of my friends meet someone and fall in love, and I'm left on the shelf like the jar of pickles nobody wants."

"A jar of pickles?"

Her mouth twisted. "Might as well be. I know I can get pretty sour and bitey at times, but it doesn't mean I don't want someone to look past that and really see me and still want me."

Wow. He'd wanted honesty, but this was levels of candor he hadn't counted on. And neither had she, judging from her flushed face and averted gaze.

"Excuse me a moment." She pushed back her chair and spoke to a staff member, who pointed to a door in the back.

Okay, so the prompting to go slow had been wise. He might like this woman, but he sensed she needed more time to hear what God said about her before jumping into a relationship and Anna trying to find validation from him. Which meant any future dates, even future conversations, needed to be threaded with caution.

He picked at the remaining cheese and crackers and prayed for her, that she'd find healing and wholeness. He couldn't afford to be the person a woman sought above God. Not again. Meghan had been a believer, but she'd had her own issues with anxiety and body image, and he'd learned the need to point to God rather than feel obliged to solve her issues himself.

Anna returned, her gaze tentative, just as a waiter asked if they were finished yet. Anna pinched the last cranberry, and after checking she didn't want it, he took the remaining cracker then smeared the last of the creamy cheese. "Thanks, that was delicious."

"It was." Anna met his gaze. "Thank you."

"My pleasure."

And it was. A pleasure, and a relief to know that God had given this time for them to get to know each other some more and cement them into being friends. And to give Tom that internal warning to take things slow and not run ahead, but to wait for God's leading with where things with Anna went next.

CHAPTER 8

"*H*ello, Muskoka Shores Medical Clinic, please hold the line."

Anna pressed hold on the phone system, and dealt with the man who had been waiting at the counter less than patiently. "Thank you, sir. Now, if you could please swipe your card here, then you'll be done."

"I don't know why this place doesn't put on more staff," he muttered.

She kept her response locked behind her lips. Employing more staff was unlikely to help him deal with his own levels of impatience.

"Thank you," she gritted out as she handed over his receipt of payment, which he snatched and walked away.

Bless.

She answered the person on hold, and caught Gabby's roll of eyes, which drew her shoulders down. The past few days had been insanely busy, as if the spring blooms had brought an increase in hay fever and half the town had decided to succumb to sneezes. Trying to fit in more appointments this week was going to be tricky.

"Dr. Strauss?" She checked with the caller. "I'm afraid the earliest we have with him is next Monday at eleven."

She braced for the abuse, but when a simple "Thank you" met her ears instead, felt herself sag in relief. "Thank you for your understanding. We'll see you next Monday at eleven."

Dr. James Wells entered the space, asked for some files which she handed him. "Who's next?" he asked Anna.

"Mrs. Brusselhorst and her daughter Jordan."

He nodded, then moved out into the waiting area and called for them, while Anna dealt with a new arrival who wanted to know what the wait time might be before their appointment.

"See, if I make an appointment at ten, I expect to go in at ten." The woman flipped her blonde bob over her shoulder. "I don't understand why I am being forced to wait sometimes for almost an hour, like my time isn't valuable or anything. If it's not ten and it's more likely to be eleven, then why don't they say eleven?"

Anna dug deep for patience. "Sometimes the doctors have emergencies they need to deal with, which is why—"

"Are you saying they've had emergencies every single time I've made an appointment?"

Lord, give me strength. "I'm sorry you've had some long wait times before. At the moment the doctor is running pretty close to time so if you take a seat, I'm sure he'll be with you shortly." She tilted her head at the chairs and smiled.

"I don't like being forced to wait like my own time isn't important."

"I understand. If you make your appointment early in the day then you'll usually find they will be more likely to be on time, or at least as close to time as they can be."

The patient grumbled and moved to the waiting areas, snatching up two magazines like she was prepared to settle in for a long wait.

The phone rang again. Gabby was busy on another call, so

Anna answered. "Hello, Muskoka Shores Medical Clinic, this is Anna."

"I have an appointment with Dr. Lewisham in ten minutes, and I'm calling to say I think I will be a little bit late."

Anna closed her eyes. "How late?"

"Maybe fifteen minutes."

She released a silent sigh as the man hung up and studied her computer, juggling appointments so the morning would not see a backlog. While most patients were given fifteen-minute time slots, some needing more specialized exams like skin checks or pap smears would need longer. And the postponement of a thirty or forty-five-minute appointment, even by five minutes, had the capacity to delay the other patients for that doctor for the rest of the day. Late patients meant doctors sometimes even missed their lunch breaks in an effort to catch up on the back-log. Patients who were late who then had the nerve to complain really had no idea.

At least that patient had called to say they may be late. That was better than the no-shows who seemed to deem everyone else's time as being less significant than their own. A low level of irritation prickled inside, as much as for the doctors' sake as for her own. She and Gabby often felt like they lived in a weird space of having to protect the doctors, while also trying to appease the patients, who often themselves were simply letting anxiety for themselves or others impinge on their manners. She knew, only too well, that stress often made people frustrated.

Which made her all the more amazed at Tom's story, about how he had coped with his fiancée's death, and come out the other side whole. Her admiration for the man had only increased, especially after his overwhelmingly generous offer to assist with her car woes.

She'd gone with him to pick it up on Monday, after hours, then been surprised to find his brother was still there. Tom had said he wouldn't be, and she'd wondered if Drew had stayed behind simply to check this new woman in Tom's life. Not that she was exactly *in* it. Not really. If she was, then surely he would've set up another date by now. And the fact he hadn't said anything more about another date made her wonder if she'd been a little too real and raw on Sunday and put him off.

Her heart dipped with familiar discouragement. She probably had turned him off, with her complaints and not-quite-hidden bitterness about Jackie. Tom was obviously looking to date again, and seemingly wanting to get married, if he'd been so eager to get married a few years ago. So why would he want anything to do with someone who couldn't move on from the past when he obviously had?

She'd heard the subtle challenge in his words, and had taken it to bed with her. His words about finding her identity and strength in God were a challenge, because she was awfully afraid she'd gotten used to playing the part of a victim. Nobody liked that. Not even herself. But the fact this came after that early morning Bible reading session on the very same day, made her wonder if perhaps God was speaking to her about letting go of the past, and finding herself in Him again.

Around her, the busyness of the clinic demanded attention, but the thought kept flickering in the back of her mind. Those words from the Bible about shining like the sun when it rose in its strength. She wasn't strong. She hadn't shone Jesus for months. Yet if she called herself a Christian, wasn't that what she was supposed to do?

The day passed, and she grabbed an apple for lunch. The clinic's busyness meant it was late by the time she had finished the paperwork and was ready to close, Gabby and the doctors having left a while ago.

She stepped from the staff door, and had just locked up when she felt movement behind. She turned. Then froze. A man she'd never seen before held a syringe, the uncapped needle pointed at her.

"Don't scream," he muttered, his breath a rush of foul air. "Don't move. Don't do nothing you'll regret."

She couldn't move, even if she hadn't frozen, wedged as she was between the man and the door. "What... what do you want?"

"You have drugs inside, don't you?"

Her limbs shook, her heartbeat racing, she was struggling to suck in air, and she was awfully afraid she might pee her pants. She'd never been so afraid in her life. "Th-they're stored in the vault. I c-can't open the vault. It... it's on a time delay."

Lord, I need Your help!

She sucked in a shaky breath, as a strange sense of stillness descended on her. The staff had trained for situations like this. Not that she could remember what she was supposed to do except to try and keep the man calm. *Lord?*

"That's a lie."

"It's not." Her voice firmed with the truth. "It's a security measure," designed for situations like this, "so it can only be accessed when the clinic is open. And n-now it's closed, and an alarm goes off if anyone tries to open it and the police get called." Would Tom come if that was the case? *Please Lord, send help.*

The man swore.

"Hey! What are you doing?" a male voice called.

The man released another foul word then shoved her away, dropping the needle in his haste. She slumped, half crouching against the door as the good Samaritan hurried across the street. "Miss? Are you okay?"

She peered up into an unfamiliar face. "Th-thank you."

He reached out a hand, his grip strong as he gently pulled her upright in the shadowed recess. "Are you okay? Did he hurt you?"

"No. Just shocked me, that's all." She heaved in a steadying breath. Another. *Oh, thank You God. Thank You God.*

The man peered down the street, took a couple of steps then returned. "I can't see him anywhere."

If she'd been the would-be thief, she wouldn't have hung around with this brawny guy looking like he was spoiling for a fight, either.

"You need to report this to the police."

She nodded. She did. "If I do, then you would likely need to come to as a witness."

"Sure." He pointed to the camera, tucked up in the upper left-hand corner of the staff entrance. "Won't they have caught him on video?"

"Hopefully." She'd have to call Dr. Lewisham to tell them to have the security footage checked.

"Okay, well, I can come now if you like. Sorry, what's your name?"

"Anna."

"Okay. Where's your car?"

She pointed to the parking lot where her Mazda was the sole occupant. He glanced at it, then at her, biceps bulging as he crossed his arms. "Nice paint job."

She nodded. "I had to get it resprayed after paint got on it."

"Looks like a recent job."

"Monday."

His mouth curved, and he waited while she got in, then assured her he'd be on his way. She drove to the police station, her hands shaky. Parked out the front. Then waited, trembling, until someone knocked on her window. She yelped, then looked up to see the big guy from before.

He winced. "Sorry about that."

She sucked in another breath, grabbed her bag then slowly opened her car door. He held it open as she exited, then opened the door to the police station building, waiting for her to enter first.

Her rescuer nodded to the front desk clerk. "Hey, is he in?"

She glanced at him. Was who in?

"He's out on a job at the moment. What's happened?"

The guy jerked a thumb at her. "Attempted burglary at the medical clinic."

The clerk eyed her. "Miss? Were you involved?"

"I w-work there and was closing up when this man appeared behind me and had a needle which he threatened me with unless I opened the safe. But I told him it's on a timer and I couldn't access it which is true, but he refused to believe me until this man yelled out, and he ran away."

"Dropping the needle," her rescuer added. "So we've got some nice evidence for the detective when he bothers to show."

The detective? How many detectives did Muskoka have? Did he refer to Tom?

"Okay, well, I'll need you both to go through to an interview room shortly. Miss, is there anyone I can call for you?"

Serena. Her mom. Tom? She shook her head. "I'm fine."

"You're clearly not," her rescuer said. "You're trembling."

"I'm cold."

"That's called shock. Hey, Jones, have you got a blanket for her? Maybe something she can eat? You don't need her collapsing."

"I'm not about to collapse," she insisted.

"Lady, I've seen my fair share of people in shock, and you might not feel it, but your body sure is, which is why you need to sit down and eat something sugary to get your heartrate back up."

Seeing Tom might help with that. She took a seat, and eyed him, annoyed. Who did this guy think he was ordering police people around?

He pulled out his phone, stabbed a number, then eyed her as he held it to his ear. "Yeah, it's me. I think you need to get back to the station asap." A pause. "There was an attempted burglary and I think someone you know was involved."

She stilled. Did this man know Tom? If so, why would this man know about her? He pocketed his phone, lips tweaking as another police officer gestured for them both to come to a room.

"Marc, you can never keep out of trouble, can you?"

"Hey, this time I was just the innocent passerby." He pointed to her. "This is the lady you should be speaking to. Anna, right?"

"Anna Morely. And sorry, who are you?"

"Marc. Marc Woodmore."

She blinked. "Tom's brother?"

He grinned, Cheshire cat-like. "Now why would you know that?"

Why would—?

"Marc, I need Ms. Morely to concentrate and tell me everything that happened. It might be best for you to wait outside until we're done."

"You're not going to wait for Tom?"

"He's out on a call."

"Still, I think he might be the best person to help deal with this situation, if you know what I mean."

Did Marc just wink at the police officer? Who did he think he was? She straightened, lifting her chin as she tried to remember the deportment lessons her mom had shelled out for her half a lifetime ago. "Thank you, Marc. I appreciate you helping me, but I don't know what you're trying to do here now. I'm happy to tell this officer what happened, and I don't need to tell Detective Woodmore anything."

"I think you'll find he'll want to know."

"I think the young lady is right," the officer whose nametag read "Jones" said. "Marc, thank you for trying to be helpful but you can leave this with me now. I will deal with you shortly."

"Deal with? Like I'm in trouble? Man, you people…." The rest of his complaint was shut off by the closed door.

"Sorry, Ms. Morely."

"Anna is fine."

"Okay, well, could you please tell me in your own words what happened?"

TOM HURRIED up the steps and entered, then strode down the hall to the public part of the station. Marc sat hunched over his phone and looked up. "She's in there."

He had no wish to know how Marc had put two and two together—he suspected it was probably their big brother who'd likely jumped on his phone as soon as Anna had pulled away on Monday evening—then quickly moved to the interview room. He knocked and flung open the door.

Anna glanced up at him, head in her hands, and he paused. "Are you okay?"

"She wasn't hurt," Constable Jones said.

Relief oozed from him in a silent exhale.

Jones cleared his throat. "We are conducting an interview here, thanks, Detective."

"And now I'm here you can continue."

Anna's mouth lifted slightly. "I just finished."

"Then tell me from the top what happened."

He studied her as she shared her story again. Anna looked pale, but not unnaturally shaky. He'd dealt with some people who had undergone similar shocking events who'd proved barely coherent. Anna, by contrast, seemed reasonably calm and assured. Whether that was because the incident had not taken long, or because she was not injured, he couldn't say. But he admired the way that she was holding her poise.

He nodded, thanked her, then looked at Jones. "What's been done about the suspect?"

"We're still getting access to the footage."

Tom glanced at her. "Who can get us the footage from the clinic quickly?"

"Dr. Wells. He lives nearest."

"What's his number?"

She pulled out her phone and sent it to him.

If Jones thought there was something odd about the fact she had Tom's phone number in her contacts he didn't say anything. Thank goodness. "Okay, sit tight for a little longer, while we make some calls. Is there anyone we can get to be with you? Your mom?"

Her lips flatlined. "She'd just stress."

"Serena?" If Serena Wakefield was anything like her husband, then she seemed the type to know what to do in such situations.

She sighed. "I can try."

"You should stay with someone else tonight. You might think you'll be okay at home but often it's helpful in these situations to have someone nearby in case you have a nightmare."

"I'll call her," she mumbled.

His heart pinged with relief. "I won't be long, okay?"

She nodded, and he turned to Jones. "I'll call Dr. Wells and get that footage asap, then get someone to survey any other public surveillance cameras in the area. If it's who I think it is, then we should hopefully be able to track him down pretty fast."

He caught Anna's creased brow and offered what he hoped was a reassuring smile. "Don't worry. We'll find him. You'll be safe."

Tom left as Jones asked her to write out a statement, then he called a suitably shocked Dr. Wells, who agreed to come in immediately to access the video. Then he caught his brother. "What happened?"

Marc filled him in, complete with a description, which he passed along to Jones. "So she wasn't hurt?"

"It didn't look like it. And she denied it. She was in shock though."

"She seems okay now."

"Hmm, says the man who's been holding out on us. How long has this been going on for?"

"It's not."

"Isn't she the one you cut a deal with Drew to respray her car?"

"I don't actually have time for this right now. I have a wannabe thief to catch."

"So go catch him," Marc called, eyes back on his phone.

It was nearly an hour later when he finally had time to return to the interview room where he found Anna talking with another woman, who he hoped was her friend Serena.

Both women looked up as he entered. "Any luck?" Anna asked.

He nodded. "We're fortunate in that there was a public camera on the intersection nearby, and judging from the description my, uh, the other witness gave, it seems likely it was who we thought. We don't have him in custody yet, but we know enough about his movements to make a fair guess where he'll be."

"So can I go?"

"You've signed your witness statement?"

"Yes."

"Then you're free to go. I know this is unpleasant, but your quick actions in reporting things means we should get a much faster result than if you'd waited." He glanced at the woman beside her, held out his hand. "I'm Detective Woodmore."

She shook it. "I remember. You were the one who helped bring in Toni's stalker." She smiled. "I'm Serena Wakefield. Toni is my sister-in-law."

He nodded. "I remember seeing you at her wedding last year."

A glance at Anna saw her eyes round. And just as he'd intended, her fear from the earlier incident seemed to dissipate as she remembered. Well, he hoped that's what that look meant. "Sorry ladies, but I need to go. Miss Morely," best he be formal now, "I'm afraid I might need to see you again in the next day or so in case we need you to identify the suspect."

"She'll be staying at our place tonight," Serena said. "Do you need our number?"

"I believe we have yours already, Miss Morely."

"Yes, Detective."

He bit back a smile, glad she was willing to play along. "We'll keep you informed on how things go. And Miss Morely, if there's anything else you recall that you feel you need to report then you know the number to call, yes?"

"Yes. Thank you."

There. The ball was in her court, and if she wanted to share with her friends about who he was to her, well she could. If she didn't, that was okay too. But judging from the way she kept sneaking peeks at him, and the way Serena looked between the two of them, it wouldn't take long before Anna was being given the third degree by her friend.

It was several hours later that he was finally able to send her a message: *Are you able to talk?*

Within a minute her number was flashing on his screen as a phone call. He smiled. Answered. "I'll take that as a yes."

"Have you found him?"

"We have. He's in custody. I thought you'd like to know."

Her exhale was loud. "Oh, thank you. Thank you so much. I know it wasn't personal, but it's still good to know he can't do this to anyone else."

"He's tried similar things in the past, which is why we had a fairly strong idea who it might be. And between the dropped syringe, the footage at the clinic, and your statement and Marc's we've got a pretty solid case."

"Thank you."

He glanced around. After the late afternoon rush of activity generated by the druggie's actions the station had resumed its usual late night quiet. "So how are you feeling?"

"Better than before. It helps to have others here to focus on instead of just running through things on my own. Home would've been too quiet."

"Tonight is not the night to be focused on true crime, okay?"

"Okay." Her laughter was shaky, sparking concern.

"Are you okay? Really?" he pressed softly.

"I will be. And I have to admit you're right. No more true crime for me. Especially of this kind."

"Good. I don't want you getting anywhere near danger, okay?"

"Yes, Detective."

"That's Tom to you."

Her giggle was as good as salve on a burn for soothing his concerns. She might be still shocked, but if she could laugh as his corny jokes, then that was a good sign.

"Will I need to come in and identify him?"

"I'll let you know."

"Just so you know, I'm not necessarily the best person at identifying people."

He frowned. "Why do you say that?"

"Well, see, I totally didn't realize that it was you who I sat next to at Toni's wedding last year. Which, well, makes me feel kind of dumb."

"Hey, if it makes you feel any better, it took me awhile to realize that was you."

"You knew? And you didn't say anything?"

"I didn't think it mattered. Especially as I barely got a chance to talk to you at the wedding, only saw this pretty woman wearing a great dress who arrived late and left early, which made me wonder why."

"Oh."

Silence stretched between them, and he wondered what she'd say next. Admit to why she'd left early to her friend's wedding when most friends would hang around? Or would she respond to his compliment about the dress?

"You thought I was pretty?"

"I still do."

He could almost hear her smile.

"Detective," she began.

"Tom."

"Detective Tom," her voice held a smirk, "on second thoughts, I'm now really feeling like I probably could identify the man. If it means coming into the station and seeing you again."

He smiled, then glanced up to see Cole Jones had entered the room. He needed to choose his words carefully. "I think we can arrange something. And if it turns out a lineup is not necessary then perhaps we can arrange an alternative meeting."

"I'd like that."

So would he. He cleared his throat, conscious his was the only voice in the room and whatever he said could be heard. "Then I trust you will have a good rest of your night. I'll be in touch soon."

"Good night, Tom. And thank you."

He placed the phone screen down on the desk, as Jones drew near. "Who was that?"

"Just following up on an incident today."

"The druggie?"

"All dealt with. He's in the lock up as we speak."

"That's a fast result. Here." Jones handed over a sheaf of papers. "It just came in. Marked for you."

"Thanks." His stomach tensed, as he accepted the sealed folder, marked for his eyes only. A quick glimpse inside revealed, as he suspected, the financial records for the Foundation. Which was exactly why he didn't want word leaking out. Who knew if the Craylings had connections with the police too?

His phone buzzed, and he flipped it over. Anna. *Thanks again. I really appreciate your support.*

He moved to write *Any time,* when he realized he didn't want her thinking that this kind of thing would happen again. So instead, he tapped out *I'll be praying for you.*

She sent back a smiling emoji and praying hands, which caused his heart to smile.

And caused his prayers to double as he glanced at the files and prayed that she would be kept safe too.

CHAPTER 9

"Anna?" Serena's voice called through the closed door. "Anna, are you awake?"

"Yes." She'd barely slept.

"Can I come in?"

"Sure." She sat up in the bed, thankful for the cozy room, for Serena's hospitality in letting her stay. She was such a good friend. Such a good, good friend. Her eyes filled.

Serena noticed as she entered, instantly wrapping her in a hug. "Oh, honey, it's okay. You're safe."

"Oh, I know. Thank you. It's not that."

Serena smoothed a hand down her face. "You look like you didn't get much sleep."

But not for the reason that Serena obviously thought. She couldn't sleep because she'd been so busy trying to strain her memory for details about Tom when she had sat next to him at Toni's wedding. And wondering about the caress in his voice when he'd asked if she was okay. And shivering as she wondered exactly what he'd pray for her about. The thought he'd do that for her made her tingly.

"I got enough. T—" she quickly corrected to, "the police called last night to say they found him."

"They got the guy?"

She nodded.

"That's wonderful! Praise the Lord."

"Amen."

"He must've called very late."

"I didn't want to wake you."

"That's the kind of good news worth waking friends for. Oh, I'm so glad you're okay."

Anna's tears spilled as she wrapped her arms around Serena. "I'm so glad for friends like you who still love me, even when I've gone astray."

"Hey, that's what love is. Always patient, always hoping."

She nodded. She hadn't loved her friends the way they had her. Her mind might understand the concept of grace, but her heart struggled still. "I'm… I'm so sorry for how I've treated you."

"Hey, it's forgiven. It's in the past. And I'm really happy that we are able to move forward."

"I want to," she admitted. Even though it wouldn't be easy. That moment yesterday had shown there were no guarantees in life. And what would that have meant if she had died, and her friends still thought she hated them? What a terrible legacy that would be.

Her phone alarm buzzed, and she glanced at it. It had been set for her usual get-ready-for-work time. Amid the fuss of last night, she vaguely recalled Dr. Lewisham saying she didn't have to come in today. Or had that been a dream?

"You know you don't have to go to work today."

"I told you that?"

"I was there when you took that call."

"Okay. It's been such a crazy twenty-four hours I barely know what's real anymore."

Serena nodded. "Would… would you mind if I told the others about this? I know they all care about you, and they would want to pray."

"The others meaning…?"

"Toni, Rachel, Staci. And Jackie." Serena said that last name slowly, like she was testing it out.

Anna's chest tensed. "You can tell them, but I don't think I'm up to talking to a lot of people all at once."

"But just those four?" Serena winced. "Not that they can all drop everything and come here. Although I'm pretty sure Rachel could."

Rachel was someone Anna might possibly cope with, if she had a little more time to get used to the idea. And Toni and Staci, she could cope with too, although she knew Staci was often in New York, and Toni was often in Toronto with Matt. But why couldn't Jackie? Not that Jackie would probably want to see her. Not after Anna had blocked her calls. But still. A tiny spark of stupidly unreasonable offense flared. Why couldn't she come? Probably because she was too busy with Lincoln.

"How about you just message them, and maybe if Rachel's around we could do something with her."

"I know she'd *love* that."

"But I don't want people feeling like they need to smother me. My mom will be more than capable of doing that if she finds out."

"You're not going to tell her?"

Anna shuddered. "I can't imagine the fuss she'll create if I do."

"She is your mother, though." Serena's expression turned pensive. "You only get one of those."

Anna remembered that Serena had often felt a little abandoned by her own mother, who had chosen the poor of India rather than caring for Serena and her sister. That comparison thing was legitimate, then.

"I'll tell her. But in my own time, and in my own way."

Serena's nose wrinkled. "You might want to do it soon before she finds out from the media."

"The media knows?"

"I suspect they will. We're not exactly rolling in big crimes around here, so the little ones will be front and center to make up for it."

Awesome. "Okay. I'll do it soon. But maybe I'll do it from here then she won't feel the need to come and visit me."

Serena smiled. "Don't forget that she might be the one who feels the need for comfort."

Oh. She hadn't thought about it quite like that. Suddenly seeing it from her mother's perspective, the thought that she might have been close to losing her only child, softened her heart toward telling her. "I'll do it now then."

As Serena exited, Anna pressed the numbers to make the call, and sure enough, her mother was shocked and declared that she would come around immediately. Anna was very glad to have the excuse of being "at a friend's" but that didn't deter her.

"I'll come around tonight, sweetie. Unless you want to come and stay here."

"Mom, they've caught the guy, and he's now behind bars, so I'm safe. It was just a random thing and it's not like I'm walking around with a target on my back."

"Oh, *please* don't say such things. You have no idea how much I worry about you sometimes."

Oh, she had some idea.

"I just want you to be happy to meet a nice young man and settle down and have a family."

She rolled her eyes. "I know, Mom. I want that too. One day." When it was the right time. God's right time.

Her mother kept on talking but she barely noticed. God had protected her last night and had sent someone to rescue her, just like she had prayed. Just at the right time. So surely she could trust Him to send the right man at the right time, too.

Lord, help me to be patient and to wait for Your right timing. Of course, such a prayer assumed a man would be in her life. She didn't feel so filled with faith to pray the alternative. Not yet, anyway.

"Tell me more about this man who rescued you," her mom asked. "Was he young? Is he handsome?"

"Why?" she asked, fully knowing the reason.

Her mother laughed. "Oh, you know I want you to find someone. And if your knight in shining armor happens to be that special someone, then I'd be thrilled."

"Then surely the more important question should be whether he's a Christian. Oh, and the basic question of whether he's single."

"Oh, I suppose those things are important too."

"Mom."

"So is that a yes?"

"I don't know, Mom. Strangely, we didn't talk about any of that while at the police station. Weird, I know."

"Well, I can imagine this has been a very stressful time so such questions might have slipped your mind. Never mind. I shall see you later today. I imagine you'll be busy at the station this morning doing important police things."

"I'm not exactly sure when or what's involved, but I'll be okay. I *am* okay, Mom, so you don't need to worry."

"I love you, darling."

Her heart softened. "I love you, too."

"Well, let me know how you go today and if I can help in any way you only need to call."

"Thanks, Mom. I better go."

"Love you, sweetie. Thanks for letting me know."

"Love you, too, Mom. Talk soon."

She ended the call, slumped back against the pillows.

Serena had returned, holding baby Caleb in her arms. "Do you need a snuggle?"

Anna swung her legs out of the bed. "Always." She had so many lost snuggles to make up for.

Serena handed her the baby, and she took Caleb carefully.

"God is so good, isn't He?" Serena said, as Anna caressed Caleb's soft-as-a-petal cheek.

"Yes." She held proof of God's goodness in her arms right now. Sweet innocence personified.

"I always trusted that God had good plans, but sometimes it was so hard to believe," Serena continued softly, her gaze fixed on her son. "And now I look back and I'm amazed at the answered prayers. But the challenge can be staying filled with faith when it all seems impossible." Serena kissed her baby's hand. "Our God always knows the right time."

Anna nodded, as Serena excused herself for a moment to have a shower, and cuddled the baby closer, drawing in a breath scented with fresh baby, her heart clenching. Oh, she wanted this one day.

But then her decision to let God have His perfect timing flitted through her mind, and she tamped down the longing. God knew what He was doing. He'd proved that yesterday, and had proved that so many times before. And she could trust Him. Whether He had someone for her, or whether He didn't, she could still trust Him to be with her, just like He had been yesterday, giving that sense of supernatural calm. Whatever happened in life, she *knew* she could trust Him.

So—her heart was shaky—if that meant no man, then okay. God had something better for her. Something that would be better for her. Because like Serena said, God had good plans.

But just in case God did have someone for her, then whoever that man might be that God had in her future, then she would pray, as she'd prayed most of her life, that God would touch him, bless him, strengthen him, help him to wait for her as she would wait for him. And trust that God would lead them into each other's paths. Soon.

~

"Woodmore, we are getting requests from media about yesterday's incident." Gabe eyed him. "I'm passing this to the media team because I'm assuming if you're still planning to do that undercover operation that you don't actually want to be showing your face on TV any time soon."

Tom nodded. He'd been careful not to give interviews for that very reason. "I think that's wise."

"Where are things up to with the case? I want you to do your undercover stint as soon as you can."

"I can only do that once the builder is called."

Gabe frowned. "Has your pastor friend called them yet?"

"Last I checked he was doing so this week."

"Okay, well, let me know as soon as you know. Oh, and good work with yesterday, it's always good to get a fast result."

"Amen," he said without thinking.

Gabe squinted at him, and Tom excused himself on the grounds he was busy. He didn't want to get into a political debate about religion in the workforce.

He called to follow up with Joel and asked if he had called the Craylings yet. Joel assured him that he had, so he asked how the house guest had fared.

"She's doing okay."

"Good."

More than that he couldn't say, especially as he didn't want to stir up any suspicions in anyone else. Knowing he needed to be careful, he hadn't sent her a text this morning. Text messages were all too easy to exchange and could stir up flirty feelings which needed to be contained. The package of documents he received last night had only increased his concern about Anna's connection to the Crayling family, proving an unfortunate distraction from his sleep. But he'd barely slept anyway, too busy trying not to imagine what fears Anna had faced. In that moment, he thought that reading the documents would be dry enough to distract him. He'd been wrong. Instead, it had only ignited fresh determination to get to the bottom of this case.

But something else last night had shown him was the need to help Anna learn to defend herself, to renew her confidence, and to help protect herself should something like that happen again. But how to do that without it being too obvious seemed yet another mystery he would have to solve. His lips flicked up. Good thing he loved to solve puzzles.

TOM DID his best to appear calm when Anna returned to the station mid-morning. She was accompanied by Serena again, and he didn't want to stir her suspicions by acting in the manner he might really like. Like to give Anna a hug. To get her alone, and ask if she really was okay and watch her face intently to make sure she truly was. She'd indicated her mother would be over this afternoon and may spill into the evening, which left his visit to her out. But still, the weekend loomed, so maybe he could organize another Sunday afternoon time that had a casual-yet-intentional feel about it.

"So you truly don't need me to do an identity parade like on the movies?" Anna asked.

He smiled. "How many of those true crime shows have you actually watched?"

Serena glanced between them, and he hoped she took his comment to mean something they discussed before. Which, technically it was. Still, he had to nip any further speculation in the bud, so he smoothed the tease from his face and hoped he projected gravity. "It would be helpful if you could point out the person in our mug book, Miss Morely. That's enough for now."

Her nose wrinkled. "I really didn't get a great look at him, but I'll try."

He led her to the interview room where the book was already waiting. Then, with little ado, she identified the subject immediately.

"Excellent. Thank you very much for your time, Miss Morely."

"You're very welcome, Detective."

Her flirtatious look drew fresh amusement, but he knew he had to tamp his expression back to neutral. "I'll be in touch if there's anything else."

"Thank you for your time."

He nodded. "Ladies."

Serena exited first, and he caught Anna's slowed step and touched her upper arm. "You are okay?" he asked in a hushed voice.

"I am. Thank you." Her upwards glance at him held truth, and his heart eased.

"Take care of yourself now," he said in a louder voice for Serena's benefit.

"You too," Anna said, giving him a final smile before exiting.

He switched off the light, and turned to walk down the hall, pausing to catch a final glimpse as they exited, and Anna gave a little wave.

He nodded, exhaling, gripping the book firmly as he tried to resume nonchalance like interacting with her didn't affect him. He'd never been in this situation before, where he had been interested in a witness, and it felt like he could trip up at any moment.

After putting the mug book away, he returned to his desk and filled out more paperwork for the case. This would now pass to the next in the chain of command, which meant he could return to concentrating on the case with the Craylings.

But working through this felt like walking through quicksand. He might be going through the motions, and looking like he was heading in the right direction, but it didn't really feel like he was making headway. Not when every thought kept flicking back to Anna, and wondering how she was doing, what she was doing. This wasn't how he envisaged working today.

His phone rang, and he snatched it up. The screen read *Damian Taylor*. He internally fist-pumped. One guess what this might be. "This is Tom Woodmore."

"Tom, you'll never guess who just called."

"I think you'll find I might."

Damian chuckled. "How soon can you be ready?"

"They want it done now?"

"As soon as possible, they said. And I've got a few hours free, so I hoped to go there today. Will that work for you?"

The sooner he got this sorted the better. "I'll need half an hour to change. Where should I meet you?"

Damian gave his home address, and Tom grabbed his suit jacket and left, telling Gabe where he was going.

"Good timing. Keep your head down and find out what you can."

"Yes, boss."

"The road's a bit rough," Damian noted as he drove down the dusty road.

Tom adjusted his ballcap, emblazoned with the logo of Taylor Constructions. He'd zipped home and changed into jeans and a navy tee and worn work boots, and hoped he looked the part. Damian was shorter, with the solid build of a man who had worked construction for years. Tom knew his own muscles didn't compare, but he hoped he looked like he possessed enough sinewy strength to play the part of Damian's off-sider convincingly.

The road curved, and he tapped his fingers against his knees.

His mission was to find a resident who might be able to talk and tell him about what was really going on, and help clarify whether there was anything of significance happening. Of course, if Kyle was there then he would do his best to avoid seeing him, but he prayed it wouldn't come to that.

The overhanging trees that had made for a tunnel-like effect suddenly halted, revealing a flat sandy looking stretch of land dotted with a variety of buildings. "Slow down a little, please."

Damian obeyed, and Tom took pictures with his camera, focusing particularly on some smaller buildings that looked like sheds or outhouses. A much larger house that had clearly seen better days drew their attention, positioned at the end of a circular drive. He studied the sagging roof and peeling paint job. It certainly didn't look much like the grand farmhouse that was depicted on the ancient website.

"This place looks like a dump," Damian muttered, as some figures appeared on the rickety porches. "If I had a relative here, I'd be taking them out right now."

That Spidey-sense that something was wrong was blaring loudly now. "Look."

A man appeared on the porch of the largest dwelling, barrel chested, arms crossed, his defensive posture plain.

"Are you ready for this?" Tom asked Damian.

"Born ready."

He smothered a smile. He liked the man's spirit. He seemed as honest and down to earth as Joel Wakefield. "Alright, well, here goes nothing."

Damian slowed the car, stopped. And Tom sent up a prayer. *God, thank You for being with us.*

CHAPTER 10

"Now, are you sure you're okay to be home by yourself?" Serena asked, looking around Anna's living room like she expected the boogeyman to jump out.

"Yes." Honestly, knowing the man had been caught made all the coddling feel a *teensy* bit smothering. But it was wonderful to feel loved and protected. To feel like she was getting back on track with God. And to have had the chance to reconnect with Serena and Joel, and by association the potential to reconnect with her friend group, felt most miraculous. Really, it seemed like the druggie had almost done her a favor. Not that she'd admit that for the world.

"Okay, well, I hope you don't mind, but Rachel messaged and asked if you'd be okay with a visit today, and I said I'd check with you. We could maybe do lunch?" Serena asked hopefully.

Lunch with Rachel. She wiped damp hands down her jeans. She had to start somewhere. "Sure. That sounds good. Where?"

"Do you want to go out? My treat?"

And see people who might ask about the incident? No thanks. "I think I'd prefer to be here. A Friday lunch at home is a rare treat. I'll need to clean up though."

"No, you don't," Serena said firmly. "You need to rest and take it easy."

Yes, but resting and taking it easy might mean she focused too much on what had just happened. And she really didn't want to be doing that. Cooking and cleaning would prove a nice distraction. "What time?"

"Twelve-thirty? One?"

"One sounds good." And would give her more time to cook something and clean up. And school pickup meant Rachel couldn't stay all day. Just in case things got awkward.

"And we'll bring everything, so don't feel like you need to. I want this to feel like a treat. Okay?"

"Fine, then." Anna mock-sighed. "How can I argue with that? Thank you."

Serena hugged her, Anna waved goodbye then faced her living room.

Her sigh was genuine this time. Serena had lied when she'd said Anna didn't need to clean up. For all it might be late May outside, it still looked like a wintry cave in here. She moved to the drapes and pushed them open, wincing as she spied previously hidden dust bunnies. How had Tom not commented about it when he'd stopped by before? The tilting stack of true crime books looked ready to fall at a moment notice, so she moved to straighten them, then paused.

No. These books about death and pain and suffering—no. She didn't want to see them anymore. In fact, she didn't want to see anything like that anymore. Now she'd had a taste of the real thing, it wasn't entertainment. It was awful. Nightmare-inducing. Other people's lived reality. And she had a new and deeper respect for what Tom did. How could he deal with such awful things and still maintain such a good attitude?

Tom. Her heart fluttered. And no, she didn't want to be the girl who kept getting butterflies and tingles whenever she thought of him, but there was something about the man that made her soul soar. He was a good guy. Doing good things. And she really hoped whatever he was doing today that he'd be safe.

But seriously. She rolled her eyes at herself. What was the point of hoping? Praying for him was much better. "Lord, I don't know where Tom is, or what he's doing, but please keep him safe. Thank You for being with him. Help him to be wise and bring justice to the world. Amen."

An exhale chased her prayer and her attention returned to tidying the room. She sorted out which books needed to be returned to the library, which should be boxed up for donations, and a few extra hard-core ones she'd bought that probably needed to be burned. Nobody else needed their hearts polluted by reading them. So she took them out the back to the fire-pit, threw them in to the metal bowl where they clanged in protest, and lit a match.

Satisfaction rolled through her as she watched the flames burn green and blue, the pages curling, the evil these books represented burned so nobody else could have their hope lost and innocence frayed. Maybe some people could cope with reading such material, but it wasn't healthy for her to indulge in. Wickedness might be an old-fashioned term, but these books celebrated wicked crimes—sin—and she didn't want that anywhere near her.

She waited until the last one had burned, then used a hose to dampen the last flames. Good riddance to rubbish reading, as she imagined Staci's grandmother, Rose, who lived two doors up, might say.

By the time she'd picked some flowers and made her living room look fresh and spring-like, she was feeling much better about herself. She eyed herself in the mirror. She still had some pounds to lose, but even that was on the improve too. Who knew that eating less and walking more helped a gal lose weight? Apparently those who actually did it.

Knock, knock.

She swallowed, her steps hesitant as she moved to the door. "Lord, please help me cope with Rachel," she prayed softly. "I really don't know how this will go, but You do. So help me to trust You."

She opened the front door, and was instantly smothered in a hug. "I'm so glad you're okay!"

Anna tentatively wrapped her arms around Rachel. Rachel only hugged her tighter, almost until she felt she couldn't breathe. But there was something so comforting in this hug, something so right, it didn't matter that her ribs might crack. This hug was what love felt like.

Love.

Her eyes pricked. How long had she been looking for love, when it had been here all this time? Sure she might still want a husband, but how could she have rejected these friends who had loved her—who had kept loving her, even when she'd rejected them? She didn't deserve them.

"I'm so sorry, Rachel."

"Sorry?" Rachel pulled back, studied her seriously. "What for?"

"For letting go of our friendship."

"Girl, you didn't let go. You just hit pause for a while. That's what I'm going with, anyway. Okay?"

Rachel's easy grace sparked new tears, and Rachel's pointed finger. "Hey, you better stop that now, because if you cry, I'll start crying, and I've got new mascara on, and Revlon might say it's waterproof, but I'm not convinced. Now come and help me get the trays from the car and let's get this party started."

Through the catch-up conversation, laughter and tease, it almost felt like old times with the three of them, well, four, including baby Caleb, who Serena had brought along as well. They ate what Rachel called their version of a "Girl Dinner."

"Except it's lunch, but I figure it still counts," Rachel said. "Because honestly, who wants to go to any great effort if they can avoid it? So we both brought our favorites, and what we hope you still enjoy too, and thought it'll be nice."

"It's more than nice," Anna said, her heart full. "It's perfect."

The trays of cheeses, dips, crackers, and fruits, also held other snacks like pink marshmallows and chocolate cookies. "If this is Girl Dinner, then it's something I've been doing for a long time," Anna admitted. Because cooking a meal for one all the time sucked. "It's part of why I enjoyed your soirees," she said to Serena. "I knew I could count on at least one good home-cooked meal."

"We're probably due for another one," Rachel said.

Anna glanced at Serena. "Didn't you have one just recently?"

"We're always due for another one." Serena smiled.

Her heart expanded. The fact that they'd say that, and likely would do it just because she had expressed such a thing, made her feel so loved.

She asked how Rachel and her family were doing, and Rachel filled her in on her children, twin boys Noah and Liam ("Can you believe they're nine now? I can't either") and her daughter, Jemima, who had beautiful red hair from Damian's side of the family.

Rachel settled back in her seat, popping a strawberry in her mouth. "Thanks so much for letting me come today. Damian and I were going to grab lunch, but he had an emergency come up. I even offered to go with him, would you believe, but he said he's got some new guy he's trialing. But he promised to take me out for dinner tonight."

"I guess a switch from lunch to a dinner date isn't a bad compromise."

"Right? My mom has already agreed to babysit, so we're good to go."

"A good excuse for a cocktail, right?"

Rachel tapped her flat belly. "I'm doing more mocktails these days, especially since I'm aware of drinking my calories. Cocktails are a special occasion thing now, not a weekly thing. Mocktails on the other hand..." She winked.

But that didn't seem to be the only thing about Rachel that had changed. She seemed softer, somehow. A little more thoughtful, took a little more care as she responded, like she didn't fling out the first words that tumbled through her brain.

All in all, it made for a good catch up, and fed hope that this teetering friendship might have a chance to settle into normalcy again.

"Thank you so much for all of this," Anna said, when Rachel said she'd have to go collect her rug-rats. "I've enjoyed our time so much. The food, the flowers," she gestured to the bouquet Rachel had brought too. "It all means so much."

"That's what friends do."

"Except I haven't been much of a friend lately."

"Well, there's no point living in the past, especially if you want your future to look different. Ask me how I know." Rachel winked.

Anna glanced at Serena. "Do you think we could have another soiree sometime soon?"

Serena nodded. "I think the others would love that. Some of them are out of town at the moment, so we could wait until they've returned, or we could do something sooner."

"Maybe sooner." While she still had her nerve. And not because Jackie might be out of town, and this way she could avoid her a little longer.

"I'll set something up," Serena promised.

"Ooh, you know what we should do is do one of those self-defense classes," Rachel said. "Wouldn't that be fun? Especially if there's a hot guy there for Anna."

Anna shook her head. "I like the idea of self-defense classes, but I'm trying to avoid the whole hot guy thing for the moment."

"Because you've already got one?"

Okay, so maybe Rachel hadn't changed that much. "No."

Was that a lie? It wasn't like she and Tom were anything but friends. Although judging from the way that Serena was looking at her, maybe she thought Anna had just fibbed.

"Excuse me, but why are we waiting until now for spilling all the best tea?" Rachel demanded, then glanced at her phone. "I've got five minutes until school pick up, so you better fill me in on what that look was about."

"I wasn't looking," Anna protested.

"No, but Serena was. Which means she knows something, and I want to know it now too. Who is he?"

"He's nobody."

"So there *is* someone. I knew it!" Rachel crowed. "Deets. Give me deets. Now."

"Oh my gosh you are so pushy."

"It's called caring. And I care about you so much that I want to make sure that if you care about someone that he is worth being cared for. Make sense?"

Sort of. "Look, I may have bumped into someone a few times, and yes, he's nice, and—"

"Is he a Christian?" Rachel demanded.

"Yes."

Rachel smirked at Serena. "Funny how for someone she's only bumped into they've had that conversation at least."

Serena chuckled.

"And I am trying *really* hard to not get caught up in all the emotion again," Anna continued. "So please don't tease me. You know I struggle with this, so what I'd really appreciate more than anything else is having you pray that I can learn to trust God."

Rachel's mouth fell open. Then she lowered her bag and opened her arms again, drawing Anna into a hug. "I'm so proud of you. Thank you for saying that. I'll zip my lip about him, I promise." She drew back. "But I also promise to pray that he realizes just what a spectacular human you are."

"I think he might already realize that," Serena murmured, which drew Rachel's "ooh" face and mimed cheering.

Anna pointed at Serena. "Please don't say stuff like that either. I really can't live in this constant rise and fall of emotions where I hope for things, and they don't happen. I'm really trying to trust God to bridle these feelings, but it's hard when that's how I've lived for so long."

"I'm sorry," Serena murmured.

Rachel nodded. "Girl, I hear you. It's a battle for me to not shoot off at the mouth like Annie Oakley every day. You should see my tongue, it's basically bloodied all the time these days because I bite it so much. And don't look at me like that. It's true I might not *sound* like I'm biting my tongue, but I really am."

"She's doing very well," Serena said, like she was Rachel's proud grandma.

Which drew their shared laughter, and knit a once-unraveled friendship closer again.

God bless her friends.

But how would a meeting with Staci and Toni go? Ugh. What was the point of wondering and worrying? She should pray instead.

And, after they'd left, she spent the next hour doing exactly that, praying for her friends, praying for herself, praying for her mom, praying for Tom again. Then a sleek silver Mercedes turned into her drive, and she braced as two figures exited.

"There she is!" Her mother cried. "Oh my dear, we're so glad you're okay."

Anna smiled and hugged her. Then smiled at Heather Crayling.

~

"Hello?" Tom knocked on the flimsy wooden door of an outside shed, which was covered in carpet tiles. Why would someone put carpet on top of a shed? Was it supposed to be insulation? But surely no humans lived inside, in what looked worse than a pig shed.

He knocked again. "Hello? Just warning you, I'm coming in."

He gingerly opened the door, which required more of a heft and a lift as he pushed it to one side, then almost gagged at the smell. Gross. Something—several things—must've died in here. He covered his nose as he moved inside the dim space. A tiny square window let in a little light, enough to see what looked like a roughly hewn shelf topped with chipped ornaments. He peered closer. A porcelain Winnie the Pooh. A fairy. A horse with only three legs. How sad. Why were they here?

Chest tight, he glanced around some more, his eyes adjusting to the shadows. There was no electricity he could see, no lamp or overhead light. The floor was concrete, littered with rags, but in the corner a pile of blankets lined what looked to be a makeshift mattress on the floor. Somebody did indeed live here. But who? This place wasn't even fit for pigs, let alone for some of the most vulnerable people in society, like those whom he'd already encountered in the past few hours as he'd "helped" Damian and fixed unsafe balustrades, steps, and sagging porches.

Each person he'd met had seemed very quiet, not responding when he had said hello. He wasn't sure if that was because they possessed medical conditions that made them deaf or mute— some others had obvious mental impairments—or because they were afraid of the manager. John Vanderman always kept close, as if he didn't want the residents here speaking to anyone. It was partly why he and Damian had split up, so Tom could "fix" things as he explored and learned what he could.

He'd prepped Damian before and was thankful that so far the builder had remembered his cues.

Damian had crossed his arms, eyeing Vanderman when he'd objected to them parting ways. "As I said on the phone, if you want this done quickly then the best thing we can do is to split up so we don't take as much of your time."

Vanderman hadn't liked it, but had finally agreed. Which meant Tom likely only had a few more minutes before the site manager returned to check up on him.

Tom couldn't blame him. If he'd been Vanderman he'd be freaking out too if anyone in any official capacity was to come here and see the dire conditions in which these residents were forced to live. How much did they pay to live here? He drew out his phone, snapped several more pics. A twig snapped outside, so he quickly shoved it in his pocket.

"What are you doing in here?" Vanderman demanded.

Feign dumbness. Something Marc had told him many times Tom could medal in. "Just checkin' the place out." Tom stayed in the shadows, doing his best to keep the guy from seeing him too closely, pitching his voice deeper to disguise himself as best he could. Who knew in what context he might come across this man again?

"You weren't asked to fix this place."

Tom shrugged. "Just doin' what the boss asked."

"I'm the boss around here, and you need to get out."

"Sure, man." Tom shuffled out, lowering his head, picking up the toolbox he left at the door. "Where do you want me then?"

The man pointed to a different structure that looked more like a house. Now this one he'd seen on the website. He nodded to another of the residents, a gnarled old man who was missing teeth and had heavy gray eyebrows and a mustache and wore a flat cap. "Hey."

The man said nothing, just looked at Vanderman, who was walking too close.

"Please don't talk to the residents."

"Just bein' friendly," Tom muttered.

"You're not being paid to be friendly, you're paid to fix things. So fix them."

"Okey doke."

Maybe that lingo was a step too far, because the man studied him a too-long moment, before swearing softly and shuffling off. Tom exhaled. This place was giving him the creeps. Imagine being one of the poor souls who actually had to live here. From everything he'd seen so far, the place was rundown, a haven for rats and mice and nothing like the promised "quiet life in Muskoka" with activities like bowling and woodwork and sing songs. Maybe it counted as a quiet life, because nobody around here talked. So far, he hadn't seen anything that indicated bowling or woodwork was on offer here. As for songs, the only songs being sung here were silent ones of desperation.

This place was a crime. Nobody should live here. Everything within itched for him to gather all these poor folk and hustle them away. But that wouldn't solve the greater issues. How many other places existed like this? How many other "facilities" did the Crayling family run? Move too soon and they would likely hide or shift their financial records to try to get away with it. Which left him waiting for justice, trusting the law would finally wind into action and shut things down. At least he could pray. *Lord, have mercy on the poor folk here...*

Tom worked on fixing a wobbly step with a few nails and hammer blows, which was about the extent of his handyman expertise. Vanderman kept watching him, and he knew he had to escape his scrutiny, so he faked an injured thumb and muttered about needing a first aid kit. Which he didn't need, but it gave him the excuse to return to Damian.

"How's it going?" Tom asked in a low voice.

"This place has not seen a fire inspection this century," Damian muttered. "It's criminal, that's what it is."

"Just keep us here as long as you can." Which wouldn't be hard as Tom's mediocre skills meant anything he did was something that Damien was going to have to fix later. Yet even that felt wrong. He hated leaving these poor people in such conditions, when if he only had a bit more skill, they might be kept safer.

"What are you two talking about?" Vanderman demanded.

Tom shook out his thumb, angling away, his baseball cap shielding his face. "Where he keeps his nail gun. Where is it?"

Damian pointed to a locker lining the underside of the truck's bed. "In the right side."

"Thanks."

Tom retrieved the nail gun, then nodded to Vanderman. "Can you show me where the power is so we can get this goin'?"

Vanderman sighed, and walked back with him. It was no wonder the guy was so lean, considering all the walking he must do constantly checking up on people. The definition of shifty.

"This won't be botherin' no-one, will it?" Tom asked, holding the nail gun up so it shielded his face.

"I've told them to keep away."

Tom bet he had. He nodded, and worked for the next five minutes, the nail gun's *rap, rap* the soundtrack to his silent prayers.

Finally, the man went away, leaving Tom to drop his pace a little, while still looking like he was maintaining his effort.

He finished the steps—nobody would be falling off these babies now—then shook the porch rails to figure out which needed attention too.

A cat appeared, its gray fur and white face kind of cute, its meow plaintive.

He clicked his fingers. "Hey, kitty."

"Psst."

Tom glanced around.

"Psst. Down here."

Tom bent, as if tying his bootlace, and saw a figure hiding

behind the lattice screening the underneath of the building. "Hey there."

"That cat was Mabel's."

"Mabel? Who's Mabel?"

"She's not here anymore."

Tom froze, that Spidey-sense screaming. He pretended to cough, and drew out his phone, and pressed record. Anything this man said would be inadmissible and wouldn't hold up in a court, but it might help sway a judge to execute a search warrant.

"Where is Mabel?" he asked, glancing over at where Vanderman stood, arms crossed, as he frowned at Damian. *Please Lord, keep him far away.*

"She was here, then they took her."

"Who took her?"

"Kyle."

Oh no. Anna's friend? "Kyle Crayling?" he checked.

"Yeah." The man spat out a blue word.

"Where'd he take her?" Tom asked.

"Where they took the others."

"Which others?"

"John. And Peter."

Dear God. How many more missing people were there? He glanced behind him again. Vanderman was looking in this direction, as if wondering why Tom wasn't working. He shifted to better camouflage the informant hiding below, pulled out the hammer again, and gave a few halfhearted bangs at the porch railings.

"And Bob?"

"Bob was my best friend."

Poor guy. "What's your name?" he muttered.

"Terry."

"Hey!" Vanderman called.

Tom didn't have time for this guy's antics. He hid his phone in his tool belt and shoved on the earmuffs, and got out the nail gun and started nailing again, ignoring Vanderman as he drew close. *Rap rap, rap rap, rap rap.*

He kept at it, even as the manager drew close and started yelling.

He finally finished, then started, as if surprised. "Whoa, man. I didn't see you there." Acting like he was half stoned would hopefully aid his disguise.

"How much longer will this take?"

"How long is a piece of string?" he asked, like his grandfather used to say.

His chest tightened. These poor people living here were all someone's relatives, quite possibly someone's granddad, someone's grandmother. How could their families not know how bad this place was? Surely if they did know they'd want to save their relatives from living here. But to help these poor souls, he needed something more concrete, something that would finally put a nail in the coffin of plausible deniability. *Lord, I need something more.*

The cat meowed again. Vanderman swore.

Tom pointed to the cat. "Nice cat."

"I hate the things. Always dragging in dead mice."

"You got a mice problem, huh?" he asked, as if it wasn't obvious.

"We used to have more," Vanderman continued, "then I got rid of them."

"How?" Was he talking about the mice or more cats?

"I shot them," Vanderman stated, almost proudly.

He had to mean he'd shot cats. But... shooting cats? What kind of person did that? Sounded like Animal Welfare needed to be called as well.

Tom really hoped his phone was still recording—and would remain undetected. He coughed. Noticed Vanderman took a step away. "Why'd you do that?"

"They're a menace, always begging for food."

Tom coughed again. Vanderman made a noise of disgust and returned to check on Damian.

"He shot them because they were Mabel's," Terry's voice from below came again.

"Why?"

"Because they kept on, carrying on with their screeching after she disappeared. He's coming back."

Tom angled a look over his shoulder, and hoisted up his tool belt, his mind spinning. Given Terry's comments he surely had enough evidence to convince a judge to allow a search warrant. He straightened, turned, scratched himself in a manner he hoped was off putting. "Hey, you got a washroom I can use?" he asked, before Vanderman could whine again.

"Uh, over there." Vanderman pointed to a far-off building.

"Nothing closer?"

"No."

Tom nodded, even as his whole soul shuddered in protest. Seriously? How did these poor people manage in the depths of winter?

Glad to escape the man's scrutiny, he tried not to hurry as he moved to the building. Inside was a row of stalls, a couple of dirty wash basins, and another section consisting of concrete shower stalls. Looked like they would provide zero comfort in minus twenty-degree temperatures. He took photos, then did his business, and exited the stall to see Vanderman loitering at the door. Creep. He washed his hands. The lack of a towel meant he dried them on his jeans.

He nodded to the showers. "Did this place used to be a campsite?"

"Once upon a time."

Except this place was no fairytale. The sooner they could find out the truth, and shut it down and rescue these poor souls, the better.

CHAPTER 11

*E*vening shadows lengthened, spilling across Anna's living room. She sat on her couch, rare contentment filling her. Saturday had passed with more reunions, this time with Toni and Staci. Dr. James had driven Staci straight to Anna's house after Staci's return from a business meeting in New York, resulting in another bone-crushing hug. That he had put Anna and her scare on Thursday night ahead of his own need to reconnect with his wife made her heart glow.

In fact, the way her friends had literally opened their arms to her gave hope that returning to tomorrow's Sunday service might even be okay. A girl had to do something when her house was clean, and the guy she'd hoped would suggest spending time together had instead messaged to say he was caught up in work again.

She swallowed a sigh. No. She couldn't afford to get carried away and start hoping for more. Tom was her friend. Besides, dating a detective would be like dating a doctor. They might have set work hours, but their after hours didn't necessarily mean they had the freedom to put down tools whenever they wished. She knew that. And on the long list of internal self-improvements, she also knew that she couldn't afford to be selfish or demanding.

"Lord, please help me to treat him as a friend."

Her words fell soft into the dusky quiet, but seeded assurance. Instead of worry about herself, she would leave her future and any possible relationship in God's hands and pray for others instead. Tom was her friend, after all, and she was now back to praying for her friends. And then she would pray for the man that God had for her out there somewhere. And if this mythical man looked a little bit like Tom, well, she couldn't help that. And then she'd pray again for herself, that the hooks and snags of the past could be released, so she could be willing to do all that God wanted for her to do. Which, she was increasingly convinced, included returning to church.

Anna's palms were sweaty as she got out of her car. She'd messaged Serena last night to say she planned to come to church today, and Serena's celebration emojis had been enough to make Anna realize just what a big deal this would be. She had practiced her story and now had it down pat: She had taken some time off and was back.

Any further explanation she didn't owe anyone. She and God were okay, and that was the main thing. Well, maybe she owed Trudy an explanation, seeing Trudy had been stuck doing Anna's load of kids' church leading. Anna and Serena had used to tag team their kids' church classes, but obviously that wasn't something she'd done in the past few months. And with Serena's time off for having a baby, it seemed to have all fallen on Trudy's shoulders. God bless the woman for not holding it against Anna.

"You came!"

Rachel's exuberant call spun her around to see the Taylor

family, and after hugging Rachel, Anna high-fived the kids and kissed Damian on the cheek. "Good to see you guys."

"Good to see you," Damian said. "It's been a while."

"Sure has." Quick, move this on. "How's business?"

"We're keeping busy." He brushed at his balding head. "It's funny just how many people suddenly remember construction jobs they want done before summer begins."

"Honestly, people." Rachel winked at Anna.

Anna smiled.

"Look, let's just say there are some people out there who really have some explaining to do." Damian shook his head. "There are some bad people in this world."

"But then they get caught, like Anna's attacker did," Rachel said.

"Hey, yeah, I was sorry to hear about that," Damian said.

Oh. Her head tilted. So he hadn't been talking about Anna's encounter with the would-be drug thief? Who would Damian, of all people, have had an encounter with who classified as bad?

"You doing okay?" Damian asked her. "You haven't had any nightmares, I hope?"

"I've been fine. I think it probably helped that he was caught right away."

"The police here are pretty good." Damian placed his hands on his boys' heads and steered them to the door. "We better get inside before these two cause a scene."

"Sit with us?" Rachel asked. "Pretty please? Then we can have an adult spacing the kids so they don't flick each other during the service."

"Like we used to do?" Anna drew her handbag's strap over her shoulder.

"Shh, you're not supposed to say that so loud," Rachel murmured. "I like to think that my kids operate under the delusion that I was a perfect child, and I have no intention for any of my friends to inform them otherwise. Even if my parents try and do that every single time they mind our kids. They like to call it reaping what you sow." She rolled her eyes.

"Your secret is safe with me."

As an only child whose parents had often used church as a babysitter, Anna had spent many a Sunday service sitting with Rachel or Serena or Jackie when they were kids. Many had been the time when she had flicked Rachel or been flicked back during particularly long and dry sermons in those days before John McPherson had taken on the church. At least the habit of church attendance had stuck. As had her relationship with God. And her friendships with others, even if it had gone through some rough patches.

Her nerves tingled as she entered the church's foyer. Sure enough, faces turned to her, some lighting with surprise. Thank goodness for Rachel's kids which gave an excuse as she pretended she needed to pay attention to them, and couldn't linger for conversations with the adults who were, as suspected, mildly thrilled or deeply curious to see her return, depending on their levels of grace.

She inwardly winced. Judging people who she strongly suspected were judging her was no way to start with her return to church. Those people who thought Christians were hypocrites might as well cast the first stone at her. She was a living and breathing contradiction.

Angela McPherson, the senior minister's wife, spied her, quickly ended her conversation, and moved through the chatting congregation to wrap her in a hug. "Welcome home."

Emotion roared, spilling down her cheeks, as one of Rachel's boys said loudly, "Why is Aunty Anna crying?"

This only caused her to cry more. As an only child, she would never be an aunt, but the fact her friend's children still called her that, even after all these months apart, well, that was truly special.

. . .

AFTER THE SERVICE, she joined the others at Rachel's, and for once did not feel like she was on the outer, as her friends laughed and teased, and they ate and drank—mocktails—and she finally felt like she was home, that she was free. As the conversation circled, she no longer felt like she wasn't good enough. John's sermon today about God being like the prodigal son's Father might've been written for her, but John hadn't looked at her once during the sermon. Serena had even said she hadn't told anyone that Anna had planned to attend today. It must've just been one of those God things, those moments of "serendipitous coincidence" which she knew was just part of God's plan. And she knew that if God could orchestrate a sermon just for her, then she could trust Him to orchestrate and divinely provide in other matters too. And if He didn't, that was okay, she would trust Him regardless.

Because as Joel had said in his communion message, faith without actions wasn't faith. So for her to actively trust God to bring the right man across her path one day meant getting actively focused on God.

Maybe Jackie had been right with those long-ago words that had cut like a knife. She thought back, the conversation still piercing in veracity.

Jackie had eyed Anna seriously. "You act like you'll never be happy until you have a boyfriend, and I hate to break it to you, but having a boyfriend won't make you happy either. Sooner or later, you're going to have to let God be the one who gives you joy. Until you find that, you'll always be dissatisfied."

Those words had burned across her soul. And truth be told, this past year, she hadn't been happy. Going on dating apps for dates that didn't show or were rude or inconsiderate always left her feeling cheap. They might work for some, but hadn't for her, instead leaving her feeling a sense of despair. Hiding, isolating herself, pining after imaginary men she'd never meet, none of that had helped. In fact, it'd probably only made things worse. And happiness sure hadn't been found in those true crime books and podcasts she used to listen to.

And yet now, while she still did not have a boyfriend, she felt better, happier, like with the return of her friends, the missing puzzle pieces of her life had been found. She was thankful for them. So grateful that God had placed them in her life. She'd been such a fool to think she could do life without them. She might as well have tried to cut off her right arm.

"Hey, did you guys hear from Jackie?" Staci asked. "I think I saw that she and Linc are—"

"Would anyone like another drink?" Anna pushed to her feet, her heart tight.

"But don't you want to hear about her?" Toni asked.

"I'm good." Although the tension inside said she wasn't. So apparently there was still some way to go before full friendship status was restored with some.

Serena bit her lip, but Anna faked a smile and collected glasses. Oh yes, she knew she still had a long way to go in the maturity stakes.

Once inside, she grasped the counter, listening as the men watched a hockey game on TV. She didn't know who was playing, she didn't care, but Damian was a super-fan, and had a framed jersey that Rachel had bought him for his birthday a few years ago enshrined above the TV.

The sounds of conversation outside provided the backdrop for the louder cheers and "He shoots, he scores!" drama from the TV. She probably should go back out there and ask about Jackie and how she was doing with Linc. She rolled her eyes. It still seemed incredible to her that Pastor Jackie had caught the eye of a Hollywood superstar, but whatever. Now she thought about it, it probably wasn't Jackie's fault, and to be fair, in all the years Anna had known her, Jackie had never once gone out of her way to catch a man's eye. So for Anna to keep holding this grudge like this, even though it was more about what Jackie had said to Anna, rather than Jackie waltzing off with the ultimate man prize, probably wasn't fair.

"Fine, God," she muttered.

After collecting a fresh jug of lemonade, she returned and this time her smile was not so fake. "Hey, I'm sorry for acting on like that. What did you want to say about Jackie?"

Serena shook her head. "It's okay. If you haven't talked to her for a while, then it's probably something you should talk with her about directly."

Oh. Sounded serious. "Is she okay?"

Serena smirked. "That's something you'll need to talk about with her."

Huh. She'd take that as a yes, then. But still, what was going on with her friend?

Her phone buzzed. She glanced at it. Oh! Her heart fizzed.

"Anna? Is everything okay?" Staci asked.

"Um, yeah. I…" Just hadn't expected Tom to contact her again today. She'd thought he'd be busy, but here he was, asking if she was free to have a walk along the lakefront. Which didn't exactly scream romantic, but probably was a little necessary after how much she'd eaten in the past two days or so. Especially if she wanted to fit into that dress for the Summer Ball. Which reminded her…

She quickly tapped out a "Yes" then put the phone back in her bag and looked up to see everyone watching her curiously. Oh, right. She hadn't ended that previous sentence. "Um, I'll need to go soon, but while I remember, I wanted to mention that my mom is helping organize this year's Muskoka Summer Ball. Anyway, if anyone feels like they have some extra cash to splash," she eyed Staci and Toni, "and would like a night to dress up I'd really like you to consider coming so I don't have to be there on my lonesome."

"What's the ball for?" Staci asked.

"My mom is on a charity board and each year they have

organized a fundraiser in support of one of the local charities. They didn't hold it the last few years so those of you who are newer to town may not have heard of it, but it's happening again this year."

"What charity is it in support of?"

"The Strong Hearts Foundation. You know, the one that supports low cost homes for the underprivileged."

"Oh." Serena's eyes rounded.

"What's that look for?"

Serena shook her head. "Oh, I heard that things have gotten a little rundown at Muskoka Ferns Lodge, so they could probably do with all the funds they can get."

"For sure," Rachel muttered.

"What do you mean?" Anna asked.

"Damian got called out to a job there a few days ago, and he said the place is terrible. He couldn't believe that all these old people were allowed to live out there. He said he didn't think a fire inspector had gone out there for decades."

Protest balled in her chest. "I've known the Crayling family for years. I thought they were doing their best to help the community."

"I don't think it counts as your best when some of those places have no electricity."

"What?"

"Right? I couldn't believe it either."

"But surely someone has contacted the authorities if that's the case," Staci said.

"I'm sure the Craylings are doing the best they can," Anna said stiffly.

"But no electricity, Anna?" Toni asked.

Rachel's head tilted. "Is that really doing the best they can, or is that just wrong?"

Clearly continuing this discussion with her friends was not the way to get back into harmony. "Well, anyway, if anyone wants tickets to the ball, I'd really appreciate having some more friends there. And yes, the tickets might be pricey, but it is for a good cause."

"Sounds like they can do with all the money they can get," Rachel murmured.

Okay, and that was her cue. If she was going to keep this hard-won accord, then she should exit now before anyone else said something that tipped her over the edge. "I need to scram. I'll see you when I see you."

"And Anna, it's been so great to see you." Toni hugged her.

"Amen," Staci said.

Anna breathed in their hugs. *Amen*, for sure.

TOM WIPED damp palms down his shirt as Lake Muskoka sparkled in the sunshine. He didn't want to do this, but everything he'd discovered in the past few days meant this couldn't go on. Either he ran the risk of compromising the investigation by revealing his involvement with one of the Crayling family's friends, or he'd hurt Anna by doing the same. Either way, there was no easy way to go forward. At least, not at the moment. And there was no guarantee that at the end of the investigation she'd want anything more to do with him either. How could she, if his work ended up putting some of the Morely family's friends behind bars? But it wasn't like he could admit any of this to her, either. Not because he thought she might potentially expose the operation and say something to them, but because experience had told him how easy it was for things to slip out, or for an unguarded facial expression to be a tell. He couldn't risk it. Gabe wouldn't risk it. And it wasn't like he could admit any of that to her either.

He stabbed the gravel in the parking lot with the toe of his sneaker. Which was why it was best to stop things progressing now before any more looks like that flirty one she'd given him on Friday morning occurred again.

Sunlight flashed off Anna's red Mazda as she pulled in. He knew it wasn't exactly chivalrous to meet like this. But he hoped that meeting in a park for a "walk" wouldn't give the impression that this was a date. Not like the other night. Thinking of her as a potential girlfriend was a road he couldn't go down. Not anymore.

He pushed away from his car as she parked in the spot one over. Forced his lips up. How to play this so they could still remain friends, but he didn't give any false hope…

"Hi."

"Hi!" Anna seemed happy, much happier than the last time they'd met. "I'm so glad you messaged me."

"Uh, sure."

Her smile dimmed a little. He felt bad so he gestured to a nearby ice-cream van. "I wasn't sure if you'd like ice-cream or a bottle of water. I'm game for both."

"Do you do that too?" she asked.

"Do what?"

"Well, you know, when you have ice-cream and then you need a drink of water after." Her nose wrinkled. "Yeah, judging from that face you probably don't."

No. He found half a smile, motioned to the van and they walked there.

"What's your flavor?" Buying her an ice-cream didn't count as a date, right? It was only food. Even if it felt a little like those times when he was a kid when his dad would buy his sons an ice-cream at the end of a long hike, in an effort to convince them that it had been fun. This… relationship… with Anna was barely even that, let alone something deemed hike length-worthy, but he hoped the cold treat might help sweeten things between them a little so she wouldn't hate him too much.

She ordered mint, he got chocolate, and he gestured to the

lakeside path where a seat was placed to take advantage of the views. But actually, a walk would be better, would allow things to be said so he didn't have to face her. He might've earned a few bravery citations along the way in his career, but he felt as weak as a used one-ply paper napkin right now.

The minutes passed in licked ice-cream and small talk about their days, and he shared about what he'd heard at his church that morning.

"I… I went to church too."

She said that like she hadn't been recently. "Did you enjoy it?"

She nodded, her gaze on the lake. "I wasn't sure what to expect, because it's been a while since I'd been, but it was much better than I thought."

"How long since you'd gone?"

Her forehead wrinkled. "Over six months."

Wow. Okay. Not what he'd expected when she'd talked about "a while" or about Joel being her pastor. "I'm glad you found it helpful."

Her gaze slanted to him. "I know this will sound weird, but I'm almost grateful for what happened the other day at the clinic, as it's brought me and my friends back closer."

"I'm really glad," he said sincerely. "I mean about you finding reconciliation. Not the attack, of course."

"I know." Her lips tilted.

But she wasn't the first to have expressed similar things after a traumatic event. He'd met plenty of others who had found positives, while some stayed trapped in that moment forever. "So, have you had any nightmares or anything?"

She gave a soft huff. "I've been asked that so many times lately that I almost feel like there's something wrong with me for not having any."

"It's a blessing to have not had any."

She nodded. "I really feel like it's people's prayers that have protected me from feeling that way."

He knew from personal experience that people praying didn't stop all the bad memories from creeping in, but it did ease things.

"Anyway, it was great to catch up with my friends afterwards, and feel their love and support."

"I bet."

"Oh, and that reminds me. I know you're probably busy, and this is probably not something you'd ever want to do anyway, but I asked my friends, and it sounded like some might go, so I figure there's no harm in asking you too."

"Asking me what?" he asked, smiling at her fluster and roundabout ways.

"Well, I think I mentioned before about how my mom is helping organize this ball—"

Uh oh.

"—and I know it's probably not your scene, but if you were interested at all in dressing up and having fun and eating yummy food then it'd be *really* awesome if you could come. But I won't be offended if you can't, or don't want to, or, um, anything."

Her gaze pinned his, and in it, he could read her hope, which twisted his gut anew.

Part of him desperately wanted to say yes. Yes, he'd love to see her dressed up, to have a night of dancing and food and firm this friendship into more. He might even be able to get insider knowledge into the Crayling family if he said yes.

But another part of him knew he shouldn't, because saying yes was like saying they could still date, when that probably wasn't helpful for either of them, or his case. He would have to decline. But he sensed declining would turn this conversation into the endgame he would've preferred to have delayed for a little longer.

The hope in her eyes faded, her face fell. "It's okay. I can tell you don't want to."

The chocolate in his stomach made him queasy. "I'm not sure I'm a ball guy." A lie, but he had to say something. They couldn't keep doing this.

"It's okay. I knew you probably wouldn't want to."

"It's not that," he blurted. Except, hadn't he just said it was? He shoved the last of the cone in his mouth, swallowing the truth.

Her steps had slowed, she was eyeing him, as if waiting for further explanation.

"It's just…" Maybe he could lead with the truth after all. Or at least part of it. "I'm involved in a really big case at the moment, and I can't promise how much I'll be around. And while I'd like to have the time to take you out and get to know you more, right now isn't a great time for that." And probably would never be, if she ever found out he was investigating her friends.

"I see."

The animation in her face faded, like a lightbulb had switched off, and he felt renewed regret for these circumstances. If it was any other case, he'd be fine. But because it was her family friends, he needed to steer away. "I'm really sorry."

She finished her ice-cream, then folded her arms, studying the path. "So, just so I have this straight, you're saying you don't want to see me anymore."

"No," he said quickly, hating the disappointment he could hear in her voice. "I do. It's just that work means it's really difficult right now." Understatement of the year.

"And yet you've still managed to meet me on Sundays. I thought that was your day off."

"It is, but, uh, I can't guarantee how much longer that will be true." Man, hearing himself try to explain sounded like the lame excuse she obviously thought it was too.

She nodded, still not meeting his gaze. "I understand." She drew in a deep breath. "So, can we still call, or message each other like we've been doing?"

"I…" No. It wouldn't be wise. If anyone discovered he'd been talking to someone associated with those under investigation, then it might compromise everything. "I… think I'll be too busy."

Her breath hitched sharply, her face averting. "I see."

Oh no, she didn't.

"Well, thanks then." Her voice was shaky. "It's been real."

"Anna…"

She shook her head. "I guess I'll see you around. Or not."

"It's just work, Anna." He winced. He might as well say "It's me, not you." Which might be true, but everybody knew it was a cop-out.

She backed away, and he could see the hurt in her posture, the way she rubbed her upper arms. "Look, thanks for the ice-cream. You know you didn't have to do that. You could've just told me straight out. I would've understood."

No, she wouldn't. His heart hurt for her. "Anna, please. I don't want you to think I'm not…" He hesitated. He probably shouldn't admit the truth.

"Not what?" she challenged, her gaze meeting his for the briefest moment before veering away, but not before he saw her eyes were sparkling with sorrow.

I don't want you to think I'm not interested, were the words he shouldn't say, even if they were true. He was interested. He wanted to know her. But he couldn't right now. "Nothing."

Her head jerked. "Okay, then. Well, I guess that's it. Goodbye, Detective."

She turned and walked stiffly away, swiping at her cheeks, and his heart cracked for her.

CHAPTER 12

She should've known this would happen. Should've known he would slip into her heart. Should've known she wasn't strong enough to protect herself from leaping into hoping for more, when really she was as newborn-kitten-helpless as she'd ever been.

She drove home, wiping at tears that kept blurring her vision. Oh, she hoped he hadn't seen her cry. Nobody wanted to be the weak woman who cried and got emotional when things didn't go her way. But once again it seemed like things never did go her way. And while part of her heard his excuse of work as truth, another part of her was awfully tempted to read into his rejection as something more. Tom might try to say he'd like to take her out but couldn't due to work commitments, but if that was so, why couldn't he meet her on Sundays, or even text her? Surely if a man was interested, he could still make an effort. Which only made her wonder whether he'd said the part before about wanting to take her out as his way to soften the blow...

Her chest crumpled, and she had to slow the car thanks to the rainy conditions inside that made driving difficult. "God?"

Her voice shook. She probably should pull over. She mightn't be drunk or on drugs, but her driving was likely a menace to others on the road.

She took a right, pulling into a little parking bay right next to the lake. Drew in a shuddery breath. Released it. Which seemed to trigger the tears to cascade. She sobbed, part of her hating the fact she got so emotional over a man, part of her wishing she was tougher than this. But right now, she simply wasn't.

Gradually the storm passed, and she placed her folded arms on the steering wheel and leaned her head on it. She was such a fool.

She closed her swollen eyelids, trying to pray, but no words formed except "God" and "why?"

Oh, she was tired. Tired of these emotional rollercoasters that always left her hanging wrong side up, her heart dangling in the air. Maybe it was time to let go of the whole relationship thing once and for all.

For so long she had been clinging to God's promises that He had her future in His hands. But right now those promises seemed about as far away as Mars. And while part of her still wanted to trust Him, another part felt like God had let her down again, and that rejection was all she should expect. She knew she wasn't as good as Jackie or Serena, so she didn't deserve a man who would surely just become polluted by her negativity. So maybe it was just best if she let go of any hope of ever finding love again. She didn't think it was what Jackie had meant when she'd said what she had about Anna never being happy while looking for a man, but it seemed awfully close.

"Fine, God. You win."

She gave up. A boyfriend, marriage, babies, all the good things her friends had, was obviously not meant to be part of God's plan for her life. So she'd let go, and let God win. And trust that He knew what He was doing.

. . .

SHE MIGHT NOT HAVE HAD nightmares, but she'd barely slept. Her return home Sunday afternoon had seen her fall into a deep sleep for several hours, then she'd woken, the rejection swirling around her heart and brain that she couldn't get rid of it. She'd tried to read her Bible, had even reread Psalm Nineteen, but it seemed removed from her reality. Still, each time she turned off her light, the rejection swarmed again, so she'd be forced to turn on the light again and read or pray. But after praying for everyone she knew, at least a dozen times, she still felt on edge, uneasy, and the words of what she could've said to Tom, kept marching through her mind.

But at least this time she sensed a fight, she wasn't going to lie down under the weight of her emotions. She was trying to cling to what God said about her. To think on His promises. The fact she was loved, that He had good plans for her, that He wanted to give her a hope and a future.

But it was hard. *So* hard. Like a test she kept failing. And the fight to keep her head above water and not drown in rejection left her exhausted. It had been her alarm that had saved her as she scrambled to make it to work on time.

She parked, pushed back her shoulders, hoping today's makeup would hide the swollen nose and red-rimmed eyes that had greeted her in the bathroom mirror this morning. She didn't want anybody thinking she was sad or sick, and should be at home instead. No way did she want to spend a second longer wallowing at home, the temptation to feel sorry for herself lurking in the corners of each minute, waiting to pounce. Far better to be distracted by filling her day with busyness and staying focused on people who were often suffering far more than she was.

"You're here," Gabby said, as Anna entered the clinic.

"Sure am."

Judging from the look Gabby shot her, Anna had to try harder for a convincing level of perkiness. She smiled wider.

"Are you okay?" Gabby asked.

Oh. Gabby meant about the druggie attack last Thursday. With everything else that had occurred, that seemed so long ago now. "Yep. Ready to roll. How did Friday go? I'm sorry you had to cover my shift."

"Hey, it was totally okay. I'm just so glad you're alright."

"Yep."

"Oh my gosh, I still can't believe it. Were you scared?"

"I was, but I'm okay now." Anna drew in a deep breath. "To be honest, I'm trying not to focus on it, so I don't really want to talk about it too much. So if it's all the same to you then I'd really like to just get stuck into work today."

Gabby nodded. "Did you check your emails?"

"I noticed that Dr. Lewisham sent something, but I'm sorry, there's just been so much going on that I can't remember what it said."

"It was about more staff training for safety procedures, so something like that doesn't happen again."

Great. "You know. I'm pretty sure I followed all the correct procedures." That's what the police had said. That's what Tom— *no.* "Anyway, sure, whatever."

"It won't hurt to go over things. I don't know that I would've been that calm in that situation."

"I wasn't that calm, but I did the best I could."

Gabby placed fresh paper in the printer. "I think maybe we should take self-defense classes."

"You're not the first person to have said that to me in the past few days."

"Well, maybe we should. What are your evenings or weekends like these days?"

"Pretty open." Especially now there was no Tom to see,

message or even think about. "If you can find something nearby, then I'll do my best to make it work."

"Great." Gabby peered at her. "Are you sure you're okay to work today?"

"Absolutely. Let's get this show on the road."

The first few hours passed as they normally did, interspersed with a few enquiries about her welfare after Thursday's incident.

"I'm fine, Mrs. Peterson," she said, when Trudy called in for her appointment.

"It was good to see you at church yesterday," Trudy said. "I'm sorry I didn't get the chance to talk with you. You hurried away so quickly."

Exactly so she wouldn't feel obliged to talk to the Trudys of this world and be forced to fumble through awkward explanations. Her lips twisted. How much better to save it for her workplace instead.

"I hope this means we'll see you back on the kids' church roster soon."

"I think I'll need a few more weeks before I'm ready for that." Anna smiled, then thanked God as the phone rang, forcing her to end the conversation with a small wave. "Hello, Muskoka Shores Medical Clinic. This is Anna speaking."

The day ended with a quick staff meeting and a refresher about safety, and Anna was—once again—asked about her encounter on Thursday night, and by turns felt validated for following the safety protocols, and also somewhat of a scapegoat, being talked about so much in this way.

The following days were much the same, save for the afternoon training session, and she was glad to reach Friday evening, when she had offered her babysitting services to Toni, so she and Matt could attend a cocktail function for the launch of a new art show at the gallery Toni ran at the Muskoka Shores Resort.

Looking after Ethan was a joy, as the boy was nearly two years old and his toddler chatter and plump-armed hugs and willingness to sit beside her on the couch while they watched Disney movies seemed to make him the perfect date. Especially if she couldn't have—

Nope! "So, Ethan, what do you think of your mommy's dress?"

"Mommy bootiful."

Anna smiled at Toni who had an "Awww" look on her face.

"He's a smart kid," Matt said, kissing his wife's cheek. "I keep saying that."

"Of course he is." Toni tilted her head against Matt's shoulder. "He gets his smarts from me."

Ethan certainly didn't get his brains from his biological father. Toni's ex was in jail, and was going to stay there for a long time, or so Toni had said. Tom had been on that case, and—

"No!" she muttered.

Toni cleared her throat, eyeing Anna askance.

"Oh, I didn't mean you. Come on, everyone can see that Ethan takes after you in every good way. No, I was just thinking about something else."

"Uh huh." Toni's smile said she believed her.

Relief filled her. "Now go, have fun. Sell lots of paintings. And if you drink too much wine and have to stay the night at the resort just let me know. I'm working tomorrow, but I might've packed a bag and have it in the car just in case."

"You didn't have to do that."

"It's good to be prepared." While it might be almost summer now, the weather in Muskoka could be unpredictable, which meant preparing for the unknown. Most of her friends had an emergency kit of food and clothes in case of misadventure. Like when Serena and Joel had crashed during a winter snowstorm and been forced to spend the night in the car. Or the poor folk who had been trapped in another wild weather event just before Christmas last year. Anna may not have been a Girl Scout, but it always helped to be prepared.

"Now go, go have fun. And don't worry about us at all."

"Are you sure you don't want to come?" Toni checked. "Ethan would probably be okay, and the others are all going. It'd be fun to have you there, like we're the old gang again."

But not if Jackie was there. She still wasn't ready to talk to her. And while it might be nice to go it was probably safest not to. "Thanks, but I'm happy to stay here with your little man."

"You're a good friend," Toni murmured.

"Sometimes." Maybe.

They left, and she soon served Ethan his mac-and-cheese. She eyed it, tempted for the comfort such food provided, but sighed and refrained. A slinky gown called her name. Which reminded her…

She tapped out a message on the group chat, reminding the girls about the tickets for the ball. She refused to think about the guy who had said he couldn't go. She forced her thoughts to focus on the task at hand. *If you still want tickets to the ball please let me know by next weekend as we need to send through our final numbers shortly.*

"Anna?" Ethan called from the living room.

She moved out and noticed his truck had fallen. She retrieved it and placed it next to him on the sofa. "There you go."

"Fank you."

She smiled, then felt her phone buzz in her pocket.

There was a new message on the group chat. From a number she didn't recognize.

What ball?

Her heart stuttered as she recognized the face.

Jackie.

Tom had never been so glad to reach Friday evening. His week had passed at a snail-like pace, even though he'd flung himself into his work in a desperate attempt to forget how his words and actions had hurt Anna last Sunday afternoon. He still felt regret, even though in his conversation on Monday with Gabe he'd been reassured that it was the right thing to do. Except it didn't feel like the right thing. It felt unnecessarily hard. But his job wasn't about feelings, but about facts and finding out the truth. So while regrets might gnaw at the edges of each day, the results of last Friday's visit to the Lodge meant he'd now collected enough information to write up affidavits to present to the judge for the search warrant for the Muskoka Ferns Lodge property. A search warrant that—hallelujah—had been granted at five o'clock today.

Returning to the station, he'd talked with Gabe about the next step. This would prove the challenging part, putting the wheels into motion to ensure that a search could be conducted, but without any of the Crayling family finding out. He felt an increasingly great concern for Terry, his helpful under-the-house informant, and prayed he'd be kept safe. The judge hadn't liked Tom's method of recording, pointing out that it wouldn't hold up in court. But that was the point. They had to find out what was happening in order to begin proceedings that would allow this to be played out in court. And while he hated the delay, he knew that waiting until next week would allow for more resources to be gathered in order to hit the Lodge with all the elements of surprise that was so necessary for a successful search.

Damian's horror at the conditions had seen him plead for Tom to call the appropriate welfare agencies, but Tom had explained the need to hold off, even though refusing to act immediately went against every one of his inclinations. But as soon as the other agencies were called then the risk for information leaks increased. And any leak might see the Craylings hide themselves or bank accounts or go on the defensive, and any chance of discovering the truth about the disappearances could potentially be lost.

So getting those other chess pieces lined up was just part of the delay. In an ideal world the welfare authorities would attend and retrieve the patients while the police executed the search warrant and John Vanderman and the Crayling family were taken in for questioning. But he'd been involved in too many operations over the years to believe in an ideal world, or that things would work out exactly the way he planned, which was why they needed contingency plan upon contingency plan to do their best to make things happen that would get the right result. *Lord, we need Your help to bring justice.*

He was in the middle of yet more paperwork when his phone rang. "Marc."

"Hey, whatcha doing this weekend?"

"Not much. You?"

"I'm going to check out this art exhibition at the resort."

"You? Since when?"

"Since now. I might've been persuaded by one of the new firefighters who's a bit of an art buff."

"I didn't think you the type to care about art buffs." Tom's lips tweaked. "Or is this art buff the new female firefighter?"

"Look who hasn't missed his calling," his brother teased.

"Have fun."

"You betcha. Right back at ya, too."

The call ended, and he studied his phone. He didn't care for art particularly, and had only really met one artist, Toni Wakefield—now Vandenberg—when she'd been stalked by an ex. He glanced at the golden ticket on his desk.

Toni had sent him a ticket for this, the first new exhibition she'd opened in a year, along with another thank you note for helping her when she'd gone through such trouble with her ex. He hadn't planned to go. But it'd be kind of fun to see Marc's face if Tom showed up unannounced. And he could score some points with their mom and fill in the rest of the family about the woman that Marc was obviously interested in. Doing so would take the heat off him in that regard, at least. And if he went out, he wouldn't be sitting here, frustrated that the wheels of justice seemed to always take an awfully long time to turn. And that he wouldn't feel frustrated with the situation with Anna.

He checked the ticket details, then tapped it against the edge of his desk. Should he? Why not? He had nothing else to do. And it would be kind of fun to spy on his brother, which was only what an older brother should do…

Within half an hour he was turning in at the drive of the Muskoka Shores resort. The five-star resort had been here for years and had hosted everything from nationally important conferences to celebrity weddings, such as the one for NHL star Dan Walton a few years ago. Tom had still been working in the city then, but had heard of the scale of that event, and some of the other events that had added to the local policing load. It was nice to visit the resort in an unofficial capacity, that ticket saying he was as welcome here as much as any millionaire.

The trees branches met overhead along the drive, and glimpses showed the lake bathed in the golden light of sunset in an almost ethereal glow. No wonder Lake Muskoka was so popular with tourists during the summer. He parked, then entered the resort's glass front doors where a buzz of happy chatter came from a room just beyond the reception desk.

He flashed his ticket, was offered champagne which he refused, then found the woman of the hour, her husband, Matt, at her side, welcoming people near the door like at a reception.

Toni smiled and extended her hand for him to shake. "Detective Woodmore, it's good to see you."

"Thanks for the invitation." He glanced around. "Looks like you packed them in."

"I'm not sure if it's the art they've come for or the free champagne."

"I'm sure it's the art," he said.

"Definitely the art." Matt shook his hand. "Good to see you again."

"And you." A passing waiter paused to offer them a tray of savories. He took a tiny meatball, savored the meat and spice, his gaze returning to Toni. "No little guy tonight?"

"He's at home being minded by a friend. I'd hoped Anna would come but she decided not to."

He nearly choked. "Anna?"

"Anna Morely. She works in the local medical center."

"I know," he said, without thinking.

Toni's brows lifted a little, then her forehead smoothed. "Of course. You probably dealt with her case from Thursday."

"Yeah." That was true. Quick, he had to change the subject. "Well, I should let you mingle with your more important guests."

"We're glad you could make it," Toni said.

He nodded, wending his way to a corner where he found another face he recognized. "Joel."

"Hey, small world." They gripped hands, and he nodded to the blonde woman who was talking to someone else. He recognized her from last week. Serena.

"What brings you here?" Joel asked. "Excuse my prejudice, but I didn't figure you for an art aficionado."

Now wasn't the time to admit to spying on his brother. "I'm here for something to do."

"Me too. I'd normally be running a youth group, but there was some school function which meant I got a rare night off. Which is good, because it's awesome to see my sister in her element."

Tom nodded, giving the paintings deeper attention. "She certainly is talented."

Each picture displayed a different aspect of Muskoka. The four seasons were evident in the lakeside and woodland scenes, scenes he'd witnessed so often, but captured in oils. The paintings were shown to greatest effect when one stood back and could see the progression from white renderings of winter through to the brighter tones of spring and summer, then the muted earthy colors of autumn. "I like how it's displayed."

"Don't tell anyone, but I think she's hoping that the display will encourage others to buy more than one." He winked. "Things I'm privy to as the older brother of the artist in residence."

Tom smiled, but Joel's words ignited the memory of why he had decided to come tonight. Was Marc here yet?

He glanced around, but still couldn't see him, then grew aware that a softer voice was speaking. "It's good to see you again, Detective."

"And you."

Joel put an arm around Serena, and he realized afresh that they were husband and wife. Man, he must be tired to have forgotten the basics.

"You know each other?" Joel asked.

"We met again at the station when Anna needed to go in for questioning last Friday." She smiled at him.

Tom smiled back, even as his stomach tensed. He really hoped she wasn't about to ask—

"Have you seen her lately?" Serena might appear sweet, but that smile suggested she knew more than he was willing to say.

"Yeah." He cleared his throat. "Just needed to clear some things up."

She nodded, eyeing him with that look that wasn't fooling anyone. He really should go find Marc. "If you'll excuse me. I need to go speak to someone over there."

"Of course." Joel shook his hand again. "I hope you'll soon get some more progress on that other matter."

"Keep praying."

"Always."

"What matter?" Serena asked her husband as Tom departed.

He hoped Joel could allay her questions. Already he could feel how there were undercurrents happening here that could easily tip into unwanted exposure.

He nodded to Damian, who stood with his arm around the waist of a loud brunette. Damian nodded back, lifting his eyebrows as if asking whether they had a result yet.

He shook his head slightly, which drew Damian's frown. Tom held his fingers an inch apart to indicate soon. *Please, Lord.*

There was still no sign of Marc, so Tom quietly made his farewells, just as someone tapped a microphone for what seemed like a time of speeches. He didn't have to be here, so he quickly departed, then paused in front of the large poster situated on an easel opposite.

The Muskoka Summer Ball. His fingers clenched. The other part of the waiting game was getting the police's financial fraud unit to check into the Crayling's affairs. There was no point putting them on their guard if it meant they were going to immediately hide their money. Most people in their situation had offshore bank accounts and crafty accountants who knew where to put ill-gotten gains.

They needed time to get those ducks lined up too, so it could be a bang, bang, bang of targets shot down. But with everyone already having heavy caseloads, people putting his case as their priority would require tricky timing.

But God could do miracles, and he hoped He'd do this one.

For the sake of the families of those who were missing. For the sake of those poor people who lived almost as savages. And because all this talk of Anna meant he really wanted this over with so he could see her again soon.

CHAPTER 13

Saturday dawned. It was Anna's turn to be on reception at the clinic, and once again she was glad for the distraction from her thoughts. Focusing on others was helping. Looking after Ethan had been fun. Toni and Matt had returned, glowing with the success—Toni had sold half her paintings—and by the time they'd finished chatting and she'd returned home and fallen into bed it was nearly one in the morning.

Now she needed to spark awareness to her brain, which meant a pit stop at The Coffee Blend. She drove there, smiled at Suzy. "An iced mocha, please."

"Good call. It's going to be a warm one, eh? One iced mocha coming up."

Anna tapped her card to pay, noticed a poster by the counter advertising the Summer Ball. "Are you going to the ball?"

"Do I look like Cinderella?"

"Come on. It's for charity and a good cause."

"Is it, though?" Suzy's nose wrinkled. "I often wonder how many of these charities take our hard-earned money and use it on administration fees. Do you know how much of the money actually goes to the people who need it?"

Well, no. In all the years Anna had helped her mom with the ball, she'd never once thought to ask this question. "I can find out."

"If you find out, and the fees are less than ten percent, then I might think about it. Because if it is actually helping people, then it would be nice to dress up and pretend I had a chance to meet a handsome prince. Speaking of…" She cleared her throat, and tilted her head at the door.

Anna froze. Then ducked her head. Then lifted her chin. Bent her lips up. Put on indifference like she didn't care. She caught the moment he saw her, his movement freezing for a second, then he too seemed to draw himself up and offer a smile as fake as hers. At least, she hoped it was fake, and that pitiful effort wasn't all he could truly muster.

"Anna. I mean, Miss Morely."

"Detective." She faced the glass-fronted display of pastry delights. Oh, forget fitting into her dress. A situation like this called for chocolate. "You better add a chocolate croissant to my order, please Suzy."

"Sure thing. Want it heated?"

"No thanks." Heating would mean she'd be forced to be in his company even longer.

Anna stilled as Tom drew nearer, and she caught his scent of Cool Water. But no. She wasn't going to let this man steal her focus. In fact, he had no right stealing under her defenses. She'd spent too much time this week reading her Bible and filling her mind with what God said about her to stumble yet again.

"How are you?" he asked in a low voice.

"Fine." *Hurry up, Suzy.* "You?"

"Busy."

Of course he was. Which was great. If he was busy with work then he wouldn't feel the need to pester her like he was doing now, demanding her attention like her every sense wanted to crawl over there to gain satisfaction.

Lord, help me. "How is your case going?"

She might have her face averted—it was so hard not to face him—but her peripheral vision noticed how his eyes dipped to the poster, then back to face her. Clearly he was stronger than she was. "It's going."

She gave a short nod. "Great."

Suzy checked if she needed anything else, and she shook her head. Nope, she only needed to get out of here, with the dignity she sure hadn't had during the last time they'd spoken.

"Hey Tom, what do you think of this ball?" Suzy pointed to the poster. "I always wonder about these things and how much of the money actually goes to those who really need it. You're a detective. You must've come across a few scams in your time."

He took a few moments to answer, then said, "I have."

Anna peeked at him. He glanced away, like she'd busted him looking at her. She rolled her eyes at herself. As if.

"Anna here said she'd find out for us exactly how much goes to administration."

"Did you?" The depths of his grave tone betrayed curiosity, like he was as concerned as Suzy. "Why is that?"

She'd said she'd find out for Suzy, not for him. She shrugged, still not looking at him directly. That way danger lay. "I think it's a shame a good cause doesn't get more support because people are worried about such things. I'm happy to find out if it appeases their concerns."

"Their" as in Suzy's concerns. Not his. He could do his own dirty work.

"Here you go, Anna."

She thanked Suzy and collected her tall to-go cup and paper bag of croissant, fake-smiled at Tom, then escaped.

Her shoulders slumped as she returned to her car and drove

to the clinic. If she'd wanted something to spark awareness this morning, she'd sure found it.

OPENING for three hours on a Saturday morning was usually limited to emergency patients who did not need to be seen at the hospital. Anna was still kept busy, fielding calls from those who insisted their case was serious, juggling appointments for those whose cases truly were, and ensuring Dr. Wells wasn't going to be forced to stay here past noon. Some of the doctors liked the Saturday shift, as it often gave opportunity to catch up on some of the paperwork from the week. Others, especially those with smaller children, tended to complain about the inconvenience. Regardless, the members of the reception team knew it was important for the doctors to preserve their own time off and be refreshed in order to be ready for another week. People could overestimate a doctor's capacity for good health, and there'd been incidences of medical staff self-medicating—or worse—to try and cope with the heavy workloads and stress.

The door to Dr. Wells' room opened with a murmur of voices, then a young mother appeared, her young son tugging at her hand. He looked perkier than before he'd gone in, which might have something to do with the maple syrup lollipop he now held.

Anna fixed up the account and smiled. "There you go, Mrs. Brusselhurst. I hope Simon is feeling better soon."

"Thanks, Anna. Will we see you in church tomorrow?"

"That's the plan."

Anna waved to Simon as they walked out then returned to her juggle of appointment making and changing, filing, and cleaning, doing all the things a team of three or four usually managed on a regular working day. Fortunately, having only one doctor available meant the waiting room was fairly quiet, and with it being nearly twelve she would soon turn the sign to say closed. She nodded to poor Mr. Watson who, as a walk-in, hadn't made an appointment, but she hadn't had the heart to send him away, knowing his mobility was limited and he'd likely struggle to return. She'd find a space for him to be seen soon.

The sliding door behind her opened, and she turned. "I'm afraid we're closing soon and… oh!"

She blinked, as Jackie O'Halloran drew near.

Jackie smiled. "Hi Anna."

No. She couldn't cope with this. Not now. Not like she was being ambushed. Oh, if she'd known this was going to happen today she would've bought all of Suzy's pastries!

She hurried behind her counter, glad for the distance and authority it gave her. "We're closed."

"I made an appointment."

"What? No. You're not on the book."

"I think you'll find I am. James knows. I spoke to him directly."

She had? Well, sometimes people did a few things off the book. Off the appointment book, she meant. She lifted her chin. "Well, if you'd care to take a seat then."

"Anna." Jackie stepped forward. "How are you?"

No. She blinked back emotion. Seeing Tom then seeing Jackie in the space of a few hours was totally unfair. "Fine."

"You look well."

No she didn't. But Jackie did. She seemed to be glowing, and had put on a few pounds that made her look far more attractive than extra curves did on Anna.

"I just got back—"

From where?

"—and I know it's been a while, but I was hoping—"

The phone rang. Anna snatched it up. "Hello, this is Muskoka Shores Medical. This is Anna speaking."

"Are you open this afternoon? I think my daughter has poison ivy."

She fake-smiled at Jackie, still not quite meeting her eyes, then shifted her stance as she tried to explain to the irate mother why she couldn't come in.

James did come in, and was all set to see Mr. Watson, but the thought of Jackie staying there, just the two of them, made her rush to say, "I believe it's Miss O'Halloran next." She snatched the file and passed it to him, and called to Mr. Watson, "You'll be next."

"I don't mind waiting," Jackie said softly. "It would give us the chance to talk."

Exactly why Jackie had to be seen now. "I'm afraid I'm busy now, and as it's almost twelve, and Dr. Wells still has another patient to see after you, I suggest you don't hold him up any longer."

"Anna," James began.

"*Please.*"

Maybe they heard the note of desperation in her voice, because they both nodded, and disappeared, leaving her to prop her elbows on the counter and slump her head in her hands.

"You don't like her much, do you?" Mr. Watson remarked.

A slow exhale pushed away her first inclination to tell him to stop being a sticky beak. Then she straightened, and smiled as sweetly as she could. "Mr. Watson, do you think you'll ever need to visit a doctor again?"

"Probably."

"Then can I please ask you to mind your own business?"

He huffed, and folded his arms. Excellent. That made three for three for people she'd ticked off today.

She busied herself with tidying everything she could, getting things ready for the Monday shift. Monday was often their busiest day, and the more organized things were here the better the start of the week would tend to be.

As she tidied, she wondered what was wrong with Jackie. She hoped nothing too bad. But surely someone who truly was sick wouldn't look like they were the picture of health.

The door opened, and James smiled at Jackie, who seemed to sparkle. Anna frowned. Jackie had never sparkled. But maybe that's what having a movie star boyfriend did. He'd probably gotten her onto using some incredibly expensive Hollywood starlet-only makeup or skin care routine, so she looked so very different to the makeup-free Pastor Jackie that Anna had once known.

"We'll schedule an appointment soon." Dr. James faced her. "Anna, would you please schedule an appointment with Dr. Schifley in Gravenhurst for a CFTS screen?"

She nodded, her focus on the computer screen as she noted that request.

"Thanks, Anna," Jackie said, moving to pay, just as the phone rang again.

"Excuse me," she muttered, and completed the transaction, while Dr. Wells took in Mr. Watson, and Jackie waited. "Excuse me, would you please hold the line?"

She handed Jackie back her card. "We'll get back to you with that appointment as soon as possible."

Jackie nodded, and clearly took it as the dismissal it was meant for as she departed, offering a soft, "It was good to see you, Anna," which caused emotion to burn at the backs of her eyes.

She cleared her throat, working to regain her professionalism, although she knew little of that had been on display today. "Thank you for calling Muskoka Shores Medical Clinic. But it's out of hours and the clinic is closed. If you have a medical emergency, please call 911 or visit Muskoka Shores hospital, otherwise please call during nine to five weekdays or make an appointment online to come see us."

"But—"

No. She put the phone down, and switched it to voicemail, the out-of-hours message giving details of their opening hours, but not allowing patients to leave messages. If people had an emergency, that's what the hospital was for. She hurried to add in the details for Jackie's appointment.

Then paused, her eyes widening as she realized just what James had asked. Seriously? Why was Miss Jackie O'Halloran scheduled to see an OB-GYN? She blinked, her mind spinning. Jackie had put on weight, was glowing. Her breath hitched. Did that mean Pastor Jackie had sinned?

TOM DRUMMED his fingers on the desk, staring at the screen. The figures were pretty much as he suspected, but a quick refresh of his email revealed no fresh messages had come in.

Great. He really didn't want to have to do this, but after what he'd heard this morning, how much longer could he put it off?

He sighed. Picked up his cell phone. Dialed Anna's number. It rang out, and he couldn't even leave a message.

Huh. Judging from that last fact he wondered if she'd blocked his number. That might account for the way she'd barely looked at him this morning.

He'd been surprised she'd bothered to acknowledge him at all, but considering they'd been on show in front of Suzy and the other patrons at The Coffee Blend he'd not been too surprised. Small towns had faster tongues than some places he'd worked in.

But still, the fact she'd promised Suzy to find out about the administration costs of the charity event had the potential to blow this wide apart. He couldn't afford for that to happen, and apart from talking to his boss, who probably wouldn't appreciate Tom coming to him yet again with his concerns about Anna, he didn't really know who else to turn to.

Except God.

His fingers kneaded the back of his neck as he closed his eyes. *Lord, I need some more wisdom here.*

He glanced at his phone again. Anna had been dressed for work in her navy blue uniform, so maybe that was worth a shot. He used his desk phone and tried the clinic. Got the clinic's voicemail, with no chance to leave a message. Okay. So maybe using the office phone to call was possible. If not, dropping around at her place might be best. She couldn't hang up on him that way.

He tried to call her cell again, but she still didn't pick up, which made him wonder if it was just a service glitch after all, and she hadn't blocked his number. Regardless, trying to talk to her like this had all kinds of potential to go wrong. At least if he saw her, he could try to explain, and unless she ran away, he might have a chance to make her listen.

He pushed back in his rolling chair, said goodbye to the staff on the Saturday morning shift, and moved outside. Gabe met him in the secured parking lot. "You leaving? Good."

"Aw, come on. You know you love having me around."

"I know that you're heading for an ulcer if you keep up this pace. You've done all you can, now it's a waiting game until all those agencies get back to us, so go and make the most of your weekend before the proverbial really hits the fan."

"Yes, sir." There was obviously no point worrying Gabe by telling him what he planned to do.

He drove, his fingers clenched against the wheel, praying under his breath as he wondered whether she'd even be home. She might've gone to the store. Or to visit someone. Except he was counting on the fact she probably didn't want to keep wearing her work uniform all day would rule out that one. *Please God, please God…*

There! The red Mazda sat in what he'd come to think of as its usual spot in her driveway. So, she was home. He had to now figure out exactly how to ask her to not investigate the administration costs of the Strong Hearts Foundation in order to avoid raising their suspicions.

He stopped outside her place, chewing his bottom lip. He really should've thought this through a little more. He couldn't exactly demand she not talk to people. How much of a red flag would that be?

His vehicle's interior heated, the sun having already warmed the air inside and causing his shirt to stick to his back. Awesome. So now he'd smell as well as appear totally unshady as he asked her not to talk—

Tap, tap.

He startled. Glanced at the passenger window. Whoa. Anna frowned at him, her hair wet, her skin glistening like she'd just had a shower. That white singlet top was nothing like the work uniform she'd worn when he'd seen her earlier this morning. It should be illegal.

She mouthed something he couldn't hear, so he powered down the window. "Sorry. What did you say?"

"What are you doing here?"

Apart from feeling embarrassed that a woman had taken him unawares like that? So much for being a vigilant cop. "I, um, wanted to talk to you."

Her eyes narrowed. "I thought you were so busy you had no time to talk. Yet you've been sitting here in your car for ten minutes, and not even on your phone."

She'd been watching him? Wow. He really needed to lift his game. Good thing that day of undercover was done. "I was having a power nap."

"With your eyes open?"

"It's a gift."

"You're a card."

And she was a peach. He really liked this banter. Way too much. It was far too easy to fall into banter with her. He had to act like the professional he was. He opened his door. Got out. "May I please speak with you a moment, Miss Morely?"

Her lip flickered, like she thought his act as ridiculous as he knew it himself, then she lifted her chin. "Fine. Talk."

"Out here?"

"Would you prefer me to come to the station?" she asked snidely.

"I'd prefer to talk inside, if that's okay with you."

"Will you arrest me if I say no, Detective?"

His lips jerked. "No."

"Then…" She studied him for a moment, and again he was drawn into the depths of her eyes. "Then okay."

He guessed from the way she abruptly turned and went back inside that she'd meant it was okay to talk in her home, and that she didn't want to be arrested. Even if having an excuse to be near her was a little too tempting for his state of mind.

When he entered the opened front door she stood just inside at the far edge of the entryway's tiles, her crossed arms warning he was going no further. Standing here, looking past her, he could see her house looked different. It seemed lighter, brighter, somehow.

Even if her face held clouds as she eyed him skeptically. "What do you want?"

Man, not this. This felt way too awkward. "Could I please trouble you for a drink?"

She sighed, like it was a huge ordeal. But standing at cross points like this was hardly conducive to the kind of conversation he needed to have. Even if it wasn't the conversation he wanted to have. The one he couldn't have until this was over.

"Water or diet cola?"

"Cola, please." It would keep him awake longer.

She pointed to a glass dining table where an opened Bible lay. His heart clenched. She was reading that? He peered at the verse, saw it was the Psalm he'd mentioned the other day. His heart softened, and when she returned with his drink his "thank you" was softer than he'd normally say.

She eyed him, as if not sure whether to trust him, then gestured for him to sit, which he only did after she had.

She crossed her arms, studying him. "Well?"

"Thanks for the drink."

Her left eye narrowed.

"Did you enjoy your croissant—?"

"Don't try and small talk me, Detective. You made it clear you don't want to spend time with me, so say your piece then you can be on your way."

"Are you always this tough on your friends?"

"You have no idea," she muttered.

Clearly, he didn't.

"Well? What was so important you had to come here, on a Saturday, then spend ten minutes getting up the courage to say something that it seems you still can't find the words to actually speak?"

She knew him too well. He placed the glass on the table. "It's what you said at Suzy's."

"About?"

"About telling her you'd find out the administration costs of the charity."

"Why on earth should something like that concern you?"

"Look, it's just that I've had some dealings with those things in the past, and I hate to admit that she's right. I know these people are your friends—"

"They're more my mother's friends, but whatever."

They were? His heart eased a notch. "And anyway, I just thought you probably didn't want to embarrass them by asking an awkward question like that."

She studied him for a long moment, clearly unconvinced by his reply. "Since when do you care about whether my mother's friend's feelings are hurt?"

He didn't. But saying that wasn't going to fly. And he couldn't exactly hit her with the truth. Except this part of the truth he truly could.

So, eyes firmly on her, he said, "Since I started caring for you."

CHAPTER 14

hat had he said? No. No, no, no. She *refused* to go down that long and painful road again. So what was the correct response to this? It still didn't make sense. How could he say that then treat her like—?

"No." She pushed to her feet. "I think you should leave."

"Anna, please."

She shook her head. "I don't know what you're doing here, but right now, I feel like I'm being gaslighted or ghosted or something, and that you're playing with my emotions. And I really hate feeling like I can't trust myself or you or anyone else right now, so could you please leave now?"

"Anna."

"No! I can't cope with any more people saying one thing then doing another. That's not who I am. I know I'm not perfect, but I am trying to do better, and it doesn't help when people call themselves Christians then suddenly act in ways that are completely contrary to what they used to preach about before."

His face showed confusion, and yes, she knew that last line was more about Jackie than him, but it didn't change the fact that she'd been sorely disappointed and confused by way too many people today and just couldn't cope with any more.

Another of her stupid bouts of emotion threatened, and she had to get rid of him before it overflowed. "Please leave." Her voice wobbled.

"I'm going," he said quietly, moving to the door. "But before I do, can I say that I'm sorry for whoever it was that made you not trust Christians. And if I've done something that made you doubt my faith, if I haven't walked the talk, then I'm sorry. And I wish you'd tell me what it was I did so I could change."

Her shoulders rounded. She couldn't tell him that, because there was nothing to tell.

She pivoted, placing her hands over her face, ignoring his final "Anna" then waiting until she heard the door open, then close, holding still until she heard his car drive away.

Then she released a shaky breath, grasped the back of the dining chair, which she used to support her until she reached the sofa and could collapse into it, tears running down her cheeks.

She didn't know how long she lay there. Thinking about Tom. Thinking about Jackie. Thinking about her own father who had first shown her men couldn't always be trusted. Thinking about her own insecurities that made her lash out instead of be gracious. So much for all the Bible reading she'd done. It hadn't seemed to stick.

"Lord, I'm not doing well, am I?"

Her chest swam with recriminations, and the temptation to sink under the weight of self-pity grew. But a lifeline called out faintly, the one she'd been trying to cling to lately. The one that reminded her she was loved, she was forgiven, that God's grace had set her free from condemnation.

"Lord, how many more hits do I need to take? How long will it take for me to ever be set free?"

She sure hoped the "seventy times seven" wasn't something meant for tests in graciousness as well as for forgiveness. Even if it felt probably necessarily true in her case.

Her thoughts flicked back to earlier. Why had Tom come all this way to speak to her face to face about that? It seemed such overkill. It didn't make sense. But she was so tired to care too much.

Her thoughts tracked back even earlier, to Jackie. Jackie. Her nose wrinkled. How could Pastor Jackie be pregnant? It seemed the most ironic of all ironies that the woman who had looked down her nose at everyone else as sinful was pregnant. Out of wedlock. Anna could only presume the father was Lincoln Cash, which didn't seem too hard to believe, as he'd had a reputation as a player after all. But still. How could holy Jackie have succumbed to his charm so easily? What about all those sermons about waiting until marriage? Then she'd gone and done the last thing anyone would have ever expected her to do. She was so different to the Jackie of a year ago.

The temptation to keep on judging rolled on, thick waves of accusations pointing out her former friend's flaws, in an effort to try to boost her own fragile self-esteem.

But no. She needed to stop this. She pushed herself wearily upright. She had to do something. Be elsewhere. Not be alone with her thoughts.

The sky beckoned her outside, to make the most of the Muskoka promise of beauty, so she grabbed her bag and went to visit Serena. She wouldn't mind if she dropped in without notice.

When she arrived, she saw a new car parked in the driveway. Another visitor? She hesitated, doubts threatening to smother her previous boldness. But she couldn't live like this, not any longer. So, just like at her house, she pushed past the fears and intimidation and knocked on the door.

Then it opened. And revealed Jackie.

She blinked. Checked outside. This was definitely Serena's house. "What are you doing here?" she blurted.

Jackie's lips curved halfway. "Talking about you, actually."

"Excuse me?"

The door opened wider, and there was Serena, looking a little shame-faced, as she ought. "I'm sorry, Anna. I didn't realize you were there."

"Because it would've been easier to talk about me if I wasn't?"

"Anna, please, let me talk to you," Jackie pleaded.

"No, I don't think I'm the one you should be talking to. I think the one you need to speak to is John and Angela McPherson and maybe you can tell them why you were at the clinic today."

Jackie bit her lip, glanced at Serena, then at Anna. "Don't do this. It's not what you think."

"No? I'm pretty sure it is. I've worked in a medical clinic long enough to know what that kind of a referral to an OB-GYN means."

Serena gasped. "Jackie, is this true?"

Anna watched in satisfaction. Let the good girl, never-put-a-foot-wrong face the fury of a disappointed Serena.

Jackie nodded. "James thinks it's ten weeks."

Wait for it, wait for it…

"Oh, I'm so happy for you!"

What? Anna watched in disbelief as Serena wrapped her arms around Jackie, who seemed to glow even brighter. Wait. Why wasn't Serena mad, or disappointed, or any of those things, considering this was their super holier-than-thou friend? Or former friend, in Anna's case, at least?

But the way Jackie laughed and—was that a tear?—simply

seemed to grow even more radiant through it all, without a hint of shame, made her rear back as a startling thought tiptoed through her mind. No. Surely not.

"Anna?"

No. Someone would have told her. Someone would've had to have said something. They couldn't be—she couldn't have—

"Anna? Are you okay?"

She swiveled and exited out the front door, hurrying to her car. She so didn't want to make this moment about herself, but once again she felt like her world was toppling on its axis. How could she not have known?

"Anna!" Serena's voice, her hand on her arm, swung her to face them.

"She and Lincoln are married?"

Jackie appeared behind Serena's shoulder, biting her lip, then nodded.

She wrenched her arm out of Serena's clasp. "Why didn't anyone tell me?" Her gaze leveled at Jackie. "Why didn't you?"

"You... you didn't want to know me, you stopped responding to my messages and calls."

Because she'd blocked her. Just like she'd blocked Tom. Because that was the mature kind of individual she was, the person who avoided others when she felt wronged by them, who focused on herself instead of others and treated them in a way that made them not trust her. And she was so tired of living like this, but it was so hard to change, and...

"I've got to go."

She hurried to her car, ignoring their pleas to stop. How could they—? How could she? Oh, she'd need to leave the country given the rate she kept hurting the people around her. She might as well have a nuclear waste dump around her so people knew to avoid her toxicity. She scrambled into her car, slammed the door, and drove away.

∼

"You didn't go to the art show," Tom said to Marc when they were having dinner at his folks on one of those rare Saturday nights when work shifts and plans permitted such a thing.

"The art show? What art show?" Drew asked.

"The one at the Muskoka Shores Resort last night," Tom said.

"Marc doesn't like art," Dad scoffed.

"But apparently he likes a certain female firefighter who does."

This tugged out Drew's smirk, as Marc jeered. "And how would you know?" Then Marc's eyes widened. "Wait, did you go to spy on me? Is that it?"

Clearly Tom wasn't the only one in the family with powers of deduction.

"Now Tom, you're not supposed to be telling tales. Aren't you a bit old for that?" his mom said, her wink saying she heartily approved this particular story.

"He's just wishing he had his own tales to tell," Marc mocked.

Yeah. Tom pressed his lips together, as his brother's laughter halted, as if suddenly remembering why Tom hadn't had any relationships to boast about in recent years.

"Sorry, man." Contrition filled Marc's eyes. "I forgot."

Tom shrugged. "It'll be four years next month."

"Some days it feels like yesterday," Mom said.

Sure did.

"But it *is* four years, son. It is okay to move on."

He glanced away as their dog drew near, wanting a head rub. He obeyed the implied request, and rubbed Pinky between the ears.

"Have you… have you ever found someone that makes you think you'd like to try again?" Drew asked.

He pressed his lips harder.

Marc whistled. "I know what that look means."

"Don't," Tom rasped.

"It's the medical chick," Marc announced.

Tom side-eyed him. Marc might as well be rubbing his hands together.

"You like a doctor?" Dad asked.

"No, it's the receptionist who got attacked at the medical center last week," Marc said for him.

Mom's eyes widened. "She got attacked? Who is she? Why is this the first I'm hearing about this?"

Tom heaved out a breath. "Because there's nothing to tell, Mom."

"He lies, Ma. There's plenty to tell." Marc smirked.

He shook his head.

"Oh, this is the chick whose car he got me to fix for 'nothing', right?" Drew asked.

"Red Mazda?" Marc said to Drew's nod. "One and the same." Marc grinned. "See? Plenty to tell."

"Except there isn't." Frustration edged Tom's words. "And I messed things up and now she doesn't want to speak to me anymore, so there's that."

"Aw, come on. What are you? A wussy little dandelion?" Marc ridiculed. "I'm sure the big tough detective can figure out a way to win her back."

"I don't know if I can afford to. Not yet, anyway."

"Not yet?"

"It's complicated, Mom."

"When is it not with Tom?" Marc rolled his eyes. "He might pretend to have it all together, but I think there's a lot going on beneath the surface."

"He's a detective, Marc. You know he can't talk about his cases."

Sure couldn't. At least their mom had Tom's back.

"There's that look again." Marc eyed him thoughtfully. "Is she somehow connected to your case?"

He stood. "Are we finished eating here?"

"She is!" Marc high-fived Drew.

"I think it's time for me to go."

"Are you going to see her?" Marc asked, eager and wide-eyed, like when Pinky was a puppy.

"I already told you, she doesn't want to see me, so the answer is no. I'm trying not to stress her by doing what she wants which is to keep away."

He collected plates and went to the kitchen, as his family's laughter continued outside in the evening cool. He wished he could be so carefree, but life and death and pain had eroded some of the simple joys in life. Sometimes happiness felt like a concept where he was always waiting for the other shoe to drop.

He started the water, filled the sink, squirted in the lemon dish liquid. Family lunches and dinners like these meant his folks cooked while the boys cleaned up. Every time. He was glad it was his turn to wash dishes today.

One plate down, upright in the dishrack. Then another, sparkling clean. Like he wished his heart could be. Without the contaminants of the past, without the swirl of dirt that he seemed to live in. If only he could so easily wipe away the stains that had marked his soul.

Too many deaths. Too many broken people. Too many lives he'd been unable to fix. Too many times when he'd tried to trust "the system" only to see the system fail and leave people worse off than before. Too many times when he'd given his heart and hopes only to see them shrivel in the face of such things as cancer, like his grandparents, or car accidents, like Meghan.

Who was he kidding? Marc was right. Tom might act like he had things all together, but he was addicted to work, he was bad at learning to rest, and in his own way, he was as broken as

Anna had once seemed. Fractured. Soul-splintered. At least she seemed more whole and at peace these days. Unlike him, with agitation rippling beneath his skin, frustration spilling from every pore.

His mom came in, placed her hand on his back, and some of his agitation faded.

"You prayed for me just then, didn't you?"

"I'm always praying for you, son."

A lump formed in his throat, and he focused really hard on the water, so he didn't do anything stupid, like cry.

"So, would I like her?"

"I don't know. Anna is nothing like Meghan." And Mom had loved Meghan. Meghan, the delicate and pretty preschool teacher who had shared Mom's interest in quilting and cooking.

"Anna, huh?" His mom's voice was soft. "What *is* she like?"

"Funny. Sweet. A little snarky."

"Oh, we need a girl like that around here."

He shot her a look. "Mom."

"No, I'm serious. Marc especially needs someone to pull him into line."

Whoa. "She's not going to go out with him." Just the thought of Anna going out with his far more good-looking, more-muscled younger brother was wrong.

"Because she's got to go out with you?" his mom teased.

Yes.

She did. The thought fired fresh determination. He'd have to trust God that she'd still want him, even once the truth of his involvement in the investigation of her family's friends came out.

"Is Anna a Christian?"

"Yes. But she goes to the community church in Muskoka Shores."

"*But?*"

He heard what that implied, and amended it to, "*And* she goes there. There are some good people there."

She nodded. "I know. Jenny Wells is one of the loveliest people I've worked with. She's always said it was a true fellowship of believers, like a family, something she really noticed when poor John died."

The Wells' family's eldest son. Killed in the Middle East a number of years ago. Tom had been one year behind him at school.

"Does Anna make you laugh?" his mom continued.

He thought back. Anna might have her issues, but she'd definitely made him laugh. And smile. And brought a joy to his heart he hadn't felt for a long time, a bit like the spring flowers that waited for the snow to melt before it was time to bloom. Gosh, his English teacher mom would be proud of him thinking in metaphors like that. "She does."

"You need someone who gives joy, and shares your sense of humor. So did you go out at all?"

"We went out a couple of times," he confessed. "Once to The Coffee Blend, and once to the cranberry farm in Bala. Then I realized there could be complications with my case if we kept going out, so I called things off. Well, I tried to put things on hold, but I messed up explaining things and she took it the wrong way and now she's avoiding me."

His mom winced. "Poor girl. She doesn't know?"

"Of course not."

"Ah."

Exactly. "So that's why I feel like I'm stuck in limbo, waiting for things to happen, and it's frustrating the life out of me, Mom."

"When did you last see her?"

"Yesterday. I had to ask her not to say something to someone, and she basically gave me both barrels and forced me out of her house."

At his mom's silence he glanced across. She had raised her eyebrows.

"Wow. No, Mom. It wasn't anything like that. I can't believe you'd think that about me."

"Honey, I know you're not your brother, but you are a man with hormones, still."

"Yeah, and someone who knows how to control them. I'd never disrespect a woman like that."

"I know."

He exhaled. "I'm just tired of feeling like I'm the bad guy as far as she's concerned, when it's the case that's the main thing coming between us. I'm waiting for all these agencies to finally get on the same page so we can get the ball rolling."

"A few too many metaphors, there, dear."

He snickered. His mom might be a retired English teacher, but she'd never stop correcting their grammar and use of mixed metaphors.

"Okay, so what I'm hearing is that you like this girl, and she likes you back—"

"No, she doesn't," he corrected.

"Oh yes she must, because she wouldn't get upset if she didn't care now, would she?"

Huh. He might be a detective, but he hadn't deduced that.

"So it's just a matter of waiting on God's timing and being patient. You may find it's not just about you learning some patience, but also it allows God to work more in her heart."

Maybe. Though God had plenty of work still left to do in Tom's heart too. "And mine," he admitted.

"And yours," she agreed softly. "God knows what He is doing, Tom. You can trust Him, all the time."

He nodded.

Lord, help me to trust You. With Anna, with the case, and with everything.

CHAPTER 15

It was a strange thing to be caught in the no-man's land between truth and lies.

Outside, bird chirps begged her to get up, but her warm bedcovers held a cozy weight that induced drowsiness. Anna might've promised various people to be at church today, but after yesterday's shock in learning about Jackie's secret marriage—which Serena had known about!—oh, how she wanted to break her word.

She rolled onto her side, her thoughts tracking through the lows and even lowers of yesterday's interactions. Seeing Tom at The Coffee Blend. Seeing Jackie at the doctors. Tom, again, at her home. Then the shock of learning Jackie was married. *Married?*

After seeing Jackie at Serena's Anna had gone home and instantly cyber-stalked Jackie and Lincoln, and whoa—there wasn't a peep anywhere about Lincoln Cash being married. There had been plenty of online articles about Jackie, and how it was only a matter of time until he dropped her, because how on earth could amazing hot him see anything in ordinary, ugly, plain Jackie? Or so his groupies claimed.

That, and the amount of abuse Jackie had been receiving, had been enough to help Anna understand why they might want to keep such a special thing private. Except, now she wanted to know how they'd managed to keep it under the radar.

And surely now Jackie was pregnant, it would only be a matter of time until people knew, and then what would people start saying? Good girl gone bad? Lincoln back to his wild ways? Conviction panged. Judging harshly, just like Anna herself had done.

Her heart was such a mess, teetering between regret at her own judginess, offense at being left out of the loop, and defensiveness for poor Jackie that made Anna long to set some of these random people straight. But before she could do that, she had to speak to Jackie herself. Anna had to apologize, beg her forgiveness, and do whatever she could to make restitution.

She'd been so selfish. So mean. As horrible and judgmental as anyone else on the internet. And she was so sorry, so, *so* sorry for what she'd thought, for how she'd treated her friend. It was more than past time to make up for it. And Sunday, the start of the week, was a good place to start.

She went to the Sunday service, arrived late, sat up the back, left early. But as she drove away, she was glad she'd gone. It had been good to see a few more friends, wave at Trudy, smile at Angela McPherson, even if it felt like she was here partly out of obligation because she'd said to them she would attend.

But no. That wasn't entirely true either. Anna had gone because she'd sensed she needed to, as much as for her to get back into the habit of regularly gathering with God's people again as to hear the sermon, and hear a perspective different from her own thoughts. Joel's message was on the Holy Spirit, and how Christians were supposed to let God's love flow into but also through them. She hadn't been doing that. She'd kept

God at arms' length for far too long, then been so busy looking to be filled with His love that she hadn't spilled any love recently. Something she was determined to change, and put into practice now.

For too long she'd been at the mercy of her moods, following her emotions wherever they might lead. But she'd had so many reminders of how much of a roller-coaster of a life that led to. The emotional rollercoaster wasn't something she wanted to ride on anymore. But she knew she'd need God's Spirit to help her to change.

She exhaled, arms on the steering wheel as she prayed, once again releasing all the hurts and offenses, letting her heart still as she breathed in God's truths. That God loved her. That His Spirit was within her. That she might not have much strength, but God strengthened her for what she needed to do. Including what she needed to do right now. "Thank You for Your forgiveness, Lord," she whispered. "Cleanse my heart. Help me love others like You want me to."

She wiped her eyes, grateful nobody had felt the need to check on her, then left the church parking lot. She turned onto the main street of Muskoka Shores, heaving with tourists on this mild Sunday. The shops were packed, although some, like Brandi's Bookstore and Annette's Florist, weren't open with their bosses usually attending the church she'd just left. Although Annette hadn't been there today. Maybe she'd had a big day doing wedding flowers yesterday. Annette always did the best flowers, and since Sarah Walton had posted about Annette's beautiful bouquets following her wedding, Annette had been in increased demand. Which reminded her... Maybe that was something she could do to make amends.

She took the turn onto Fir Avenue, then followed the road to the familiar apartment complex, as memories rose from the last time she'd been here. She winced. How petty, how juvenile had she been? Another exhalation. But that was the past.

God had forgiven her. And she'd pray and trust others would too.

She knocked on the door of Jackie's apartment. No response.

The door across was opened by Annette. "She's not in."

"Has she been here recently?" Or did she now live at the giant house on the lake that local rumors whispered Lincoln had bought last Christmas?

"I saw her arrive a few days ago, but she went out again this morning."

Maybe she was back at Serena's. "Um, Annette, what are the chances that someone could whip up an enormous bouquet of apology flowers for me?"

"Apology flowers?"

"Yes, please."

Annette studied her. "Finally come to your senses, have you?"

She winced. How many others in the town knew of her petty behavior? "I know I've done a lot of dumb things, but I'm trying to do better."

"We all do dumb things, but it's only really with God's help that we can do better. Otherwise, it's really us just stumbling in the dark in our own strength, and we all know that will fail, sooner or later."

So true. "I know."

Maybe Annette understood the reason for Anna's red eyes or the shakiness in Anna's voice, because her face softened. "It may just be that I have an appropriate bouquet that I was working on here."

"Really?"

Annette smiled. "It may be that God told me that I should expect a visit from someone who might need to apologize."

Anna exhaled. "Did God tell you they had to be the most beautiful, expensive, loveliest flowers because I hurt one of my loveliest friends?"

"I think you'll find what's here will work well."

And when Annette brought the creamy roses and orchids to the door it was exactly that. Beautiful, perfect, lovely. Everything Anna had not been. But everything she would—with God's help—work to become again.

Her eyes filled with fresh tears. "How did you know?"

"Like I said, I had this sense that God was telling me to work on this today." Annette traced a delicate petal. "As for you, I guess God knows it's all about timing. If you force a flower to bloom too early, it never lasts as long as one that blooms when nature tells it too."

Was Annette subtly referencing Anna's overdue apology? Or something else, like Anna's ill-fated push to find validation and acceptance in a man? Regardless, it still held true. "How much do I owe you?"

"That's the other funny thing God told me," Annette said.

Uh oh. She had a funny feeling what this was going to sound like. "No, don't you go telling me that they're really cheap or something like that. I can afford to pay, I promise."

"Yes, but here's the thing. I'm trying to be obedient to what God tells me, and He said to trust Him. So they weren't cheap, but you could have them"—she placed the tissue-wrapped stems held in a squat glass vase in Anna's arms—"for free."

"What? No, I can't accept that. I don't want to give a gift that costs me nothing."

"And I can't afford to disobey God, so I guess we've got a problem now, don't we?"

"But it cost you. The flowers and your time all cost you."

"They did, that's true, but the older I get the more I realize that everything I have is because God was so generous to me. And I've learned to follow those little promptings I feel because I believe it's God leading me. So I have to do what He says, when He says it, as part of my obedience to Him."

"But it's too much. This must be worth hundreds." Anna shook her head. "I can't accept it."

"But that's the thing, Anna. If you can't accept the gift of grace, how can you ever really understand the depths of God's love and the richness of His grace to you?" Annette smiled. "I'm pretty sure that's what He was saying."

Anna shook her head, but Annette retreated and shut the door, leaving Anna holding the flowers, looking at them with awe.

God's gift, freely given, just like His love, His mercy, His forgiveness. It wasn't designed as a one-stop, one way, fill-her-up-to-the-top one-time deal. She wasn't designed to be a vase, but was meant to be a fountain, just like God's living spring. A spring where water flowed in, then out, and life could continue. The living wells of God's life and love within her was meant to run freely into other people's lives. And she'd tried to unblock things, but the grit of life kept blocking things, and she'd been dammed inside for months, feeling the pressure only increase.

God wanted her to live freely, and share His life and love, just as He did with her.

ANNA PRAYED ALL the way to Serena's, where she saw the fancy car, which must be Jackie's, was there again.

She knocked on the door, then hid behind the flowers, figuring the occupants inside might not open it if they knew it was her.

The door opened. Then she heard, "Anna?"

She peeked between the roses. The tentative smile on Serena's face tugged at her emotions. "Oh, Serena, I'm so sorry. Please, forgive me. Jackie is still here, isn't she? I can't believe I've been so mean. I hope she'll forgive me."

"Of course I do," Jackie said, drawing into view.

Anna quickly handed the roses to Serena and hurled herself

at Jackie, wrapping her in a big hug. "I know I should be on my hands and knees, but I couldn't with the flowers, and I want you to know I'm so sorry," she said into Jackie's neck. "I'm so, so sorry. And I know I've pushed you away and said some awful things, but I didn't mean them, and please would you—"

"I forgive you."

She was pretty sure those streams of living water weren't supposed to consist of her tears. All she seemed to do these days was cry. But there was something healing about tears, something that released within, like the dams of twigs and muck and silt had been set free through the force of her tears. The result of her repentance. The realization of what God's grace actually meant in her life.

Jackie's arms tightened around Anna. Her hug felt different now, a little softer, less bony, more relaxed.

Anna pulled away. "You're so beautiful, Jackie. Marriage suits you. As does being pregnant. I thought that earlier, and I didn't say anything, because, I don't know, I was dumb and jealous, but you really are glowing. Don't you agree?" she asked Serena.

"Absolutely. Marriage suits her. And pregnancy."

"Oh, and I'm so sorry for spilling the news about that," Anna rushed to add. "I really shouldn't have said that. Apart from anything else it was so unprofessional. I was just shocked, and—no, I won't make excuses. I was wrong. Please forgive me."

"It's already done."

She exhaled. "Thank you. I'm so sorry—"

"It's okay." Jackie smiled. "You can stop with the apologies. It's in the past, okay?"

Anna nodded. "So, can I ask you about when you got married? I can understand why you kept it secret, but I want to know all the details."

Serena handed the vase to Jackie and gently pushed Anna

toward the living room. "Go sit down. I think we're all going to need some tea to hear this."

Over cups of hot tea Anna soon learned about Jackie and Lincoln's secret wedding just before Christmas, at the time of the biggest snowstorm to hit Muskoka in years.

"So tell me about how he proposed. I imagine the man knows a thing or two about how to deliver a romantic line." She winced. She hadn't meant that to sound snarky, even if it was true. If the man ever took up voiceover work for commercials, he could probably sell ice-cream to Santa, his North Pole helpers, and all the reindeer.

Jackie's cheeks pinked. "He, um, does."

She knew it. "And then what? He decided you had to get married then and there?"

"Actually, I think it was more the other way around."

Anna's jaw sagged. "You told him you wanted to elope?"

"It wasn't really eloping."

As Jackie explained, Anna found herself reluctantly impressed. She'd never have thought Jackie had it in her to suggest a quickie wedding.

"And we agreed that we might as well make the most of it, because otherwise it was going to be months before we could see each other again, and we both agreed that was simply too long."

"Wow."

"So it was only John and Ange McPherson, and then we needed another witness or two, so we asked Joel and Serena. I'd wondered about asking Lincoln's grandfather, considering he's really the one who brought us together, but it would've been too hard to organize things with him so quickly, and probably too hard to keep as a secret as well."

"So who else knows?" Rachel? Toni? Staci?

"Lincoln thought it was wise to let the local police know, at least some of them, in case there were questions about why I might be at Linc's place. But apart from that, only Linc's granddad—and he's sworn to secrecy—his agent, our folks, and that's it. Oh, and James Wells now, too."

"Wow." Okay. She felt a little better now. It wasn't like everyone else had known and she'd been the weakest link nobody wanted to tell. "And you quit your job?"

"I love the residents, but couldn't guarantee to be available for shifts. I suppose I didn't want to have my life hampered by work when it meant not seeing Lincoln for ages, as I'm trying to be with him as much as his schedule allows. I'm still working at Golden Elms but on a casual basis when I'm available."

"Wow."

"I know, right?" Jackie smiled.

"And now a baby."

"I can't believe how much my world has changed in such a short time."

"Right? I remember you sitting there telling us that you didn't need a husband, and now look at you. Happily married, jet-setting around the world, glowing."

"It surprised me as much as anyone," Jackie said, humble as ever.

"But what happens when you start showing? Aren't you worried about what people will say?"

"Well, that's the beauty of it. We've had these months of peace and quiet, just finding us in the middle of all of Lincoln's spotlight, and when I'm showing he'll be back filming in Toronto, so he'll be closer. Then we can stop sneaking around and just tell people we got married last Christmas. All of which is true. I'm hoping that we'll have missed so much of the drama."

"I think it's amazing that with somebody as famous as Lincoln you've really managed to keep this off the radar," Serena said.

"It definitely hasn't been easy, and I know there have been plenty of people who have judged me for sneaking off for romantic rendezvous with my boyfriend when I'm supposed to be a good Christian girl." Jackie's smile faded as she glanced at Anna.

Oh no. Did Jackie know Anna had done exactly that? She'd been such a bad friend. *Lord, help me to do better.*

Jackie sighed. "It's hard to ignore some of the magazine covers out there, even if I never read what's inside."

Oh, she hoped that was what Jackie meant.

"People can be so wicked, can't they?" Serena said. "Feasting on other people's lives purely for their own entertainment."

It wasn't only celebrity gossip, Anna thought ruefully, thinking about her true crime phase.

"I understand that a lot of that came from people not knowing what they thought they deserved to know," Jackie said. "But it's tricky figuring out the line between privacy and giving the hordes enough to keep them happy, especially for Lincoln to keep his fans onside." Her nose wrinkled. "I get the impression that his agent wasn't too happy Lincoln married me."

Indignation roiled. "What gives him the right to determine who makes Lincoln happy?"

Jackie smiled. "That's exactly what I say, and what Linc says too."

Huh. Warmth filled her to think the Hollywood megastar might think the same way as she did.

"Anyway, enough about me. What's been happening with you?"

Not much, then a lot, but compared to what she'd just heard… "Same ol', same ol'."

"Come on, that's not exactly true," Serena said. "You had your own excitement just a little while ago. Remember?"

"What happened?" Jackie asked Anna.

"There was an attempted robbery at the medical clinic. I was locking up when this druggie tried to break in."

"Oh my goodness!" Jackie's hands flew to her mouth. "Were you hurt?"

"No. God was faithful, and sent someone just at the right time."

The right time. The words from that prayer she'd prayed rose again. She could always trust God to be there, because He always was. He'd never left her or abandoned her, even when she'd tried to walk away from Him.

She tuned back in to what Jackie was saying. "...really feel like we should take self-defense classes. Lincoln has mentioned it before, not because he thinks anyone will actually do something, but it's better to be prepared and have that confidence than freeze and be at the mercy of a would-be attacker."

Like Anna had done. "I've thought that would be good too."

"I think a lot of us have thought the same." Serena nodded. "We should mention it to the other girls and see about a class."

"Oh, I'd *love* for us to get together soon, all of us," Jackie said. "It'd be good to tell them all the truth about me and Linc, especially before they find out about the baby. Maybe we could have another of your soirees soon, Serena."

"Actually…" Maybe Anna could make it up to her friends by hosting a proper event. "Could we have it at my house? Serena has done so much for me that I'd love to host something as my thank you, and apology, and oh, everything else it needs to be because I know I've been a bad friend. I hope hosting something like this will show I've changed."

"That sounds lovely," Jackie said. "But for the record, you don't have to do this."

"Except I really feel like I do. We can have nice food, although it won't be as good as what Serena makes, but I'll follow her recipes. And we'll have cocktails for Rachel—"

"Mocktails, these days," Serena said.

Okay. She'd double check that with Rachel. "And a movie or two. Just like we used to."

"Sounds perfect!" Jackie's grin could light candles.

"The tricky thing will be finding a time we can all do it. Especially if someone keeps having these romantic rendezvous with her celebrity husband," Anna teased.

"I'll tell him certain things take priority." Jackie winked.

Oh. She loved her friends.

"And if he happens to have that weekend off, I'll tell him to hang out in Toronto. He can prep for his next production."

"What's he filming?"

"A police detective show for TV. He says he can't wait, and I can't either. It'll be so good to have him living nearby again. He's already bought an apartment in the same complex as where Dan and Sarah Walton live, so they will be neighbors both there and here."

"Lucky them." Serena smiled. "I still remember their wedding like it was yesterday. It was the best day."

"Linc's still got some more scenes to shoot back in Morocco, then some more stuff to do in LA, but he'll be back in a few weeks, which will be wonderful. And he's always looking to get some real-life inspiration. So if you know any police in Toronto…" Jackie teased.

Anna blinked. Actually, she did. Or at least one who had worked there, not so long ago.

Jackie paused. "What's that look for?"

Anna glanced at Serena who gave a "go on" gesture. She sighed. "I do."

"Really?"

"And you know him too. Remember Tom, the police officer who worked Toni's case? He used to work in the city as a detective there too."

"Did he? I didn't know that. Why do you know that?"

"He, uh, worked on my case, and…" God bless the gene that gave away her emotions and was right now pouring heat into her cheeks.

Jackie's eyes widened. "Oh, don't tell me—you and him. Oh, Anna, he'd be perfect!"

"Maybe to tell Lincoln about detective stuff, but not for me. I... I'm trying not to keep living like I need a man. Just like you told me last year. I, um, didn't appreciate it at the time, but I see now what you meant by it. And I know my happiness has to be found in God, rather than in someone else."

"God will never let you down." Jackie's voice was soft.

"Amen." She knew that now. God never had let her down. His love was both the baseline and the peak example for how she wanted to live her life. "So I'm trying my best to get secure in God so I don't need a man."

"I'm so proud of you, Anna," Serena said.

Jackie said nothing, only getting up to wrap her in a hug.

Anna clung on, relishing her friend's acceptance, her love. Oh, why had she thought herself unloved, when love had been here all the time?

Jackie pulled away, wiped away tears. "Oh, I'm so hormonal all the time these days."

"It's to be expected," Serena said.

"Lincoln calls it Jackie 2.0. The softer version of me. I think he can't wait to be a dad." Jackie blew her nose, then resumed her seat. "Well, I'll be sure to tell him there's a detective here he could interview. I know there are plenty in the city he could ask, but I know he wants to meet Tom because of what happened before, so that would be perfect. Thanks, Anna, for the suggestion."

"It doesn't mean Tom can. I know he's got some big case he's working on."

"Well, it won't hurt to try. I can't believe I didn't think of that."

"That's probably because you've been too busy buying all those designer handbags and clothes," Anna said, with a pointed look at Jackie's battered handbag she was pretty sure she'd seen Jackie buy on a long-ago shopping trip to Target.

Jackie blushed. "I really don't like that stuff. I think that's partly why Richard, Linc's agent, doesn't think I make a good match for Linc because I don't care about my image. It seems so pretentious to me, and I can't wrap my head around why people need expensive status symbols to feel better about themselves."

Anna laughed. "You must be like a breath of fresh air to Lincoln."

"I think that's part of why he loves me. That, and apparently, I am the best kisser he's ever met."

These words, so shocking from once-prim Jackie, spiraled through Anna sending her into a fit of laughter, and Serena and Jackie joined in. Oh, laughter was like medicine, good for the soul. And their restored friendship was balm for her heart.

THE WEEKEND PASSED, the next week too, as frustration lined Tom's heart. So much for trying to get a quick result. Tom's fears about the Craylings catching wind of the planned bust was apparently echoed by the higher-ups, and now Legal was involved, which had ground his plans to a near halt. He woke each day dreading to find out what newest hitch awaited.

Gabe caught his eye, and Tom's heart sank. This didn't look like good news.

And sure enough, Gabe's murmured words were exactly what he'd feared.

"What do you mean there's another delay?" Tom asked. "How much longer are we going to have to wait?"

Gabe sighed, steepling his fingers as he leaned back on his chair behind the desk. "You know how these things go."

"But if we delay much longer, the fundraising ball will happen, then all that money that well-intentioned people are donating will likely go offshore, and we'll have even less of a chance of tracking it."

"I've also expressed that to the powers-that-be. The ball is only two weeks away, so we've still got time to get all of our ducks in a row."

"But how can we let those poor people keep living out there?" He couldn't get the memory of those broken souls from his mind. *Lord, be with Terry. Let him be okay.*

"They've survived so far, so we'll have to hope they can last a little longer. Remember, the whole point of doing this as a huge operation is because we want to shut these people down for good, to leave no loopholes so they can do it again. That's why Legal is taking so long to make sure every T is crossed, and I is dotted."

Tom scraped his fingers down his cheeks.

"In the meantime, you have other cases you can work on. Oh, and I got a request from one of Lincoln Cash's representatives. Apparently, he wants to meet you."

"Really? Why?"

"I don't know. He's probably wanting to get the low down on police work for some new and incredibly inaccurate TV show about police."

Amusement poked out. Realistic TV police shows were rare. "I met his wife. Remember her? She's the one who took down the ex-partner of Toni Wakefield with a Muskoka chair."

"Oh yeah. The Muskoka miracle or whatever it was they called it."

"Could you throw a Muskoka chair? Those things are heavy."

Gabe shrugged.

"She's so skinny and petite so that's why they called it a miracle. She couldn't have done it in her own strength."

His boss scoffed. "Fifteen minutes of fame girl."

"Not quite fifteen minutes if she's married to Lincoln Cash." But whatever. Gabe was a staunch non-believer. At the moment, anyway. *Touch his heart, Lord.* "I guess I'll go work on these things then."

"Do the service proud."

"I always try."

Tom returned to his desk, saw the message on his laptop keyboard, and called the number. Spoke to Jackie herself, heard her surprising requests, which he found himself reluctantly agreeing to.

He hung up, leaned back in his chair, hands clasped behind his head.

Had Anna ever reconciled with Jackie? He hoped so, for her sake. Jackie seemed as genuine and down-to-earth as what he remembered from their interviews early last year. Being married to a movie star hadn't changed her at all. He was glad that things were working out for her and Lincoln.

Lord, if there is any way You can make things work out for me and Anna, I'd be forever grateful.

Then he exhaled and refocused on his case.

CHAPTER 16

"Oh, I can't believe how good it is for all of us to be together again!" Jackie said.

Anna glanced around her living room, every seat filled with her friends. Some friends, like Serena, Jackie, and Rachel, she'd known all her life. Other friends, like Toni and Staci were newer. Some of the other women, like Brandi and Camille were newer still, but they had all come today, happy for the excuse to gather.

"Cherry sends her apologies," Serena said. "She's working at a wedding today, but says she'll try for the next one. Except, we're in the middle of wedding season, so that might be a while, unless it's an earlier-in-the-week event."

"I was glad to have the night off," Camille said. "Alphonse told me I deserved a night off, so this is rare for me."

"We're so glad you could come," Serena said. "I'm sure he's keeping you busy making all those pastries for all these weddings."

Camille nodded. "And prepping for the Summer Ball."

"It's going to be spectacular." Serena clapped her hands.

"Cherry and I have been working on it, and I know your mom will love how the ballroom will be decorated."

Anna nodded, then wondered again how much it would cost holding it at the Muskoka Shores Resort. They didn't do things for free, she knew. Well, for someone like Serena who had worked there forever and was a linchpin in the whole operation they may, but she bet most of their employees only got a discount. So how much of the cost of the ball was because of the venue and food charges? Was this some of the administration costs that Suzy had wondered about? She really should ask her mom, or maybe even Heather about it.

It just seemed weird. Why had they insisted on one of the most expensive venues in the Muskoka area? And why did it always have to be a ball? A more cynical person might wonder if the Craylings did this kind of thing simply because they wanted an excuse to dress up and impress people, or have it as a tax write-off or something.

"Speaking of the ball, it's for a charity, right?" Jackie asked.

Anna explained about the Strong Hearts Foundation.

"So are there any tickets left?"

"A few. Why, do you think Lincoln can make it?"

"How is Lincoln doing?" Rachel interrupted.

"He's great, but is really looking forward to moving back this way." Jackie looked at Anna. "I don't think he can make it to the ball, but I'm happy to buy a ticket just in case."

"I still can't believe he's your boyfriend," Brandi said.

"Actually…" Jackie glanced at Anna, then at Serena, who gave her a nod.

Anna waited, sensing this was the time. Just wait for the squeals…

Jackie pulled out a silver chain that held two rings. One, a big fat square diamond that she'd showed Anna last weekend. The other, a smooth gold band.

"Oh my gosh! Oh my gosh!" That was Rachel.

"You're married?" Staci's eyes were huge. She was probably wondering how to use something similar in a story one day.

"I knew it!" Toni nodded with satisfaction.

Brandi was fanning herself. "I'm too young for a hot flush, but I need air."

Anna joined in the laughter, and the next minutes were filled with excited questions, all of which were ones she'd asked Jackie not so long ago.

"So did you enjoy the dessert?" Camille asked.

"How did you know?" Jackie's eyes rounded. "Wait. Did you make it?"

Camille nodded. "It took time, but we knew it had to be very special."

"Oh, it was! It was divine, and I don't use that word often."

"She doesn't," Anna confirmed.

"But honestly, I think it was the best thing I've ever tasted," Jackie continued. "Even better than what I ate in Paris."

Camille looked pleased, as Jackie was then inundated with questions about Paris. Apparently, Lincoln had flown her there for a special honeymoon rendezvous.

"And I'm sorry I've been distant." Jackie glanced around the group. "But working things around Linc's schedule makes things a little tricky for planning things here. It'll be easier when he's here."

"Especially when—" Anna bit off the rest of those words. Then mouthed a "sorry" at Jackie.

"Especially when what?" Rachel asked.

Jackie took a drink of her pink lemonade. The fact it was non-alcoholic hadn't raised anyone's suspicions. Nope, Anna managed to put her foot in it again.

"Especially when he's here for his TV show, right?" Anna said to Jackie.

"Exactly."

"What TV show?" Brandi asked. "Sorry, I read more books than watch TV."

"It's his new police detective show. They're filming in Toronto as a stand in for New York. Like with *Suits*."

"I thought that was filmed in New York," Camille said.

"There's a bunch of shows and movies they film in T.O. because it's easier and cheaper," Staci explained.

"So that's why I couldn't find the right street when we were there last Christmas," Rachel mused.

"Oh, and your friend Tom has agreed to help Linc, so that's good," Jackie said to Anna.

Anna froze, conscious all eyes had switched to her. But no, she didn't need to make this weird. And for both Linc and Tom it *was* good. "Good."

"You have a friend called Tom?" Rachel asked, eyebrows raised.

"Not really." Not anymore. "He's more an acquaintance, really. But I'm trying not to get caught up in wanting a boyfriend, so please don't lead me astray and let's keep the focus on the main thing. Which is Jackie here, am I right? So Jackie, you were saying about Lincoln?" she prompted, ignoring the look Staci gave her.

"Um, yes. That's right. So it'll be great to have him nearby in Toronto." Jackie glanced at Anna, then placed a hand on her non-existent stomach. "Especially when the baby comes."

"Get out of here!" Rachel cried. "No way. No way!"

"Yes way."

"Ahh! I'm so happy for you girl!"

Jackie was swarmed with new hugs, and it took some time before everyone had calmed again.

"Here's to you," Toni said, lifting her glass. Hers was sans alcohol too. "We're so thrilled, even though I know it means little Ethan will miss having his favorite Aunty Jackie around as much."

"He won't miss me, as I'll still be around. I have to learn from you all how to do this baby thing."

"You'll be fine."

"A natural earth mother." Staci winked.

"Please." Jackie rolled her eyes. "Ethan will have a new playmate."

"Actually, he won't be the only one." Toni smiled.

There was a collective gasp. "You're pregnant too?"

"It's much sooner than what I imagined, but yes. Well, according to the test I took yesterday." She glanced at Staci. "I'll probably need to go see your husband and confirm it."

Anna sighed as there was another round of congratulations and clink of glasses.

Serena caught her eyes and mouthed, "Are you okay?"

She nodded, smiled. She genuinely was so happy for them all.

Serena smiled back, and Anna's heart swelled with joy. She was content. These friends of hers were living their best lives, and she finally felt like that was possible for her too. The more she read her Bible each day, the more she stood on God's promises, the more she felt hope firm in her heart, and a greater sense of peace layer in her soul. Maybe God didn't have a husband or children in her future, but His promise that He had good plans for her still was true. She could trust Him. She smiled. She *would* trust Him.

Jackie clapped her hands, drawing their attention. "Anyway, back to what I was originally asking. Gosh, we're good at side tracks."

Rachel lifted her glass. "Amen!"

Jackie laughed. "I wanted to know about the ball, because I wanted to buy tickets to the ball for all of us."

"What?" Rachel's eyes rounded.

"You don't have to do that," Serena protested.

"I'll be working," Camille said regretfully.

Staci's face wore smugness. "I've already bought mine."

Toni nodded. "And Matt and I got ours too."

"Well, Damian and I would be more than happy to take you up on your generous offer," said Rachel.

"Joel and I too. Thank you," Serena said.

Brandi blushed. "I can see if Marcus is free. That sounds fun."

Which left Anna, flying solo. But that was okay. She'd be so busy helping her mom that she'd barely notice she had no partner. And despite her recent antics, she had a feeling that her friends would all let her borrow their husbands for a dance if need be. And there was always Kyle Crayling, she supposed.

Serena ate a grape. "I got a call from Leanne Waterman. *Toronto Living* magazine is coming to do a big spread on the event."

Anna nodded. Mom had mentioned that during their last catch up.

"James tells me that she and Michael have really hit it off," Staci said.

"Michael?" Toni asked.

"The paramedic. Maybe you should invite him too," teased Rachel.

Jackie shrugged. "If it's for a good cause, then why not?"

But was it for a good cause? Suzy's question rang softly through her mind. How much did the Craylings actually give to the folks who needed it? For all of Heather's talk of charity, she wondered sometimes if it was more for show and name dropping and status and tax breaks than because of genuine compassion. Which was probably as judgy a statement as anything else she'd been doing over the past months, but there it was. Somehow Suzy's words had wormed their way into her mind and now she couldn't let them go.

"Hey, are we ready for the movie?" Toni asked.

"What are we watching?" Brandi asked.

Staci held up a DVD. "I know it's old school—"

"The movie or the fact that it's an actual DVD?" Rachel asked.

"But as the one charged with movie selection, I thought we could watch *Miss Congeniality*."

Camille clapped her hands. "I love Sandra Bullock."

"This is fun. And the hero guy, I forget his name, he's not hard to watch at all. He's almost as good looking as Damian," Rachel winked.

But as Anna watched Sandra's antics, she couldn't help but once again compare the leading man to a certain detective in Muskoka, and decide that he was almost as good looking as Tom. She drew in a breath, released it slowly. Prayed a blessing on Tom. Refocused on the movie.

The scene where Sandra used him to demonstrate her Miss United States "talent" drew chuckles, and Staci's considered look. A look that was still there when the movie ended, among happy sighs and talk of their favorite scenes, and this film being among people's favorite movies.

"What's going on, Staci? Why are you looking like that?"

"That scene before reminded me again that we should do self-defense."

Wow. How many times would this come up?

"It wouldn't hurt," Rachel agreed.

"Actually…" Jackie shot Anna a quick glance. "After hearing about Anna's story, I made a call to the local police and asked for tips on local defense classes. For us and any of the other local women who might be interested."

"What a great idea! When do you think we could?"

"Well, actually, they were able to fit something in next weekend. I didn't want it to clash with your ball, Anna, but I also sensed we should do it sooner than later."

"Ooh, will this involve a handsome police officer some of us might know?" Rachel winked.

Please Lord, no. Anything but that.

Except, that wasn't really true. She'd be okay. And there truly were plenty of things worse than seeing Tom again.

Jackie glanced at her. "Don't worry. It's someone else."

Phew. "I'm not worried."

And now she thought on it, apart from that tiniest of moments, she really wasn't as concerned as she once might've been. God had been working with her to remove Tom from her heart. She lifted her chin. She'd be okay to face him.

Tom gripped the steering wheel as he drove. This was so not how he'd expected to spend his Saturday. But then, when their community liaison officer, Wendy Martene, had pulled out, and nobody else had been free, Tom's still-playing-the-waiting-game meant the task had somehow passed to him. He half suspected Gabe had arranged things to stop Tom complaining about the continued delay, but whatever. In two hours, he'd be done.

He pulled into the community church's parking lot. Parked. Got out. Then paused.

His stomach tightened. Uh oh. He recognized that red car. Anna was here? But of course she was. When he'd prayed for God to give him an opportunity to reconnect with Anna, he sure hadn't anticipated this. Even though, now he thought about it, it seemed maybe God had had a helping hand courtesy of Jackie. Not that he was the one anyone expected today. A groan escaped and he internally braced. Given their last few encounters, he doubted this would go well.

He followed the signs to the hall and pushed open the door, and was met with a cacophony of noise as more than a dozen women laughed and chatted. All of which ceased as every head swung to face him.

Serena Wakefield's jaw drew closed, then she moved toward him, closely followed by Jackie and Toni. "Tom? Uh, I don't mean to be rude, but what are you doing here?" Serena asked.

He hid his wince. Yep, this would go really well. Had Anna told this trio about his fumbled attempts at connecting with her? He didn't dare look for her. Not yet. "I'm what's known as the last resort. Wendy, our community officer, was supposed to come, but got sick and couldn't make it at the last minute. So rather than cancel today, my boss sent me." He swallowed, then asked in a lower voice, "Is she here?"

"There are plenty of women fitting that description here. Which 'she' could you possibly mean?" Serena's head tilted, her look knowing.

"Oh, don't pick on him," Toni said. "Good to see you again."

"You too." He nodded to Jackie, who put out her hand. "Ma'am."

She chuckled. "Oh, you don't need to 'ma'am' me. Just Jackie will do. It's nice to see you again."

"You too." Jackie looked so different to the last time he'd seen her. "You're looking well."

"Thanks."

"It's amazing what the love of a good man will do," Serena murmured, eyeing him.

"I'm not here for trouble, Mrs. Wakefield."

"Stop it. Call me Serena. You know I'm only teasing."

He sure hoped so.

Just then the sea of women parted, and he looked up and saw… "Mom?"

"Oh! Hi honey. I didn't expect to see you here."

"Same."

Wow. This was getting surreal.

But Serena was now drawing him to the center of the room, asking the women to take their place in a circle around him, was introducing him, which meant he had to look around the circle of women, and see—

Anna. Dressed in another of those singlet tops and yoga pants that made him swallow. His gaze fixed on hers, and he drank in the sight of her greedily. It might've only been two weeks since he'd seen her, but it felt much longer, and he wanted to trace every feature, even though he feared she'd still hold him in contempt. But no, her face held no flash of storm or fire, instead holding a peace he hadn't seen before. She offered a small smile, which drew his own, and a measure of comfort that this might go better than he'd feared. Maybe she might even be willing to listen to him after, while he tried to tiptoe around his explanations, and see if they could somehow reconcile enough to be friends.

He vaguely recognized some of the others here from Toni's wedding he'd attended. And yes, then there was his mom. Smiling at him, like she thought this the biggest joke in the world. He wondered if she'd noticed how his gaze had locked on Anna before.

The women broke into applause forcing him to refocus on why he was here. Hopefully, there'd be time for reconciliation after.

"Thanks for having me today, ladies. I know this is as unexpected for some of you as it is for me, including my mom. Hi Mom."

His mom waved. "Hi sweetie."

Anna's gaze swerved to his mom then back to him.

He cleared his throat. "So, the safety of women is something that we in the police take extremely seriously. Given recent local events, many of us are even more aware that women's safety should be prioritized, and that women should feel confident in their movements, especially in how that pertains to self-defense. So when Jackie called the local station and asked for some tips on self-defense we were glad to help."

"Yay Jackie," someone called. He thought she might've been called Rachel.

"Anyway, I know this is something that many feel is best taught over weeks or months, but when the preference for a quick start was expressed, and given everyone's busy lives, some tips are better than none, right?"

"Right," the women chorused.

"So, let's get started."

When Jackie had first explained what she wanted on that phone call, he'd figured passing it to Wendy would be the smartest thing to do. The community liaison officer had done countless of these kinds of things before. With Wendy getting sick and pulling out last-minute he'd had to quickly revise the reams of notes she'd prepared for moments like this.

He glanced at his instruction card, then began. "One of the first things people should do is to be aware of their surroundings. Pay attention to what's going on around you, so put the phone down and don't be distracted. Predators are looking for easy targets. If you think someone is following you, then cross the street or step into a store. If that's not possible, look the person straight in the face and ask them what the time is. This helps you to identify the person in a lineup, which makes you less of a desirable target. And by showing yourself as confident and unafraid, you also show that you will stand up for yourself and fight back if attacked."

"Go girls," his mom called.

He smiled, then got them to pair up, and practice turning, chins up as they faced their "attacker" and practiced projecting confidence.

Once he was satisfied, he looked at the next point. "If you're walking to your car, have your keys in your hand and hold a few of them between your fingers so they can be a kind of weapon. Don't unlock a car from far away, or sit in it for too long before driving."

A glance around showed nods, and focused expressions.

He talked about pre-incident indicators, the signals some men used to coax a woman into a situation where she was forced to give up control, using all kinds of tricks like charm, insults, requests for help, unsolicited favors, or refusing to accept rejection.

He talked about being vocal, loud and proud, and ran through them yelling, "Back off!" and "Go away!"

"Come on, ladies, let's do that again, louder this time."

"Back off! Go away!" they yelled.

"Whew, that felt good," Rachel said, fanning herself. "And I was only imagining saying that to my kids."

Amid the women's laughter, he caught Anna's smile, and wondered if she was thinking of what she'd said to him not so long ago. He sure hoped she didn't see him as some kind of creeper.

He talked about phone location awareness. "It's always good to let people know where you're planning to be. If your phone has a location-finding device, switch it on. In fact, let's do it now."

He led them through that process, helping some of the older women find the correct settings.

"Are we going to learn the stuff like in *Miss Congeniality?*" Rachel called.

"I'm sorry?"

"You know. The attack stuff, like when you sing."

Huh? "I'm afraid I don't really know what you mean."

"You know, when you hit your attacker in the solar plexus, instep, nose and groin."

"Clearly he doesn't," someone muttered.

This felt like it was getting out of hand. "You want to talk about what to do if you're attacked?"

"That's why we're here, isn't it?"

"Um, okay." This was a bit off script, definitely not in

Wendy's notes, but he'd go there. "Self-defense means having the confidence to know what to do in different scenarios. So if someone attacks you from the front, know his weak spots. Eyes, nose, throat, feet, fingers, knees, and er, crotch. Ladies, if you're attacked, you have permission to scratch, bite, kick, bend, punch, spit, elbow, claw, and do whatever you need to do to protect yourself."

He got them to pair up, then led them through the potential scenarios, the options women could do to disrupt the attack to help them break free and run. "Use your palm and strike his chin, kick him in the groin area, then strike his face while he is bent down. It's not the time to be polite, or act ladylike or anything. You need to do what you can to protect yourself from being hurt, or worse."

After they practiced those maneuvers for a while—sans the actual striking and kicking—he moved on to effective reactions when grabbed from behind.

"Elbows into his torso makes a great point of contact. If you're wearing heels, rake it down his shins or stomp on his foot. A backwards headbutt can also be effective. Remember, you are doing all you can to create a scene, to get the attention of witnesses, to create space to escape so you don't get taken to a secondary location." Because that's where the really bad stuff happened. *Lord, protect these women here.*

"But what about like what they do in *Miss Congeniality*?" Rachel asked.

Huh?

"Yeah, we want a demonstration," someone called. He thought her name was Gabby.

"I do like that scene in that movie," his mom said, her head tilting as she studied him "You know I always thought the hero reminded me a bit of you, Tom."

Several of the women eyed him, nodding, and he caught a trace of a smile on Anna's face before she glanced away. His heart sank. Maybe she didn't see anything heroic about him these days.

"It needs two people," Rachel objected.

"Then get him a helper."

"I, uh, really don't think—"

"Oh, come on, Tom," his mom said. "I'm sure he'd be okay for someone to practice on him."

"What?" Mom, no. He recognized that expression.

"Except…" His mom looked around the room. "I think the best person to demonstrate it would be you." She pointed to Anna.

Anna shook her head. "No. I don't want—"

"Come on." Serena's expression held more than a little smirk.

"But I don't know what to do—"

"Yes, you do," someone else—Staci?—said. "You said just the other week how funny that scene is, even though you've watched it a million times before."

He had no idea what they were talking about, but he didn't like where this was going. "Ladies, I really feel—"

"I really feel like she's right," his mom said, smiling at Anna before grasping her hand and leading her to the front. She turned Anna to face the front, and he glimpsed apology in Anna's eyes. So, she hadn't put them up to this. Looked like it was a giant set-up. Mostly of his own mom's doing. Traitor.

"Now, stand there, son, and we'll instruct you."

Whoa. This definitely wasn't how his self-defense class was supposed to go. Not with Anna standing so close he could see the sweat beading between her upper shoulders. Nor smell her vanilla scent. Or see the way her hair had curled in the heat.

"Ready?" his mom called.

For what?

"Tom, pay attention," his mom complained, to a titter of laughter. "Honestly, you'd think he'd never done this before."

There was a reason for that.

"Now, I want you to pretend to grab—Anna, was it?" his mom asked sweetly, as Anna nodded.

Oh, she fully knew who Anna was.

"Ah, so you are the poor girl who was attacked from behind the other day?" His mom patted Anna's arm. "I'm so sorry that happened to you."

"It's okay," Anna murmured.

"Oh, you're so brave." His mom looked at him. "Isn't she brave, Tom?"

"Very brave, yes." Although… He angled and murmured to Anna, "If you don't want to do this because it might renew memories then it's fine."

She glanced up at him, her face only inches away. "But isn't that the point? We have to face our fears sooner or later, and I'd rather be prepared and know what to do, rather than let something in the past hold me prisoner forever."

He felt the challenge in her words, but sensed she was making a statement for herself. "You're right."

"I am. And I'm also alright now."

"That you are," he murmured.

His mother coughed. "Are you two ready?"

Anna nodded. "I'm okay."

"I'm ready."

"Okay, then you need to sing, like in the movie," his mom said. "S stands for solar plexus. Go on Anna, show us where that is."

Anna's elbow jabbed him lightly in the stomach.

He faked a wheeze, but kind of knew where this was going now.

"I stands for instep. Which is great, especially if you're wearing heels."

Anna trod down on the inside of his foot. He didn't have to fake the wince. She might be wearing sneakers but that hurt.

"Can anyone guess what N stands for?"

"Neck?" someone called.

"No, N stands for nose. Come on, Anna, you can demonstrate that too."

She lifted her hand up and in a backwards motion tapped his nose.

He coughed. She twisted. "Sorry, did I get you?"

"It's fine," he said, rubbing it, to the women's smirks and laughter.

"And now for the best one: G stands for—"

"Great," he mumbled.

"What was that, Tom? Did you say groin?"

Anna moved away. "I'm not going to go there."

"Well, I should hope not. Not unless you're married, of course."

"Mom!"

His mother's cackles seemed the signal for the other women to fall about laughing. Anna's cheeks were red, and he knew his face must be that color too. Awesome.

He cleared his throat. It was way past time to get this demonstration back to where it was supposed to be. "I think we all have a good idea of what to do. So if someone was to come from behind, then you know what to do."

He demonstrated—with his mom—a few preventative measures to stop a bag snatcher, and several other techniques, and got them to practice in their pairs.

Rachel's hand waved in the air. "I'd really like to see the SING technique again, please."

"Did you want to try that out the front now?"

"Me?"

He nodded.

"No. Anna did a great job last time. She can do it."

"I'm not sure if she wants to."

Anna studied him, arms folded, then shrugged and moved

forward.

"Are you sure?"

"Are you worried I might hurt you?" she murmured.

"I don't want to do anything that might hurt you is more my concern."

"Like I said, I'm okay. So let's do this," she added in a louder voice, taking her stance in front of him.

"Solar plexus." She jabbed him in the stomach with her elbow.

"Instep." The women joined in the call, as Anna pressed down on his foot.

"Nose." The back of her hand touched his nose.

"Groin."

Before he'd realized what was happening, Anna twisted, and lifted her knee between his legs. And he bent over, again not feigning pain as he collapsed to his knees and wheezed.

"Oh my gosh, I'm so sorry!"

Amid the gasps and murmurs of sympathy he heard muffled laughter, some of which sounded a lot like his mom's. He winced, hands on knees, and carefully straightened, and exhaling slowly.

"I'm so sorry, Tom," Anna said. "I *really* didn't mean to do that."

"I know," he gritted out. "I should've been more aware and… yeah."

"I hope you haven't done my son a permanent injury," Mom said. "I'm still waiting to become a grandmother, you know."

Anna placed her hands on her cheeks. "I'm so sorry, Mrs. Woodmore."

"It's okay dear. That was the funniest thing I've seen in years. And it seems you certainly know how to protect yourself."

Anna bit her lip, her look apologetic.

"And it seems that's the end of the lesson," Serena said.

Sure was. And he'd never be doing this again.

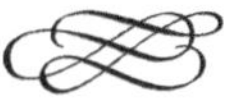

$\mathcal{A}$nna wrapped one foot behind the other as she waited for the others to leave. How humiliating. Even if a part of her had felt empowered. If she could bring a man bigger and stronger than her to his literal knees, then she felt braver than before. The last of the fears from the attack had left her.

Her shoulders pushed back, and she smiled as Tom's mom drew close and put out her hand toward Anna. "My dear, it was so nice to meet you."

"And you. I... I really didn't mean to hurt him, you know."

"I know. That's why you're still here waiting to apologize, isn't it?"

"How did—?"

"I hope he apologizes too. I know he's been struggling with his case, but you know he likes you, right?"

He did? "I don't know if he still does after..." She winced, and made a circling gesture at her mid-section.

Mrs. Woodmore laughed, as Tom drew near. "Oh, that. He's been hurt many times in the line of duty, which is why I was so glad to hear he'd found someone again. So I really hope the two of you won't let a little bit of pain come between you."

"Mom, what are you saying?"

"I'm saying that I like your young lady—"

His young lady?

"—and I think we should invite her to lunch after church one day soon."

Lunch?

"Mom," he snuck a peek at Anna then angled his shoulders away, dropping his voice, "I'll invite her when it's the right time."

"It better be soon. I'm not getting any younger."

"Mom, stop. You're embarrassing me."

"Well, you weren't even supposed to be here today, were you?"

Anna bit back a smile watching the interaction between the two of them. Tom's mom bossing him around was kind of adorable.

He glanced up, his gaze snagging Anna's, and mouthed a "Sorry."

She smiled. Said farewell to Mrs. Woodmore, who trotted off, looking pleased as punch, then nodded as Rachel, Staci, Toni and Jackie left with a mix of winks, smirks and praying hands gestures.

Then as Serena finished locking up, she finally murmured, "Um, Tom, have you got a minute?"

"Sure."

They followed Serena to the parking lot, waiting under the shade of a tree as Serena hugged Anna goodbye, then silently gestured behind Tom's back for Anna to call her.

Anna nodded, then faced Tom. "Look, I just wanted to say sorry again. I *really* didn't mean to hurt you."

"Hey, it's okay. Stuff happens, especially when you're close."

It sure did. She hadn't realized exactly how close they stood right now. She backed away. "I probably got too near."

He shook his head. "Like I said, I should've been more aware."

Was he talking about today, or earlier? His mom had said he liked her. Had called her "his young lady." Which wasn't exactly true, but it must've meant he'd talked about her to his mom before. She shivered. And while she didn't want to have her hard-won confidence defined by whether a guy liked her, she also wasn't going to look a gift horse in the mouth and walk away.

He studied her, his dark eyes holding a plea her foolish heart wanted to chase down. But no. She would be strong. Let him make the first move, yet be clear about what she wanted, and not misinterpret anything. Her life was hers—and God's—but she couldn't, wouldn't, blame others for what she allowed inside her heart. That was on her.

She wasn't helpless. She wasn't a victim. Today's session on self-defense had reminded her of that. She could put in good and godly boundaries and own her attitudes and actions and find contentment in trusting God and His plans for her. With the strength and guidance of the Holy Spirit.

"So what do we do now?" he asked.

"Well, you probably have work," she said.

He nodded.

Of course he did. Her heart dropped a little, but she picked it up. "I have some stuff to sort out with my mom for next week's ball."

He wet his bottom lip. "How... how is that going?"

"We're doing seating plans today. The tickets are pretty much all sold. I think there's one or two left, in case anyone you know might like to come."

He bit his lip, and she wondered what he'd do if she rushed in and kissed him. Probably a defense move he hadn't taught them today.

"You know I'd like to come," he said finally.

Her heart leaped, then she tamped it down. Feigned nonchalance. "Like I said, there's still room."

"But I can't. I… I'd really like to see you all dressed up, but I can't. I'm sorry."

"It's okay. I know you have work." Her lips twisted wryly. "I mean, I really do know that. I guess it must be important."

"It is. But…" He stepped closer, tucked a strand of hair behind her ear.

His touch sent shivers rippling down her spine.

"But if you can be patient with me, and still want to talk to me once it's done, then I hope you know I'd love the chance to take you out again."

"Really?"

He nodded, picked up her hand. "Really."

APPARENTLY, she still had a very long way to go before she could find contentment in just waiting. She'd thought she'd found it, but all week since the self-defense class she'd wondered just what Tom had meant. What did he mean by wondering if she'd still want to talk to him after "it" was done? He meant his case, right? What else could he mean? So did that mean yes, after his case was finished, she could maybe expect an invitation to the Woodmores for lunch, like his mom had hinted at?

No. She tamped down the rush of nerves. She wouldn't get carried away. She had to focus on setting up for the ball today, and let him make the first move later, if he wanted to. And if for some reason he didn't, then that would be okay too. It would have to be.

She walked back to her car, admiring the paint job, then reached in to collect the table decorations. They had the use of the resort's grand ballroom all day, something which had surprised her as surely it had to cost more than just the hours booked for tonight, but when she'd murmured that to Serena, she'd said it was part of the initial quote, designed so that Heather could spend the day at the spa getting charity function-worthy. Which seemed wrong. How could people really justify spending so much when surely it would be better for the whole amount to go to help support the charity?

The charity had received so much local support, especially with the auction prizes on offer, all donated by local businesses with vouchers from everything from Annette's Florist and Merill's boutique, to Alphonse's five-starred restaurant, to the resort offering a weekend accommodation package. Nothing from The Coffee Blend, she noticed.

Her mind tracked back to that conversation with Suzy about the administration costs. There had to be a lot of money involved, and who kept the Craylings accountable?

After returning inside and placing the table decorations, she moved to her mother. "Do you know who does the accounting for the Foundation?"

"Of course I do. I've been involved in the board for years."

"Yes, but who checks the accounting? Do you?"

Her mom laughed. "Oh, I never look at the figures. I know we can trust Heather."

But surely blind trust in someone simply because they were friends was exactly that: blind. Her stomach tensed. "So who does the accounting?"

"They have an accountant who does it. Everything is above board."

"But who is the accountant, Mom?"

"Oh, Julian Vanderman."

Anna puzzled that over. "Isn't he Heather's cousin?"

"I believe so."

"And the brother of the property manager there?"

"What of it?"

"But doesn't that mean it's a conflict of interest?"

"I don't know why you're worrying about this, Anna. Or why

you feel the need to bring it up today of all days. Why haven't you mentioned anything until now if that's a concern?"

"Because I didn't know, and I do know that some people, like Suzy at The Coffee Blend, were worried about how much of the ticket price was swallowed up by administration costs."

"Well, such events are obviously not for everyone. Not everyone can afford such things, it's true."

"So true," she muttered. She'd barely be able to afford to come if it wasn't for the fact she was on the committee and her ticket was subsidized.

But it wasn't just the ticket price, with the cost of a gown, getting hair and makeup done adding up too. For tonight's event she was re-wearing a gown, and she'd do her hair and makeup herself. She'd figured that instead of a spray tan she could sit outdoors in the sun.

"I don't know why it's bothering me today, but it just seems weird to spend all this money on an event when surely things could be a lot cheaper. Like if all the prizes that were donated were auctioned off online."

"Yes, doubtless that is true," her mom said. "But where is the fun in that?"

And that seemed to be the key factor here. What was fun for the Musko-cheers and the ladies on the board seemed to be the motivator in how the charity funds were handled. And it seemed that putting on the Summer Ball was more about fun for them, even if it came at a literal cost to the amount of funds raised.

"Please don't worry about the finances. You know as well as I do that we can trust Heather. After all, they've been family friends for years. Now, enough of your worry, look who's just come in." Her mother nodded to Kyle who had just come in, carrying some of the bouquets from Annette's.

"Where should I put these?" he asked Cherry, who was helping Serena.

Cherry pointed to the corner where the silent auction would be carried out.

He placed them there, surveyed the ballroom, hands on hips, then smiled as he saw Anna and her mom. "Hello, Mrs. Morely."

She smiled at him. "How are you, Kyle?"

"Looking forward to tonight. I hope you'll save me a foxtrot."

Her mother laughed. "Go on with you. You know I don't foxtrot anymore." She glanced at Anna.

No, Mom.

"But Anna here is still single, and would love the chance to dance with a handsome young man such as yourself."

"I'm looking forward to at least one dance tonight," Kyle said to Anna.

She might be making an effort to own her decisions, but sometimes it was necessary to keep the peace. "Sure."

Her mother moved to a nearby table and switched two cards. "I don't care if the tables are already organized. I think you two should definitely be sitting together."

Anna kept her protest behind her teeth. She only had a few more hours, then the ball would be done and hopefully she wouldn't have to worry about being "still single" soon.

"Thanks, Mrs. Morely." Kyle smiled at Anna. "I'll see you tonight."

"Can't wait."

"There. Isn't he a nice boy?" her mom said, as soon as Kyle left. "Really, I think you and he would make a perfect match one day."

But Anna didn't want him. And in learning to be clear about what she wanted and needed in life she knew she had to be clear about this too.

"Mom, you do know that I don't like Kyle in that way, don't you?"

Her mother made a moue of protest. "I don't know how you can say that. Kyle is such a lovely boy."

"He might be nice, but he's not for me."

"Well, if you can say no to Kyle then I'd like to know just who you think is good enough for you. I have to say, Anna, I'm not seeing an awful lot of candidates standing around here."

"Mom," she swallowed. "I… I have met someone that I like a lot. And he likes me."

"Good heavens! Why haven't you said anything? You need to bring him to meet me. I'm sure we could squeeze him in to attend tonight if you like."

It probably wasn't a matter of whether Anna liked, but whether her mother liked once she found out what Tom did for a job. A police officer was not her idea of a suitable career. Respectable yes, but not of sufficient status for her only daughter.

"What is his name? Where is he from? Who is his family? What does he do with himself?"

"His name is Tom Woodmore, and he's a detective, and—"

"A what?"

"I beg your pardon?"

"You should be if you said what I thought you just said."

"Sorry, Mom, I'm confused."

Her mother huffed. "Did you say detective? As in, he's a police officer?"

Anna nodded. "He's the one who helped Toni when she had that trouble with her ex. He basically solved the case, and he's something of a hero."

"No." Her mother shook her head. "No, that is not what I envisaged for my daughter."

"But, Mom—"

"No. I don't care if you think you may have feelings for him. Dating a police officer is not something I ever countenanced in your future."

"But it doesn't matter what you countenanced. It's *my* future, Mom. I'm the one who gets to decide."

"Anna, I really don't want to discuss this right now."

"Mom, I'm thirty-one. I'm plenty old enough to know what I want, and who I want and what I don't want. And I don't want Kyle Crayling."

"How can you say that? He's such a nice boy. He'd make such a wonderful husband."

"For someone else, maybe. Not me."

Her mother huffed. "I cannot believe you've waited until now to mention somebody else. And why he is not coming tonight when you seem adamant that he is the one, well, I cannot comprehend."

No. She barely understood that, either. "He has work." *Lord, bless Tom wherever he is. Keep him safe.*

"He's choosing work, over a ball?"

"Believe it or not, not everyone can get the day off." Like she had. God bless Dr. Lewisham for agreeing to get in a casual to cover her today.

Her mother scoffed. "I still don't understand, but let's not talk about it anymore. Let's finish this off so we can get ourselves ready and be ready for the night of our lives."

ADRENALINE RACED as Tom gripped the side of the door as Jones sped up the drive to Muskoka Ferns Lodge. They had to get in fast, seize all phones and communication equipment, and finally execute the search. It was unbelievable that it had taken this long, but he was trusting that God knew what He was doing. And the fact that the legal and fraud departments had wanted to wait until the day of the ball meant they could chase down the leads and see where the money was going. Raids on the Craylings homes were due to happen tonight, when they were at the ball, and had no place to hide.

But in order for the ball to go ahead, and for the parties

involved to have no suspicions, he had to stop word of the raid from reaching the Craylings' ears. Which was why they'd struck at noon, during the midday lull, today.

"There it is." Tom pointed to the main building as it drew into view. His was the first car, and behind him was a motley array of vehicles with everything from ambulances to backhoes and a flotilla of police and rescue vehicles. He opened the door as soon as the car slowed and snatched the warrant, moving quickly to the manager, who was scowling at them.

"What are you doing?" John Vanderman demanded.

Tom flashed his badge, then thrust the warrant in his hands. "Detective Tom Woodmore of the Ontario Provincial Police. I have a search warrant here to search these premises to look for several missing residents."

"I don't understand. That was dealt with years ago."

"I don't know if 'dealt with' is the correct term if the person remains missing without a satisfactory explanation."

"I need to see my lawyer—"

"Actually, you're going to sit in the back of the car over there and nice Constable Jones will keep you company."

"You can't do that."

"This badge says I can."

He saw Vanderman reach for his back pocket, and as soon as the phone was in his hand, Tom snatched it. "I'm sorry. I'm going to need that as evidence."

"What? You can't do that. This is a free country! I have rights."

And so did the residents here.

The afternoon passed in a flurry of activity as everything from the offices to the manager's residence to the outbuildings were searched. The residents themselves were checked over by medical staff, and the most vulnerable, including a man who appeared to have broken his hip and had bed sores from spending too much time in bed, were loaded into ambulances.

Regrets kneaded that Tom hadn't been able to help them until now.

"He has to go straight to the hospital," Dr. James Wells said, their triage medical associate who had been roped in to help.

As the hours passed, more truth about the neglect at the Lodge became evident, especially as some of the residents shared their horror stories.

"I only had rice and pasta to eat, and I pay $700 a month to live here," one elderly woman whispered.

"It's not all bad, they took us into town once in a while," another elderly gentleman said. "But I don't really know why. Because I don't have any money."

"Where is your money?" Tom asked.

"They take it."

"Who takes it?" he pressed.

"John Vanderman, the manager."

"Detective Woodmore, come look at this." One of the welfare officers pointed to the bathroom, and noted how the septic system drained directly from the building onto the ground. "That's illegal. We have to shut this place down. Nobody can stay here anymore."

Tom nodded. Gabe had mentioned that part of the delay was to ensure there were enough spaces in various institutions to help accommodate displaced residents. It looked like every available space would be needed.

Inside the Lodge's office, forensics found traces of blood in a filing cabinet. There were pension and old age security cheques, including some that dated back decades.

One of the fraud investigators showed him what he considered a forged cheque. "See the loop on the signature there? Obviously different to this one." He pointed to a different signature.

Tom exhaled. It seemed most of what they had hoped to find they had, but he still needed to find Terry. He was a crucial witness, and if Vanderman had learned he'd spoken to Tom…

He went outside to where the fleet of ambulances waited, as James helped organize the residents by their needs. "Has anyone seen Terry?"

"Terry? No."

Tom got on his radio, alerting the search teams to find Terry ASAP.

He was called to another building where a stash of alcohol, some obviously home-made, was waiting. "Aren't there supposed to be recovering alcoholics here?" the officer asked.

Tom nodded. From what he'd learned, it seemed these people had preyed upon the vulnerable and marginalized in the city, often those in homeless shelters. It pointed to a fraudulent operation where the Crayling family moved the helpless to the Muskoka Ferns Lodge and then got them to sign over their bank accounts and have their pensions deposited directly into the Craylings own funds. These people made him sick.

A loud whistle drew his attention outside again, where search dogs were whining, pawing at the ground. Several of the rescue crew gathered, shifting sheets of metal to reveal a hole in the ground. His stomach tensed. No. As one of them bent, Tom broke out in a run, skidding to a stop beside the bricked surrounds of what looked like an old well. Inside lay Terry. His stomach heaved. He wished he was simply asleep, but the bullet hole in his forehead showed otherwise.

Murder. Tom's fingers clenched. He was going to make the Craylings pay for this.

CHAPTER 18

"Oh my dears, everything looks wonderful," Heather Crayling trilled.

"You look marvelous, Heather," Mom said.

"Oh, stop it. No, do go on. I want to know that all my hard work today has been worth it."

All Heather's hard work? Anna begged to disagree. The woman had done nothing but get pampered in the Muskoka Shores Resort's spa. The hard work of someone—several people probably—was definitely on show though. Every inch of Heather seemed to glow. But there was nothing to do with pregnancy about her. Heather's glow was simply the glisten of money. Hers, and quite possibly a hefty percentage of the tickets sales.

"You look lovely, Anna."

"Thank you, Mrs. Crayling," Anna said automatically.

"She looks fantastic." Kyle grinned at her.

Anna moved her hands down her black gown. The off the shoulder sweetheart gown was one she'd worn before, but she knew it suited her, even if it felt a lot more snug than when she'd last worn it a couple of years ago.

It was such a shame that Tom couldn't see her looking this good. It was such a shame that Kyle could. Kyle seemed to think that because they were sitting together it was his right to ogle her in a way that made her want to SING. But a girl couldn't pull out her best Sandra Bullock moves when she was biting her tongue to please her mother. Not that her mother was making things any easier.

"Oh, Kyle, you and Anna looks so good together," her mother cooed, as if she'd completely forgotten what Anna had said before about Tom.

"We're just friends, Mom." And barely that, right now.

"But we could be more," Kyle said, with a wink, drawing her onto the dance floor. "You know, I never understood why you and I haven't made things official," he murmured, twirling her out in a spin.

Anna spun back in, hoping her dress would stay up. There were definitely a few more curves than the last time she'd worn it. "Because we wouldn't suit. You know that."

"You know I've always liked you."

Her feet stumbled. "You have?"

"I'll take that as you didn't." His lips tweaked ruefully.

"I… I thought that we were just friends."

"Not just friends, Anna." He pulled her close. "Never just friends."

Her tongue must be close to being bloodied with all the biting she was doing. But honestly, after tonight, she'd be happy if she never saw Kyle or his parents again.

Which reminded her. Own her choices. She wasn't a victim. She pulled away, catching Kyle's surprise as she did so, and eyed him firmly. "Just friends, Kyle. That's all we'll ever be. Okay?"

He might've muttered acquiescence, but his face said it wasn't okay. Well, too bad.

The dance ended, and she murmured an excuse and quickly moved away. Thank goodness she had her friends here, that they provided opportunity for her to mingle away from Kyle, his mother, and the Craylings' cronies.

"The evening is going really well," Serena said, glancing around the room.

"You look so beautiful," Rachel said, hand in hand with Damian.

Anna forced her lips up. She wouldn't let Kyle spoil things. Not when her friends had made the effort to come. "You all look gorgeous." Anna smiled at them. "But where is James?" she asked Staci.

"He got caught up in work. He messaged to say he'll try and make it, but it sounds like there was an incident somewhere today that's made it hard to get away."

"He always works so hard."

"All of you guys do," Rachel said, kissing Damian's cheek. "But I, for one, am glad that you made it tonight. Especially as it gives me the chance to feel like Cinderella."

He wrapped an arm around her. "I don't mind putting on a penguin suit if it means I get to spend the night with you."

"Ooh!" Staci teased.

"I meant dressed up, but..." Damian shook his head and stalked off to find more food.

Rachel joined in the laughter. "Don't worry. I'll make sure it's the other as well." She winked.

Anna smiled, catching Matt and Toni's look, as Matt gently moved his hand across his wife's stomach. It was so good to see her friends enjoying themselves.

A photographer's flash drew their attention to a slightly older woman. Toni, Matt and Serena went and spoke to her, before Serena drew her over and did introductions.

"This is Leanne Waterman from *Toronto Living* magazine." Serena smiled. "It's so good that you could come all this way again."

"I'm happy for any excuse to come up here these days." A blush tinted Leanne's cheeks.

So maybe that rumor about a paramedic beau was true. Jackie had mentioned she'd sent him an invitation, but he'd also been caught up in some drama just north of town. Seemed it was a big day for drama.

Leanne asked for a group photo, which they obliged, then asked for their names, before turning to Anna. "So, Serena tells me you're one of tonight's organizers."

"Oh, not really. I just helped my mom out a little."

"Still, it's good to see people supporting an important cause as helping the disadvantaged find low cost accommodation. How much money do you think they'll raise?"

"I have no idea, but I think I heard Heather say it could be over a hundred thousand. I think it depends on what's happening with the silent auctions."

"That's awesome."

"And definitely necessary." Joel frowned. "I couldn't believe the state of the Lodge when I was out there a few weeks ago."

"What do you mean?" Leanne's face lit with curiosity.

"I mean, I don't feel like it's safe for the residents who were there, many of whom seemed sick or immobile."

What? That didn't seem right. "I didn't know they had people like that at the Lodge. I was always told it was only a few elderly people."

"Have you been out there recently, Anna?" Joel asked her.

"Not for years. I remember a house near a lake with a few other cottages on the grounds. The people I saw were happy and didn't seem sick."

"Maybe the Lodge was like that a decade ago, but it's definitely nothing like that now."

"Perhaps that's why they need to raise funds."

"Hmm."

Joel's comments seemed to dampen the festive feel, and she

snatched a mocktail from a passing waiter. How terrible if that was the case. Her chest creased. *If?* But why would Joel lie? And if he wasn't mistaken, then how could the Craylings let things get so bad? She glanced across the rim of her virgin margarita. Did her mom know?

Leanne had been busy jotting notes, then excused herself, then went to speak to Heather and Spencer Crayling.

"What do you think she's going to ask them?" Toni murmured.

"Do you think she'd dare give Joel's description of the state of things at the Lodge?" Matt asked.

It seemed perhaps she did, as Spencer Crayling raised his voice, before stalking off to some of his cronies, Heather trotting close behind.

"Wow. That looked like it went well." Serena's nose wrinkled. "I might go check that Leanne is okay."

"Well, I didn't come to a ball not to dance." Matt held out a hand to Toni. "Would my beautiful wife care to join me on the dance floor?"

"Why certainly, sir."

That seemed to be the cue for Damian to ask Rachel, and Joel to follow Serena, and Anna spent a wistful moment watching the couples dancing. It would've been so good to have Tom here, to have him hold her close, to let him know how she truly felt. Because there was something rather wonderful about a man who let his care for the community come before a chase for riches. And Tom's patience and humor and faith made him someone she could easily fall for.

But who was she kidding? She *had* already fallen for him. If only he was here, and she could show him what he meant to her. At least the ball would be over soon, and and hopefully his case too, and this Cinderella might be able to finally secure her prince.

The music shifted to a more upbeat song, as the singer

started a Sarah Walton song, one of her more secular hits that Anna had heard played on the radio.

"I think we need to dance."

She glanced at Kyle, not really wanting to touch him let alone be held by him and dance. But curiosity also itched to learn whether he knew about the state of affairs at the Lodge. She allowed herself to be led into the dance. How could she ask him such a question?

He studied her, his gray eyes dipping to her neckline, sending a shiver down her spine. She tried to pull away, but he held her hands tight. "Kyle? What's wrong?"

"I can't believe you think that we don't suit," he muttered. "We're so similar. Your family has money, so does mine, so there's no difference there."

Except she had the funniest feeling that how their families earned their money wasn't exactly in the same way. She hated thinking this about people whose place she'd dined at, whom she had known for so long, and it seemed unbelievable that they might exploit others for their personal gain. But why else were conditions at the Lodge so bad? And how could she ask this without upsetting him? She couldn't.

"I'm sorry, Kyle, but I just don't think we're compatible. I want a guy who lives out his faith, who makes a real difference for people—"

"I'm making a difference, I help people," he insisted. "What do you think tonight is all about if it's not about helping people?"

An excellent question. But one she wasn't now game to ask judging from the nasty look in his eye.

Ugh. Her skin crawled. The time for pretense was done. She tugged her hands away. "Look, Kyle, you're a nice guy, but I think we both know we have to tap out as friends. It doesn't matter what your mother or mine think." She swallowed. The time for truth was now. "Besides, I have a guy that I'm interested in, and I want to explore things with him."

His face sagged. "I don't believe you."

"It's the truth. And I'm really sorry I have not been more honest with you in the past. But I'm trying to do better now."

"Who is he? What's his name?" His eyes narrowed. "Don't tell me he's that guy from the coffee shop all those weeks ago?"

When—? Oh. "Well, actually, he is."

"Wow." His hands fisted, then relaxed.

She took a step back. What could she say? She prayed for wisdom to tell him how she really felt, when a commotion drew her—and everyone else's—attention to the door.

Her eyes widened. Was that—"Tom?"

Her heart leapt. He'd come, after all! But... why was he wearing a dusty-looking suit and not a tux? And why did he look so serious? And why was he holding his badge up to Mr. Crayling?

Beside her, Kyle tensed, and she glanced at him. "What is it?"

He shook his head, his cheeks pale. "That's him, isn't it?"

"Tom?"

He huffed. "That guy is your boyfriend?"

"Well, yes." Maybe technically not yet, but as soon as his case was done that was a solid yes.

He swore. "Are you serious? Is he a cop?"

"A detective."

"Did you say anything to him about me? About us?"

"Of course not. Why would I? There's nothing to tell."

Except from the way Kyle was scowling, maybe there was something to tell.

Her pulse ratcheted up. And why would Kyle ask that unless there really was something to tell a detective about?

She moved to wave, to get Tom's attention, but Kyle snatched her hand down, and tugged her away.

"What are you doing?"

"It's called insurance," Kyle muttered.

Fear rose, and she glanced around. But everyone's eyes were on Kyle's father who was yelling at an inscrutable-faced Tom. Even her mom—no, her mom turned around to face Anna. Her brow pleated. Her mouth fell open. Her eyes widened.

"Anna," Kyle hissed, dragging her so fast she stumbled.

"Ow!" She leaned down to rub her ankle, but Kyle grabbed her again. "Stop it, you're hurting me." She tried to twist her arm away, but Kyle gripped it more firmly.

"What is *wrong* with you?"

Faces swiveled their direction. Murmurs, pointed fingers.

"Shut up, Anna," he growled, his fingers pinching around her wrist.

"Stop it." She tried to wriggle free, but he held her tight. *Lord, help me!*

Snatches from last week's self-defense class rose to the fore. Make a scene. Do whatever she could to prevent herself from being taken to another location.

"Tom! Tom!" she shrieked.

Tom finally looked across, and then everything seemed to slow. She dug her heels in, fighting against the momentum as Kyle tried to drag her away, leaning forward, twisting away. She tried to tug her arm free, but Kyle's grip was like steel. She was vaguely aware of Tom rushing to her aid, while two police officers restrained Spencer Crayling.

"Sing, Anna!" Rachel screamed.

Sing? Yes, that's right, SING. This was exactly what they had run through last week. And she wasn't going to be a victim. Not again.

She twisted forward, then rammed her left arm back, using her weight to propel her elbow into Kyle's stomach. Then, as he wheezed, she turned, lifting her knee to slam into his crotch. He gasped and she heard a loud rip as she slammed her pointy heel onto his toes, as Tom finally reached her.

Kyle screeched like a wild cat, before Tom's punch seared the air beside her cheek, sending Kyle toppling backwards. Kyle clutched at her dress and took her with him to the floor. She was only conscious of a blur of faces, and that her neckline was now dangerously low.

She slammed onto the hardwood boards, but within seconds was upright again, scooped up by Tom who immediately thrust her at Serena. Then he joined Damian, Matt, and Joel who were using their weight and height to restrain Kyle who was using words she was sure should not appear in *Toronto Living* magazine.

"Honey, here." Her mom covered Anna's décolletage and shoulders with her own silk wrap, stopping Anna's bold display from becoming any bolder, then wrapped her in a hug. "Oh my goodness, Anna. Are you okay?"

She might've nearly exposed her chest to half of Muskoka's elite, and her arm and hip throbbed, the earlier surge of adrenaline was fast waning, but seeing Tom's fierceness to protect her made the other pain fade. She straightened, ignoring her aches and her mom's protests, and drew her silken cloak around her shoulders to march over to where Kyle had been dragged upright by two police officers, and stood, head bowed, nose bloodied, crumpled.

"Anna?"

She ignored Tom, her focus fully on Kyle, waiting for him to look up at her. Then, as soon as he did, she slapped him, hard and fast, drawing cheers from what sounded like Rachel and Toni, gasps from others, and a smattering of applause.

She shook out her hand, then looked at Tom. Smiled. "Yes, Tom?"

His smile was crooked. "Are you okay?"

Forget the chaos. Forget the drama. In this moment she knew exactly what to do. So she stepped closer, closer, until she was in his personal space. And there, in front of everyone, she lifted her hands, pulled his face to hers, and kissed him.

252

Tom pulled up outside the house and drew in a breath. Rubbed a weary hand down his face. Then got out. Rapped on the door. Prayed this interview would go as he hoped. Waited. Prayed again. Prayed some more.

The door opened. Anna. "Detective."

His smile flickered. "Miss Morely."

He shifted his weight, studying her as she stared back. After the craziness of the past however-many-days, it was so good to finally be in this moment when he could just breathe. Just be. And finally take this to a place where he hoped it should go.

"May I speak with you a moment?" he asked.

"Only if it's a really long moment," she said, stepping back, allowing him in.

"That's my plan—oh. Mrs. Morely. I didn't realize you were here."

Anna's mom held out her hand. "Nice to finally meet you properly, Tom."

He grasped it. Let go. "And you."

"My, you're handsome, I'll grant you that."

"Uh, thank you?"

Mrs. Morely smiled, and he caught a glimpse of Anna in the way her mouth curved. "I don't think I ever said thank you for what you did for my daughter."

"You didn't need to. She did a great job of protecting herself." He glanced at Anna. "But I was glad to do what I could. I'd do the same a million times over for you."

Her lips tilted as her mother gave a swoony-sounding sigh, which drew his attention back to her.

"She was right you know." Mrs. Morely glanced at her daughter. "You really are a hero."

His heart warmed. Anna thought that about him? Judging from her pink cheeks that probably matched the heat rising up his neck he guessed so. He flattened his lips that itched to smile. "I know it's been a difficult time, Mrs. Morely."

She fanned herself. "One likes to think they know a person, but I was cruelly deceived by Heather and her family. To think they stole so much money from those poor, poor people." She shook her head. "I'm just grateful that there are good people out there in this world like you."

"Just doing my job, ma'am. Serve and protect is what we do."

"Oh, please don't 'ma'am' me. Call me Linda."

He glanced at Anna. So his fears about her mom disliking him had been unfounded. He cleared his throat. "Ah, Linda, I wondered if it might be okay if I had a word with your daughter."

"With Anna? Please, be my guest. I was about to leave anyway. But Anna, I hope you will bring your nice young man around to the house sometime for a meal. You like salmon, don't you, Tom?"

"Yes."

He caught Anna's sigh.

"Then I'll look forward to seeing you soon." She kissed her daughter on the cheek. "Take care of yourself, darling." She glanced at him. "And you take care of her too, Tom."

"Yes, ma'am." That comment was probably worth a "ma'am."

She smiled, patted his cheek like his grandma used to do, then departed, judging from the click of the door.

He guessed she had departed because his eyes hadn't left Anna's.

"You wanted a word?" Anna asked, her head tipping. "Is a girl allowed to guess?"

He took a step toward her.

"Is it hello?" She paced back.

He stepped closer.

"Beautiful?" she asked hopefully.

Mm, definitely that. He moved forward again.

She smiled and stepped back, eyebrows arched. "Darling?"

That was closer. He drew nearer.

She didn't move, lifting her face as he got into her personal space, just as she'd done to him at the ball. She placed a hand on his chest, slid it up his shirt to his neck, and smiled, her tilted mouth a dare. "Is it just one word or is it possibly three?"

"It's this," he growled, then bent his face and pressed his lips to hers.

Her beautiful, just-as-soft-as-he-remembered, luscious lips, that had stolen through his sleep, been the subject of every dream, and crept into a few waking moments as well.

He wrapped his arms around her, and she pressed close until she was flush against him. She sighed, melting into him, as they kissed most thoroughly. There was a rightness here, a sense of connection far deeper than that shared by their lips. Far deeper than what he'd even felt with Meghan. Maybe it was too soon, but he could already feel how well he and Anna matched, two imperfect people made right by God, whose love was whittling away the past and honing them for His plans and purpose. Whose love was stirring his heart to even deeper affection for the woman he held in his arms.

Finally, she pulled away, fanning herself. "Mmm. I think I really like that word."

"I *definitely* really like that word."

She laughed, and leaned back in the cradle of his arms. "My hero."

"You did okay yourself, you know."

"I know! I can't get over the fact that we did that training so recently, and boom, I needed to use it the very next week."

"I think that's called God's timing."

"As is this."

She tugged his head down and the next few minutes were filled with more bliss, until it was his turn to need air. He exhaled. "Has anyone told you that you're an exceptionally good kisser?"

"You're the first."

"Well, those other guys don't know what they're missing."

"Let's keep it that way, huh?"

"Definitely."

It was a little while later they sat on her sofa, and he finally felt a sense of real ease. He'd been glad to finally get a day off, although the fact it was a public holiday had helped. He was so glad to sit here, to hold her, to know she was okay. And to now know her family was accepting of him as he knew his would be of her felt like a million answered prayers.

"What are you thinking of?" she asked, snuggling into his side.

"I'm thinking how good it is that God knows what He's doing. That even when we can't see what He's doing He is working things out for our good."

"Am I something that is good?" she purred.

"You are one of the absolute best parts."

She beamed. "You mean that?"

"I do."

Her happy sigh was all he could ask for. To be here, to hold each other, was perfection.

She wriggled against him. "How is the case going?"

He tensed.

"Actually, no. Don't tell me. I can't believe we ever had anything to do with those awful, *awful* people. I can't believe Kyle would kill a man."

"He's a terrible human being."

"That's an understatement."

"But I really don't want to talk about that right now. Because that's all I have been thinking about for the past weeks." He shifted to face her. "I just want to know if we're okay. And whether you can see a future with me."

She gently drew a finger down his jaw. "Oh, now I know you must be tired, Detective. Didn't that kiss give it away?"

"Sometimes this man doesn't need more mystery and just needs to have it made plain."

"Well, in that case, yes. We are more than okay. And yes, I can definitely see a future with you."

He leaned closer. "Is that so?"

She nodded slowly, the lights from the TV glinting in her hair. "Because I know that we might be new, but the more I'm discovering about you, the more I feel like I could very well love you."

His heart expanded, threatening to gush with emotion. It was a good thing Marc couldn't see him now. He might pop a cork and start spouting mushy stuff he'd never live down. "Well, I'm glad."

The light in her face dimmed a little, like his response wasn't what she'd hoped. "Why's that?"

"Because I feel like I could very well love you too."

"Love me very well?" she asked playfully, the light back in her eyes.

"Exceedingly well," he said, moving to kiss her again, in

another long and wonderful moment. This kiss held friendship, passion, and a promise. And showed that God had good things for those prepared to wait.

The End
If you've enjoyed this, please check out the last (for now!) book in the Muskoka Romance series, *Muskoka Miracle*

A NOTE FROM THE AUTHOR

Thank you for reading *Muskoka Promise,* the sixth book in the Muskoka Romance Christian contemporary romance series. This series is based on my visit to the beautiful Muskoka region of Ontario, Canada, and springs from Muskoka Blue, the sixth book in the Original Six contemporary romance series, that enters on Sarah and Dan's romance story (grab your copy of *Muskoka Blue* here). If you've enjoyed this book, please check out the pictures from my visit to Muskoka on my website at www.carolynmillerauthor.com

The Naioth Children's Home is a real ministry in India. To find out more about this work and to donate please visit the Kids for Christ Jesus site.

~

Reviews help other readers find new-to-them authors, so if you can spare a moment to write a quick review at Goodreads / your place of purchase, I'd be very grateful.

Make sure you check out Sarah and Dan's story in the last of the Muskoka Romance series (for now!) *Muskoka Miracle.*

If you've enjoyed this taste of small town life, make sure you read the other books in the Muskoka Romance series, that starts with *Muskoka Shores*.

If you enjoy Christian contemporary romance you may want to check out the books in the Original Six hockey romance series, a sweet & swoony, slightly sporty Christian contemporary romance series.

The Breakup Project
Love on Ice
Checked Impressions
Hearts and Goals
Big Apple Atonement
Muskoka Blue

I'd love for you to check out my other books and to sign up for my newsletter at www.carolynmillerauthor.com where you can be the first to learn all my book and contest news, and discover more behind-the-book details and photos. Newsletter subscribers can also get an exclusive bonus book free, so grab your copy of *Originally Yours* here.

ABOUT THE AUTHOR

Carolyn Miller lives in the beautiful Southern Highlands of New South Wales, Australia, with her husband and four children. A long-time lover of romance, especially that of Jane Austen, Georgette Heyer and LM Montgomery, Carolyn loves to write contemporary and historical romance that draws readers into fictional worlds that show the truth of God's grace in our lives.

To find out more about Carolyn's books, and to subscribe to her newsletter, please visit www.carolynmillerauthor.com

You can also connect with her at

ALSO BY CAROLYN MILLER

<u>The Original Six hockey series</u>

The Breakup Project

Love on Ice

Checked Impressions

Hearts and Goals

Big Apple Atonement

Muskoka Blue

<u>Muskoka Romance series</u>

Muskoka Shores

Muskoka Christmas

Muskoka Hearts

Muskoka Spotlight

Muskoka Holiday Morsels

Muskoka Promise

Muskoka Miracle

<u>Northwest Ice hockey series</u>

Fire and Ice

The Love Penalty

Pointe, Shoots, and Scores

Faking the Shot

<u>Three Creeks Ranch Romance series</u>

A Cameo for a Cowgirl

A Valentine for a Vet

<u>Trinity Lakes collection</u>
Love Somebody Like You
Tangled Up in Love
Only You Can Love Me

<u>The Independence Islands series</u>
Restoring Fairhaven
Regaining Mercy
Reclaiming Hope
Rebuilding Hearts
Refining Josie

Historical:

<u>Regency Wallflowers</u>
Dusk's Darkest Shores
Midnight's Budding Morrow
Dawn's Untrodden Green

<u>Regency Brides: Legacy of Grace</u>
The Elusive Miss Ellison
The Captivating Lady Charlotte
The Dishonorable Miss DeLancey

<u>Regency Brides: Promise of Hope</u>
Winning Miss Winthrop
Miss Serena's Secret
The Making of Mrs Hale

<u>Regency Brides: Daughters of Aynsley</u>

A Hero for Miss Hatherleigh

Underestimating Miss Cecilia

Misleading Miss Verity

'Heaven and Nature Sing' from the Joy to the World Christmas
novella collection

'More than Gold' from

the Across the Shores novella collection

'Convincing the Circuit Preacher' from

The Courting the Country Preacher novella collection